LIGHTHORSE JUSTICE

Segeeyah Oaks raised his Colt and put a .44 ball into the back of the Leatherleg who had laughed and spat on the Indian boy's face.

His comrade, who had shot and killed the boy, turned in surprise. Looking down the barrel of Oaks' smoking Model '60, his face underwent a transformation from blood-lust to abject horror. He dropped his compact .45 Derringer to the blood-stained ground and spread his hands in a pleading gesture.

"I . . . I give up. I . . . I ain't done nothin' wrong. Please, don't shoot."

"Are you a Christian man?" Oaks asked in English.

The Leatherleg's face was suddenly illuminated with understanding and renewed hope. If he answered correctly, he might get out of this alive. "Why . . . why, yes, brother. Yes, I am!"

"Then tell it to your Jesus," Oaks snarled as he shot the child-killing Leatherleg between the eyes.

MARK K. ROBERTS

WAR DRUMS

ZEBRA BOOKS
KENSINGTON PUBLISHING CORP.

ZEBRA BOOKS are published by

Kensington Publishing Corp.
475 Park Avenue South
New York, NY 10016

First Printing: August, 1993

Printed in the United States of America

Foreword

In the tempestuous days of the late 1850's, which led to the secession and formation of the Confederacy, far-seeing men already recognized the tremendous potential inherent in the people of the Indian nations. Nearly all had been forcefully removed from their native environment, or descended from those who had. Feeling ran strong against the United States and what was perceived as a betrayal of trust on the part of American politicians. Some of those visionary men, in fairness from both sides, made particular overtures to the Cherokee nation.

At the outbreak of the Civil War in 1861, the Cherokee nation remained divided in sentiment. Being slave owners, like the other Indians removed from the Southern states, and surrounded by Southern influences, a significant party in the nation was disposed to take an active part on the side of the Confederacy. The old Ridge Party, headed by Stand Watie and supported by a secret organization that favored secession, known as the Knights of the Golden Circle, declared for the Confederacy.

The National Party, headed by Chief John Ross and supported by the patriotic organization known as the Kitoowah Society, declared for strict neutrality. No faction in the nation held out for support of the United States, although Union sentiment was held by a few. At last the pressure grew too great to be resisted. Gen. Albert Pike, commissioner for the Confederate States, arrived at Park Hill on October 1, 1861. A consensus convention was called, and the meeting proved fruitful for the Confederate sympathizers. On October 7, 1861, a treaty was concluded at Tahlequah with General Pike, in which the Cherokee nation cast its lot with the Confederacy.

Two regiments were organized for the Confederate service. Stand Watie was commissioned as brigadier general of the Cherokee Mounted Volunteers, and Colonel Drew commanded the First Regiment of Mounted Rifles. According to the treaty, the Confederate soldiers of the Cherokee nation were not to be employed outside the confines of the nation or "Western Arkansas." The Confederate States won the right to contstruct military posts, roads, and bridges in the nation, and other concessions. At first it worked that way. Then Gen. Stand Watie's regiment was pressed into service with the Army of Tennessee. Another blow fell when Col. John Drew surrendered his regiment at Fort Gibson, which was quickly paroled by the Union commander. That left Union troops on the border of the nation at Gibson and in Kansas. This placed a tremendous drain on the manpower of the Lighthorse in their task of policing the nation. Added to the dangers was the presence of deserters, both Union and Confederate, who preyed on the land.

One

Lt. Segeeyah Oaks was exasperated. Dust boiled up from the corral in a cloud so thick one could not even discern the upright posts that held the rails in place. At his headquarters outside Park Hill, in the southern corner of Tahlequah District, the Lighthorse lieutenant had recently received a draft of new recruits.

"What a sorry lot they are," he complained to his senior sergeant, *Wayah Unoli* (Wolf Wind).

Of an age with Oaks, in his mid-20's, Wolf split his brown, leathery features with a smile. "Oh, they are not so bad. Think what they would have been like if they had not gone through Captain Conroy's schooling up at Downing."

"Don't remind me," Oaks replied ruefully. "Tell Charlie I want to see him," he added, referring to *Jali Didekanosgi'a* (Charlie Singer), who commanded One Patrol. "It's about that kid I assigned to him. I'm having some second thoughts."

"*Ayo!* I was wondering if you'd gotten the same feeling. He is either the most baby-faced kid I've ever seen, or someone is not telling the truth about someone's age." Laughing, he went off to deliver the message.

Segeeyah Oaks scratched idly at his left ear, hidden

7

behind a long, wavy wing of near shoulder-length jet black hair. Ouch, indeed, he thought. The undirected motion dislodged the green turban that sat at a jaunty angle on his large head. He uttered a harsh curse in English as the breeze caught it and sent it off his head.

Quick reflexes allowed Segeeyah to recover his headdress before it had dropped below center of his wide, barrel chest. He swiftly glanced around, self-conscious over the loss to his dignity. No one looked his way, or at least gave no indication they had seen his moment of clumsy scramble.

"Too full of myself, I am getting," he muttered.

Charlie Singer approached with the kid in tow. "I thought you'd want to talk to him, too," he offered.

"Not right away," Oaks responded with a fleeting frown. The kid sprinted back to the corral. *"Jali,* are you satisfied that he is sixteen?"

Sergeant Singer crossed big forearms over his chest and raised his chin. "Are we ready to call him untruthful?"

Oaks forced a smile. "Not exactly. Wolf said he was either the most baby-faced sixteen-year old he had ever encountered——or he might have forgotten exactly which year he had been born."

"Are we going to lose him if it turns out to be the latter?"Charlie prompted.

Green flecks sparkled in the brown eyes of Lieutenant Oaks. He rubbed large, dry palms together. "Let's go see how he handles himself down there," he suggested. "Those horses that we rounded up are only half-broke. It's going to take some tough men to top them off. If he does all right, then I suppose we'll have to accept that he is at least sixteen."

"You can be as hard as an acorn in *Dulisdi,*" Charlie observed lightly.

"'An acorn in September,'" Oaks repeated. "I haven't heard that in a long time."

Together they walked to the corral. Lieutenant Oaks acknowledged the greetings of those Lighthorsemen they met on the way. As they neared, the shouts and jeers of the men seated on the top rail could be distinguished.

"Get up! You'll never ride for the Lighthorse if you quit now," one old hand challenged the hapless rider in the dirt of the corral. Gray shot through the hair of the Lighthorseman.

"Send in *Saloli*," another suggested.

"*Sgidv, sgidv!* Put the kid on that one," a third advised.

Lieutenant Oaks watched as a ripple of jostled shoulders marked the passage through the throng of the youth they had been discussing. Too large by several sizes, his hat avoided covering the boy's eyes by the good offices of his big ears. He wore a long-sleeved paisley shirt in orange-yellow-green design. The trousers were intended to be worn with high-top boots, with buckles to keep the legs in place below the knee. His legs were bare from knee to moccasin top.

"He looks like an urchin," Segeeyah blurted, then flushed dark red for his rudeness.

A squeaky voice answered the laughing, experienced Lighthorsemen. "I'm ready. Let me at him."

"Go ahead, boy, get your butt broke," the detachment field cook cackled.

Squirrel Three-Skulls (*Saloli Juska-jo'i*) tugged up his trousers and advanced on the gate. There, instead of opening it and letting the half-wild horse escape, he bent low and squirted through the lower two rails. An approving murmur ran among the onlookers. The boy came close to a swagger as he approached the sweating, trembling animal at the snubbing post.

Two men held it tightly in place. A blindfold covered the big, soft, brown eyes. Squirrel approached and began to pet one of the large, velvety ears. He spoke quietly into it for several seconds. Then he blew into it, bent and blew into the flared nostrils. In the blink of an eye, he had rounded the horse's flank and sprung into the small leather pad of the saddle.

"Kam!" he yelled, repeating with firmness, "now!"

At once, the Lighthorse pair let go of the ropes that held the beast. For a moment, it stood, spread-legged, head down. Then it sensed the weight on its back and its freedom at the same time. A snort became a squall as the horse arched its back, drew legs under and exploded off the ground. The blindfold and Squirrel's hat flew away on the first buck.

Groaning and squealing, the remount became liquid lightning. Atop it, the small boy flailed back and forth with each crowhop. The half-wild animal blew itself up with air and tried to sunfish. Squirrel gripped the single rein in desperation and squeezed his knees into the churning shoulders as best he could.

With each violent contact of hooves with the ground, the game little lad felt his spine compress. His belly muscles burned like fire. Earth and sky whipped past his eyes in a dizzying jumble. Unacquainted with the white tradition of one-handed rides, he clung with his free hand to the coarse mane. Hard hooves pounded the ground as the big horse tucked its head against the right foreleg and began to spin in small circles. Suddenly, Squirrel came free of the big, surging beast.

He landed hard, rolled clear of pounding hooves and caught a mouthful of corral bottom. Laughter trickled through the men all around. Slowly, painfully, Squirrel came upright on his moccasins.

"Ni! Ni!" Steve Medicine Pipe shouted, pointing.

They looked, expecting to see streams of tears from the boy's eyes. However, his shoe-button black orbs reflected only excitement and determination. The wranglers had recovered the horse by then. They had barely snubbed him down when Squirrel took off with a blur of flying

10

moccasins and vaulted onto the quivering animal's back.

"*Si!*" Charlie Singer shouted at the boy. "Wait!" he yelled again. After all, the kid had been assigned to him, and he felt responsible.

Squirrel Three-Skulls affected not to hear him. This time he lay along the stallion's thick neck and whispered into the twitching ears. Still making soothing sounds, he gave the command to release the big animal. It quickly became a repeat of the previous ride.

Whipped back and forth, Squirrel fought to keep his cries of pain from escaping his lips. A red haze grew behind his eyes. His belly got stretched and compressed so rapidly it became a ball of constant agony. Snorting, the horse spun in a tight circle, its wicked hooves pounding the dirt. With a huge squall and frantic leap, it flung the annoying burr from its back.

Squirrel hit hard and flopped on the ground. Three Lighthorsemen ran to his side. Panting, his small face smeared with dirt, blood, and horse dung, Squirrel looked up at them and smiled. He came slowly to his feet.

"I want him," he chirped. "He's mine. I'll call him Blasting Powder."

"By *Yoah!*" Charlie exclaimed, and it sounded like a prayer.

This time the wiry youth ran to the untamed horse, grabbed an ear and twisted lightly, enough to get it to stand still. Then he flung himself atop the beast and once more lay along the neck. His words of assurance tumbled out. For a long, tense minute, the trembling animal remained stationary. Then he erupted with the same ferocity as before.

Ignoring the rein, Squirrel clung tenaciously to the mane and one ear. All the while, his words of calm and soothing jolted out of him. He had bitten his lip the last ride, and blood still trickled from the corner of his mouth. Now Blasting Powder flung his head violently and gave

Squirrel a nasty crack on his right cheekbone. Cherry red showed through his coppery complexion. Still the boy clung to the powerful stallion.

Now the jeers changed to words of admiration. "Hold on, boy! Hold tight. You can do it!"

Their laughter had a friendly tone to it, Segeeyah Oaks noted. Hats sailed into the air as Squirrel stayed with the plunging animal. His flat, narrow bottom pounded the saddle with each bound. This third ride took a terrible toll. Despite himself, Squirrel began to squeak in hurt each time his crotch slammed into the withers of Blasting Powder.

"Ayo! . . . Ayo! . . . Ayo!"

"Let go, kid. Let go!" Lieutenant Oaks found himself shouting.

Blasting Powder decided that for him. Squirrel went heels over head in front of the berserk stallion. He tucked his shoulders and rolled, spitting grit and dirt in outrage. He lay like a man pole-axed. Slowly his skinny chest began to heave and, by the time the wranglers had calmed Blasting Powder, he was on his feet and headed for the stubborn animal.

"Ease off," Steve Medicine Pipe counseled. "You're tough as bullhide, we can see that, son, but he's too much for you."

"Hla," Squirrel spat. "No," he said again, "I'm going to make him mine."

Afire with his determination, Squirrel took to the saddle a fourth time. Blasting Powder shivered and snorted, shook his head. By increments, he began to gather his powerful legs for a bolt into the air. Instead, he gave a sort of half-hearted hop that drew shouts of amazement from the Lighthorsemen gathered at the corral. Squirrel bent and retrieved the rein. His moccasined heels drummed into the stallion's ribs. Blasting Powder began a leisurely walk around the inside of the pen. Then Squirrel urged him into a trot. Cutting zig-zags across the center, the boy worked his mount into a canter.

"Open the gate. I want to feel him run," Squirrel requested.

To accompanying cheers, Squirrel let out on Blasting Powder, who jumped into a fast run, then a shoulder-churning full gallop. He streaked across the hilly landscape outside Park Hill until he showed as only a small black dot atop the horse. When Squirrel returned, Lieutenant Oaks summoned him into the Tsalagi pole lodge that served as his office.

"No small boy could have mastered that killer," he prefaced his decision. "Far as we're all concerned, you're man enough to be in the Lighthorse."

"Thank you, sir," Squirrel squeaked.

"Now, we have to get you signed in." Lieutenant Oaks reached for the One Patrol roster. "You can write, can't you?"

"Oh, yes, sir," Squirrel responded and reached for the steel-nibbed quill pen. Carefully, he inscribed the characters of the syllabary that spelled his name:

ᎤᏣᏛ ᎭᎵ ᎤᎴᏴᏗ ᎯᎢ

"Put your gear in the sleeping lodge and go cool down your horse," Lieutenant Oaks directed.

"My . . . horse," Squirrel said in a tone of awe.

A shadow darkened the doorway. Slender, dark-haired, an attractive young woman entered. *"Ulogili,"* spoke Segeeyah to his wife.

"Segeeyah," she said, then turned her attention to Squirrel. "You poor thing. I saw the terrible pounding you got. Come over to our lodge later. I have some elixir for your sore parts, some herbs to ease the ache."

Lieutenant Oaks shot a sharp glance at his wife. "Cloud," he said softly and gave a small shake of his head.

To Squirrel, "Go tend to those things and fall in with the rest of the men."

Squirrel drew himself up. "Yes, sir." He bolted out the door, past Cloud Oaks.

Ulogili Oaks had a stricken look. "Segeeyah, he's just a little boy."

"No, dear, he is a Lighthorseman. Such as there are these days, with that war going on. He has spirit. He's brave and unafraid of pain. If you mother him, it will weaken him."

"I—I'll never understand your men things," Cloud surrendered.

"No, dear, nor will we men ever understand your women things," Segeeyah responded, and they laughed together.

Gentle as a child's breath, a light breeze set the cottonwoods to chattering among themselves on the breast of a hill outside of Siloam Springs, Arkansas. Fat cattle grazed on the late summer grass. Beyond, a rooster stridently celebrated his afternoon conquest. Insects buzzed in the crystal air, and from behind the halted riders a flock of crows loudly engaged in naughty conversation.

At the center of the loose formation, a hard-faced man perched on the saddle of a huge charger. He wore a thoroughly out-of-place black suit, with swallow-tail coat, and a quasi-military cape. A plumed gray hat sat on his small head. His booted legs stuck straight out from the bulging sides of his mount. Smaller even than Squirrel Three-Skulls, he cut a ludicrous figure.

Not that the others saw him this way. His cold, blank gray eyes burned with an inner fire of implacable hate. He had a thin, knife-edge of nose, his mouth a nearly lipless purple slash. For all his diminutive size, he had an air of command.

14

Outside of his blazing ire, the horsemen seemed at peace. At least until the crows rose in a black cloud of noisy alarm and flew rapidly away. Following the crows came the rumble of many hooves. Gray-uniformed figures topped the rise, and the one in the lead let out a halloo to indicate the quarry in sight. At once the Confederate troops spread out in a line of skirmishers.

Sabres flashed in the sunlight, and Enfield carbines came off the saddle spyders. Alarmed glances went among the men further down the hill. The man at the center raised an arm to give the command to ride.

"Those Rebel hellhounds have found us again," he snarled bitterly.

"Colonel Moritus, where are we going?"

A sneer practiced from portraits of Napoleon formed on the face of Augustus Moritus. "Why, where else? Into the Indian Territories, of course."

Rifle balls and conical bullets cracked through the trees above them as the band of grimly determined men spurred their horses to a gallop. Many guts tightened as a fearful sound came from their pursuers.

"Whooo—eeeee! Whooooo—eeeeee—aaaaaaah—whooo!"

Two

The Confederate troops reined in sharply on the northern bank of the Illinois River, where it crossed into the Cherokee nation. A parting shot from a Georgia sharpshooter took one of the fleeing men from his saddle.

"We've got to stop here, boys," the officer in charge announced.

"Ain't the Cherokees on our side, Cap'n?" a gangly corporal in butternut and gray asked.

"They are, at least most of 'em. But officially they're considered a friendly foreign nation, not part of the Confederacy. Even though we've got treaty rights with them to have military posts in the nation, we have to notify their government in advance of any troop movements. Wouldn't do to have troops chargin' into *their* country, even in hot pursuit of Yankee trash like that."

"Gol—ly, Cap'n," the company trumpeter drawled. "I heard ol' Brax Bragg had some Injuns with him, but I never knowed they had their own country."

"Oh, they do," said the captain, and he chuckled. "You know, I wonder if Moritus and his damned Leatherlegs guerrillas know what it is they're ridin' into?"

"How's that, Cap'n?" the trumpeter inquired.

"Bein' a native Arkansawyer, I've learned a little about

16

how things are over there. The Cherokees have them a thing called the Lighthorse. They're part policemen and part soldiers—ah—warriors, I'd guess. An' mean as Billy-beat-Hell." He slapped his right thigh with a gauntleted hand. "Ol' Moritus just might be on his way to gettin' his butt whupped right good and proper."

Self-styled "Colonel" Augustus Moritus halted their headlong flight from the Confederate cavalry just south of Albert's Prairie, in the Going Snake district of the Cherokee nation. This time they stopped on the military crest of a ridge, thus giving them a clear view in all directions. They would not be surprised again. Colonel Moritus and Quinten Danvers, his second-in-command, duck-walked to the top of the rise and looked down through field glasses at the pastoral scene below.

"Outrageous," Moritus hissed minutes later. "These cursed red savages living like real people."

"They've got reg'lar little houses," Quint Danvers observed, surprised by what he saw. "An' barns, haystacks, even an outhouse."

"Unnatural, an abomination. God's wrath will fall on them," Moritus vowed darkly. "And I intend that we shall be the instrument of that wrath. Go back and get the men ready. We'll attack this farm at once."

"What if there's a whole lot of these *civilized* Injuns around here?"

Scorn bubbled around the colonel's words. "Do you think they would be any match for us?"

"Uh—no, no, reckon not," a chastened Danvers responded.

Twenty minutes later the Leatherlegs streamed down the concave face of the ridge toward the Cherokee farmstead. Howling and whistling, they thundered through the garden plot, fire flashing from the muzzles of their weapons.

Asʋnoyi Ayʋgi looked up from the anvil, where he had been sweating over forming a hinge. Even over the ring of the hammer, Nighthawk Nail had clearly heard the rumble of fast-approaching horses. The first shots caused him to drop the tongs and wrought-iron plate. No one should be shooting around here, he thought in confusion. He hurried his thick-waisted body toward the old Damascus-barreled 10-gauge shotgun in the rack beside the shed door.

Two riders, white men, Nighthawk Nail recognized at once, flashed past the smithy shed, on their way to where his two hired hands forked hay from a wagon bed onto the stack. The big revolvers in the riders' hands crackled, and one worker cried out as he fell from the wagon.

Asvnoyi blew a Leatherleg from his saddle with a load of No. 2 goose shot. Another guerrilla whirled and caught the second barrel full in the face. He went over backward, his shrieks of agony loud and clear in the smoke-laden air. Sudden fear gripped Nail as he saw his seven-year-old son running, barefoot and panic-stricken, across the farmyard.

"*Hla, Kiyuga!*" he shouted. "No, Chipmunk," he said again, "get back!"

Ruthlessly, one of the white men bore down on the small boy. With a shout of laughter over his accomplishment, he bowled little Chipmunk over and reined in his mount to a prancing halt atop the child. Sharp, iron-shod hooves quickly stomped the youngster into a bloody, broken pile of human debris.

His face a mask of horror, Nighthawk Nail dodged back inside the shed and put shaking hands to work reloading his Parker. He had powder and shot cups down both barrels by the time any of the marauders realized he was in the smithy. He thumbed caps onto the nipples as a snarling Leatherleg kicked at the door and filled the opening.

Hammers already back, Asvnoyi triggered the shotgun and blasted the guerrilla back out of his smithy. He dimly heard his wife screaming at the invaders. He started for the door when strong arms grabbed him from behind and pinioned his arms to his sides.

"Not so fast, Injun," a growling voice demanded. His captor's breath stank of rotting teeth and tobacco juice. "I got me one," the Leatherleg shouted to his friends.

"Bring him out. We got the woman," came the reply.

Nail feigned not to understand English, hoping it would give him some advantage. The man who held him wrestled him outside. Nighthawk's eyes widened in surprise when he saw the gathering in his farmyard. These white strangers wore a variety of hats, shirts, and coats, but all affected leather trousers and leggings.

All except one very small man, on a extremely large horse. He appeared ready for a formal event of some sort, in a dressy suit and short cape. He also gave the orders, Nail found out a moment later. "Good. Take him over by the woman. Some of you round up those other brats."

"Who are you?" Nighthawk asked in Tsalagi.

"I assume you are inquiring as to our identity," the little leader responded, looking down a long, thin nose at Nighthawk. "In answer, I am Col. Augustus Moritus. There are my Leatherlegs. We have come to the conclusion this land is much too nice for heathen savages to occupy. We've come to reclaim it. To do so, we have to remove the likes of you from it."

Moritus paused a moment and raised himself in the saddle. He brightened when five of his Leatherlegs frog-marched as many squirming, yelling children into place in front of the cluster of guerrillas. "Ah! I see you have been successful. Now, in order to achieve what we wish, we are going to eliminate all of you, starting with the next generation." To a ferret-faced Leatherleg, he commanded, "Line their git up over there and shoot them."

Nighthawk Nail cast aside his pretense of not understanding English and pleaded for the lives of his children. "No, please. Not my children, not my sons. You have already killed one. Please, I—I beg you."

Augustus Moritus could see the anguish in this red barbarian's face, heard it clearly in the tone of voice. He well appreciated the desperation that had brought the man to humiliate himself by begging. And it affected him not in the least. He leaned forward and looked down sneeringly, pale gray eyes icy and remote.

"Your heartfelt petition has moved me to reconsider," said Moritus offhandedly. He inwardly rejoiced at the expression of relief and gratitude that washed over the savage's face. He raised his voice, "No, men. Don't shoot them. Strangle the little monsters."

With a howl of terror, Nighthawk Nail launched himself at Augustus Moritus, arms wide, fingers clawed. He longed furiously to get his hands on this inhuman beast with the face of the dead. A Leatherleg prevented it with a hard slam to Nail's back with the butt of his rifle.

Pain burst inside Nighthawk Nail's body. He dropped into the dirt and writhed while he listened helplessly to the frightened screams of his children end abruptly as hard, calloused hands closed on their throats and crushed the life from them.

His wife began to wail, and then to sing. "*U ne La nv-hi U We tsi*/Ee ga gu yu-he yi/Hna Quo tso su-Wi yu lo se."

"Take everything useful," Moritus commanded. "Burn the buildings, and kill these two."

"*Ogidoda galvla dihehi*," Nighthawk Nail began to pray. "*Galvquodiyu gesesdi detsadovi.*" Then he felt a stunning pain in his head and the beginning of a loud crash . . .

Wolf Wind entered the small office lodge at the Park

Hill station with a grim expression on his broad face. "We don't have those boys half-trained, and already Tahlequah wants us to go into the field."

"What's that all about?" Lt. Segeeyah Oaks asked.

"Messenger just came. There's been some trouble in Going Snake. An entire family wiped out. We're to go assist the two constables from Going Snake Courthouse."

For a moment, anger flashed on the face of Lieutenant Oaks. "One long, hard day's ride, and for what? We get there and find out it's feud business and nobody remembers anything. That is, if they even talk to us."

"Look on the bright side," Wolf proposed, his mood shifting. "We can use the time to shake down the horses, get the new men used to riding trail, even practice tactical formations on the way."

"Hummf!" A thought struck Segeeyah. "The orders say for the entire detachment to go?" At Wolf's nod, he went on, thinking aloud. "That don't sound like feud troubles to me. It's been twenty years since there have been any large-scale battles over the Echota question."

"Want my best guess? I'd say some of those Confederate guerrillas went stray and thought they were in Kansas."

"Too far south, *Waya*. Oh, I know how you feel about the nation siding with the Confederates. But they let our people keep their slaves, and dangled the possibility of reclaiming some of our old territory in North Carolina, so the politicians went for it."

"And I suppose you go along with it?" Wolf challenged.

Segeeyah gave him a level gaze. "I follow orders, like everyone else."

Wolf produced a rueful grin. "Enough said on that, then. I'll go alert the patrol leaders. It does say right away."

"*Damn!*" Lieutenant Oaks swore unaccustomedly in English. "Cloud is fixing blackberry cobbler for tonight."

Wolf Wind laughed. "Take a piece along."

"Not the same," Oaks said with a blush. Blackberry cobbler night was his wife's way of inviting romance. "Well, duty calls."

They had ridden southwest for two days after the attack on the Cherokee farm. Augustus Moritus expanded nightly on his quest for a secure haven for the band of guerrillas he led. Some place from which they could raid with impunity.

"In a dream I saw the ideal place," he harangued them this evening after the cook fires had been banked. "Lush with grass, tall as a horse's belly. Plenty of water, a stream running through a canyon, or a valley floor. High hills all around, so none can tell of our presence."

"How do we take care of our other needs?" Long Tom Longdon asked slyly, with a wink to his companions.

Moritus correctly interpreted it and made a face of distaste. "For our sustenance, we can pluck the riches from these heathen savages with ease, now the war is on and their menfolk mostly gone off to fight. For those with more basal needs," he added in a tone of contempt, "you are free to amuse yourselves with the red-skinned women."

"Where is this place?" Boston Harry prompted. "We done made more'n eighty miles into Cherokee country."

"Perhaps south of here," Augustus Moritus offered. "Or north. It could even be west into Creek land. I'll know when we find it. It will be grand, I promise you that."

Quint Danvers came to his boots. "The colonel's asked me to inform you that tomorrow we hit another farm. The scouts found it some five miles to the west of us. This time we take the farm equipment, also."

"Sounds like we're gettin' close to that happy valley of yours, Colonel," Long Tom Longdon surmised.

"It could be, Mr. Longdon, it could be," Moritus responded with a beaming smile.

Lieutenant Oaks and his detachment rode into the farmyard in late afternoon the next day. Two older men stood in the clearing, beside a grave they had been digging. Segeeyah judged them to be in their late 50s from the amount of gray in their hair. They watched in silence as the Lighthorse trotted near the burned out house and dismounted.

"*Sio,*" Segeeyah greeted them. "I am Lieutenant Oaks, Lighthorse."

"*Didaniyisgi* Monroe," the elder answered.

"Well, Constable, can you tell us what happened here? We have been cutting sign of a large body of horsemen, headed in the opposite direction from our approach."

"Yes. *Diyoniga.*" he spat distastefully. "All white men. They were here. They killed a whole family. Six little ones," he added, eyes filling with tears.

"How long ago?" Lt. Oaks asked softly.

"Two days, maybe three. If I were younger, I would crush them with my bare hands. Where are the marshals? Why haven't they come to catch these men?"

"The war," Segeeyah offered lamely.

Anger clouded Constable Monroe's face. "Oh, yes, the war. Why is the Tsalagi nation at war with the United States? Tell me that."

"Surely you have enough years to know how little love we have for the Americans. They . . . removed us here," Segeeyah Oaks reminded patiently. "The marshals have become an enemy, rather than the steadying force that protects all the nations from invasion by such *devhyugi anisgaya.*"

Old Monroe's face lit up. "You have said it true, 'diseased men.' Does the Lighthorse act now for the marshals?"

Lieutenant Oaks' face tightened. "As best we can. We

23

are under-strength; there are many inexperienced men with us. We are barely able to police the normal workings of the nation, let alone deal with a large number of bandits and border trash."

"Why have they done this?" the old man appealed.

"Apparently they are bent on a rampage through Tsalagi land. Now, we must make our investigation. I'll detail some men to help with the graves."

"You are kind, Lighthorse Oaks."

Lieutenant Oaks looked at him sadly. "They were our people, too."

"He was called Nighthawk Nail," Constable Monroe offered.

"His spirit and those of his family will be sung about at our fire tonight," Segeeyah Oaks promised.

Half an hour later, Segeeyah Oaks had learned all he believed he could from examining the scene of the murders. Such sights sickened him, sapped his spirit and left him feeling oddly confused as to what moved men to act in so savage a manner. He sat on the stoop of the burned out house and drafted a report on his findings, then summoned Wolf Wind.

"Pick a messenger and have him take this to Tahlequah. I want one patrol to set out now to follow the trail of the murderers. We'll spend the night and leave in the morning."

"Isn't there something more we can do for those people?" Wolf asked.

"We're going to. We'll find the ones who did it and see that they hang."

Three

Funny business, Walt Reiley thought to himself as the wagons rolled along on the highroad between Tahlequah and Fort Gibson, gateway to the Creek nation. He said as much to the young swamper on the seat beside him.

"Why's that, Mr. Reiley?" the youthful apprentice inquired.

"I've been a teamster for neigh onto fifteen years. Had this run for the last four. Supplies from the government to the Indians. Now the Cherokees are fightin' with the Confederacy, yet we get safe passage. Even if we did have to come down outta Kansas. How do you figger that, Kevin?"

Kevin Lowery shrugged. "I s'pose it's because we're takin' food an' stuff to other Injuns. We might be haulin' freight for the Union government, but we're helpin' those Cherokees' brothers."

Walt Reiley gave Kevin Lowery a long, speculative glance. "Y'know, you've got quite a head on those shoulders, boy. Don't know of all that many people could figure it out so quick."

"Oh—oh, what's this?" Lowery asked, glancing ahead to where three men sat their horses, blocking the highroad. They all wore leather trousers.

Reiley studied on them while he hauled on the reins of

the twelve mules that pulled his high-sided freight wagon. Behind him the other three teamsters called to their teams and slowed also.

"They appear to be white folk," Reiley remarked. "Doggies, I don't like the looks of this," he added as four more men rode abreast up out of a draw on their left.

Reiley started to say more, to be interrupted by a meaty smack and a sideward jerk of his head. Splattered with gore, young Lowery made a dive for the reins. He also let out a bellow of fright and alarm. Only then did his mind register the gunshot that had killed his friend and mentor. A second later, pain exploded in his chest and side, and a great wave of darkness crashed down on him.

Quickly, more of the Leatherlegs closed in on the wagons. None of the other drivers offered resistance. The cargo they hauled didn't belong to them. It did them little good. With cold determination, the hard-faced members of the Moritus Gang shot them one by one.

"Good job, boys," Long Tom Longdon praised when the last teamster and his swamper died. "Be careful around those mules; we're gonna have to haul this stuff off."

"Where we takin' it?" a young guerrilla asked.

"Along. Least 'till we find that valley the colonel's always talkin' about," Long Tom told him.

The youthful outlaw looked dubious. "Ain't there a fort just west of us? The one Danvers told us about yesterday."

"Right you are, boy. That's why we're headin' south to join back with the main company. These wagons will travel slow, so I want four good men to drive them. The rest of us will light out due south. I reckon you'll catch up day after tomorrow."

"Colonel Moritus should be glad to hear about this," another mean-eyed guerrilla observed.

"I'm sure he will be," Long Tom said through a snicker. "That's why we're goin' ahead to let him know. Now, dump them bodies, and the four of you who think you

26

know the most about mules pick swampers to help and get the wagons started."

With only thirty miles to cover, Long Tom and his crew of murderers reached the main column well before sundown. He went directly to where Augustus Moritus had his tent erected for the night. The self-styled colonel looked up expectantly when Longdon entered.

"You have brought me good news?" Moritus asked.

"Sure have. That feller with the loose jaw turned out to be right about the wagons. We got four big freighters loaded with supplies. There's flour, sugar, beans, corn-meal, barrels of corned pork an' beef. Better condition than what we used to get in the army, too."

"Any powder or ball?" Moritus probed.

"Nope. No sign of any. Did find some coffee beans. They need to be roasted."

Moritus beamed. "You've done well. I knew I'd made the right decision in putting you in charge. What about the drivers?" he asked, eyes narrowed.

"They won't be talkin' to anyone."

"Splendid. As my former inspiration used to say, the Lord provides."

"Who was that?" Recently come to the guerrilla band, Longdon did not know of Moritus' background.

"Why, John Brown, of course. Yes, I rode with the Jayhawkers in bloody Kansas. It was a splendid adventure."

"How'd you survive Harper's Ferry?" Longdon asked, unbelieving.

"Simply because I did not go. Shortly before that ill-thought expedition, I was asked to end my association with the group."

"Oh? What for? Couldn't handle all the preachin'?"

"No, Mr. Longdon. It appears I was too blood-thirsty for old John Brown's sanguine appetites. He didn't mind gunning down slavers. Or their wives and grown young-sters. But he drew the line at killing children too young to be any threat. He didn't seem to understand that they would become the next generation of slave-owners."

Suddenly uncomfortable, Tom Longdon made to leave. "Well, Colonel, I thought you'd want a report right off. I've got to go find my men something to eat."

"Yes—yes, you're excused. And, thank you again for a job well done."

"Uh—tell me, Colonel?" Longdon found himself asking in spite of his resolve not to. "Do you really feel that strongly about abolition?"

A small smile played on the thin, purple lips. "Not at all. In fact, I don't have any strong feelings either way. It was the killing I enjoyed."

Shocked, as though by a cold hand laid on his spine, Tom Longdon got out of the tent and as far away from Augustus Moritus as the camp would allow. No wonder Moritus had ordered those Cherokee children killed. The thought haunted Tom through the night.

Segeeyah Oaks sat by a small, low fire and considered the unseen enemy they followed. Wisely, the white intruders had bypassed Tahlequah to the north, then began to angle to the southwest. They left behind them a trail of wanton slaughter and pillage. Late that afternoon the Lighthorse had come across signs that indicated that a number of the party had diverted and taken the highroad that led to Fort Gibson and on into the Creek nation. What would that be for?

Rising, he spoke to Friday Whittler. "*Junhgilosdi,* take your patrol and Tom's and continue to follow the main body tomorrow. Charlie will come with me. We'll look into what these men intend by heading toward Fort Gibson. Are they Union soldiers?"

"Killing that family doesn't suggest that," Friday replied.

"We are at war with them," Segeeyah reminded him softly.

"But I don't see even Union soldiers killing children. Those kids had been strangled," Friday protested.

"To them, we're just wild Indians," Segeeyah stated bitterly.

"There's more to it than that."

Oaks looked sharply at Whittler and suddenly saw the matter clearly. "Yes, that's right. We're dealing with border guerrillas. I feel it in my bones. Men so depraved they don't give a damn about anything or anyone."

Heads nodded around the fire. Lieutenant Oaks bent to pour fresh coffee into his cup. "A good night's sleep, then, and we head out in the morning."

At mid-morning the next day, Lieutenant Oaks and Charlie's patrol came upon the bodies of four dead men and as many youths. All of them where white. Their bullet-riddled bodies had already begun to bloat. The Lighthorsemen looked on the scene expressionlessly. At last, Segeeyah Oaks spoke.

"It appears they don't care who they kill. From their clothes, I'd say these were teamsters."

"Where are their wagons?" *Jali* Singer asked.

"Taken, no doubt," Oaks said. "Charlie, it shouldn't be hard to find out which way they went. Have someone check it out, and we'll go after them."

Within ten minutes, Segeeyah Oaks and One Patrol set off in pursuit of the loaded wagons. Six men remained behind to take care of temporary burial for the victims. By late afternoon, Segeeyah came to regret his decision to leave them behind.

"They're right over that swell," Charlie Singer informed

Segeeyah Oaks. "I can hear the trace chains jingling."

Oaks brightened, though his smile was grim. "What say we take them now, before they have time to join up with any more."

Apparently being alone in hostile country had unnerved the guerrillas. Two of them opened fire the moment the Lighthorse appeared over the rolling prairie horizon. Encumbered with the heavy wagons, escape was impossible. Quickly they formed a quadrangle with the thick-sided vehicles.

"It's Injuns, by God," one border bandit blurted.

"Danged if they don't look like some kind of soldiers," another remarked.

"Don't give a damn if they're Reg—u—lars, they're comin' after us," a third advised his friends.

"It's them Cherokee policemen, I reckon," Silas Tanner suggested.

"Oh, shit, the Lighthorse. They're pi-son mean," Slick Willie Hillery advised in fright. An Arkansawyer, he had reason to know of the reputation of the Lighthorse.

"Less talk an' more shootin', idjit!" Yank Putnam, the man Long Tom Longdon had put in charge, snapped.

Lt. Segeeyah Oaks rode down on the laagered wagons with a sense of wonder. This was like fighting the whites on the plains, as told to him as a boy by Cheyenne and Kiowa visitors. For a moment, the unreality of it bemused him. Then bullets began to crack past overhead and to the sides. The Sharps came to his shoulder with ease.

A sharp blast and recoil and a spurt of smoke that wafted away on the rushing breeze sent a sudden charge through Segeeyah. Riding and shooting made for little accuracy, yet he reasoned it might keep down the heads of those bent

30

on killing him and his men. He levered open the breech block and inserted another paper cartridge.

Closing the lever, it sliced through the base of the fresh round, and Segeeyah fitted a cap on the nipple. With the hammer back, he gave little attention to his aim. The steel butt-plate kicked him again, and Segeeyah saw the bullet tear a shower of slivers from the side of one wagon. Not good, but it helped. The pair mounted on horseback made a sprint for an opening between the team of one wagon and the tailgate of another.

"Datli! Datli!," Segeeyah shouted, indicating the men who were making a run for it.

Three Lighthorsemen, including young Squirrel Three-Skulls, set off to intercept them at once. Light in weight, and on his powerful horse Blasting Powder, Squirrel quickly closed the distance. He ducked low on the neck of his muscle-churning mount as one guerrilla turned in the saddle to fire a revolver at the boy.

Quick as a rattlesnake, Squirrel came upright and swung the butt of his rifle. It impacted solidly in the bandit's rib cage and broke three bones before he tumbled from the plunging, frightened horse. At once, the boy reined in, reversed the weapon, and fixed the muzzle on his stunned captive.

"Osda dulvhwisdaneha," Oaks complimented the youngster as he trotted up close. "Good work, indeed. Keep an eye on him." Segeeyah drummed heels into the flanks of his horse and set off for where Johnny Walks-around was wrestling with the other fleeing brigand.

Johnny had to be in his 50s, and in respect for his age and for his prowess as a Lighthorseman, the men called him "Uncle." Through a laugh now, Segeeyah addressed the older man that way.

"Uduji, why don't you just hit him in the head with your war club?"

Walksaround grunted and slipped a hand from the grip

31

of his enemy. He grasped the haft of a war club and brought it free of the wide sash around his waist. With a solid rap, he subdued the white guerrilla. Then he turned a bleak expression on Segeeyah Oaks.

"It is not wise for a younger man to tell an older one his business. I fought tougher men than this when you were only a dream in your father's head."

Segeeyah took on a pained expression. "You wound me, Uncle. I know you will tie him securely. We have other work to do."

The matter of forcing entry into the square of wagons rested heavily on his mind. Sooner or later, one of those afoot, secure behind the thick walls, would get lucky and put a bullet into one of his men. Segeeyah Oaks wanted to prevent that if at all possible. He had a force of nine, against seven. No, make that six, he noted as one outlaw defender jerked backward and made three staggering steps before he fell face-first in the dirt.

"Charlie," Segeeyah yelled in Tsalagi over the din of the conflict, "keep them busy over on that side." He picked Robert Runningdeer and *Dlayhga* Mooney. "Come with me. We're going in the way they went out."

Bluejay Mooney grinned. "I don't think they will like that."

Segeeyah Oaks rode straight for the small gap, the two Lighthorsemen hard on the tail of his big-chested horse. All three tried to ignore the whipcrack of bullets around them as they drew near. Urging his mount in a gentle tone, Segeeyah Oaks forged through the gap.

"Easy, *Udehosati*, don't stumble now." Segeeyah had no idea why he had chosen to call his horse Bashful; he was anything but that. The snorting stallion, wall-eyed in fright from the nearly constant crash of discharging weapons, plunged into the open square formed by the stolen wagons.

Immediately, Segeeyah dismounted and slammed the

butt of his Sharps into the gut of a man who spun in an attempt to shoot the Lighthorseman. At such close range, the rifle became more of a hindrance than an aid. He laid it on the ground in a ducking move that had him on the run in the same instant.

His .44 Colt leading the way, Segeeyah headed for another of the killers. A slug popped loudly through the top of his turban, and Segeeyah sought the man who had fired it. He quickly found his target.

A huge, grinning lout of a man, Yank Putnam hastened to ear back the hammer of his Model '56 Remington. A ruptured cap hung up between the recoil plate and the cylinder, and the weapon failed to index. Cursing, Putnam fought with his free hand to manually turn the bulky piece of steel. While he did, Lt. Segeeyah Oaks closed and drove the guerrilla from his feet with a diving bearhug. They landed painfully on the malfunctioning revolver.

Oaks recovered first. He rolled to one side and made a grab for his sheath knife. It came free at the same moment Putnam swung the Remington, his fingers wrapped around the barrel. The buttgrip connected with the side of Segeeyah's head. Stars and ribbons of varying colors went off inside the Lighthorse officer's skull.

Blackness raced in to replace the fireworks. Oaks went to one knee and shook his head while he gasped to recover. He no longer held his knife, didn't know where it had gone. Slowly, vision returned to near normal, and he saw where he had left his blade. It rested to the hilt in the chest of Yank Putnam.

Slowly, the huge white man formed a soundless "Oh," went slack-limbed, and pitched forward onto the churned up ground. Segeeyah had recovered enough to stand. He did so to his regret as another of the white bandits leaped on his back. He clung with the tenacity of a cocklebur.

Segeeyah's powerful fingers dug into an iron bar

forearm in an attempt to fling the man off his back. His throat burned like he'd swallowed coals, and big, black snowflakes danced behind his eyes. Segeeyah could feel the strength flowing out of his body.

With the speed of an eyeblink, he considered and rejected possible means of dislodging the man who hung his whole weight on the arm around Segeeyah's throat. It seemed a day-long internal debate to the Lighthorseman, yet only seconds passed before he set his heels, flexed his knees, and surged upward. Arching his back, Segeeyah went over backward.

He landed with his full weight on the desperate white man. Air, and the sour odor of whiskey, gushed from the man's full lips. His grip on Segeeyah loosened. Segeeyah's hand scrabbled across the crushed turf to where his .44 Colt lay. Long fingers curled around the butt grip, and he hefted it. The man under him gathered his legs and made a violent lurch. Segeeyah flew off to the right and sprang to his feet as the guerrilla snatched a .36 Colt Navy from his waistband.

Oaks fired first. The .44 ball struck the white bandit in the breastbone and shattered it. Suddenly numb fingers released the small caliber Colt, which thudded on a tuft of trodden grass. Still highly charged from his struggle for life, Segeeyah eared back the hammer and put another .44 round into the dying man, who still stood on his rubbery legs. Sighing out blood bubbles, the Leatherleg sank to his knees and then toppled to one side, to curl in a tight ball.

Segeeyah discovered the fighting around him had ended. Three of the new recruits in Charlie's patrol gawked at him as though they had never seen two men fight before. Panting, Segeeyah Oaks surveyed the scene of battle.

"How many alive?" he queried.

"Only the two taken outside the laager," Charlie replied.

"Good enough. We'll get what we need to know from them," Segeeyah decided aloud.

After an hour of rough handling, Slick Willie Hillery decided to talk. "The man running our outfit is Augustus Moritus. He's supposed to have rid with John Brown. Tough as whang leather, so I reckon he might have at that. Funny thing, he never uses a cuss word. Not a one. Oh, he's no sissy-boy, but he don't hanker after women a-tall, nor does he swear or drink. Don't abide by any of us doing it in his company."

"Where is this band headed?"

Hillery shook his head and stared at the toes of his boots. "Don't rightly know. The colonel—ah—Moritus is always talkin' about this valley of promise he's lookin' for. Say, you speak mighty good English for an . . ."

"An Indian? We're civilized, Hillery. Compared to what your outfit has done, we're just about the most civilized people you'll ever see. Now, tell me, why did Moritus bring you here, to our nation?"

"Again, I don't know. 'Cept some Johnnny Rebs was chasin' us in Arkansas. We crossed over a river, and Colonel Moritus said we was in Injun Territory, an' the law would be no trouble to us any more."

Segeeyah gave him a tight smile. "You learned how incorrect that is. If anything, your fellow border trash are in for more trouble from our law than any they could imagine."

"You mean you folks have lawmen an' all like that?"

"Yes."

"Then you're gonna turn me over to the sheriff?"

"We don't have sheriffs. And we don't need to turn you over." Segeeyah showed Hillery his badge. "We're the Lighthorse. We are the law."

"Then what you gonna do with me an' Pete?"

"You'll be taken to Tahlequah and held for some disposition. If the authorities are seeing our current situation with the United States the way I am, we'll try you and execute the both of you. Along with your Colonel Moritus and the rest when we catch them."

Hillery recovered his courage enough to get a snotty tongue. "You talk mighty big for an Injun."

"Friend Hillery, you were knocked clear and the hell off your horse and made captive by a boy I'm willing to bet is no more than fourteen. What do you suppose one of us who is full-grown could do to you?"

Hillery swallowed hard and lost his moment's bravado. "I see what you mean."

"Which reminds me," Segeeyah said, rising from the prisoner. "Saloli, you'll ride along with Corporal Tall-corn and two others to escort the prisoners to Tahlequah. I want you to accompany the corporal when he reports to Colonel Hood. You made your patrol leader proud today, and made me mighty proud, too."

Young Squirrel swelled his chest with a hot gush of well-being. His sergeant and his detachment commander talking about him like he was a man full-size. He thought he would burst with how good it made him feel.

"Yes, sir, Lieutenant," Squirrel chirped. Then he frowned. That *damned* squeaky voice.

Desperation at the outlook for his future, Slick Willie blurted, "Ain't no gawdamned Injuns gonna torture me."

"You won't be tortured," Segeeyah assured him. "Worst that'll happen is you'll be stood against a post and shot. Or hanged."

Four

Dawn broke clear, and with a touch of coolness, over Fort Gibson. Right on time, the little six-pounder at the base of the flagpole banged off a blank, and the trumpeter released a cascade of shivery notes. The flag glided smoothly up the lanyard toward its place below the big brass ball. Standing on the only rampart, over the equally useless main gate, Col. Owen Bledsoe stiffened to attention and touched the brim of his plumed hat with fingertips in salute.

He shouldn't be here, Bledsoe told himself for at least the thousandth time. He belonged with the Army of the Potomac, facing those Rebel fiends. McClellan continued to hand the Union delay after delay and disaster after disaster. What was needed was an officer with dedication. Owen Bledsoe saw himself as such a man.

At a height of five foot eight, he did not cut an impressive figure. His receding chin and wispy, straw-colored hair, around a large expanse of bald pate, did little to aid such an image. Yet, he had about him an air of command and control that had earned him the nickname of *Colonel Ice* among the troops.

It amused him to know of this and know that the troops did not know. Which brought him back to the agenda for this day. The problem with desertions was a familiar one at any frontier outpost. Living and working conditions were appalling; dysentary and other diseases epidemic; danger from hostile action an almost constant. Small wonder some men found it all too much to endure. Yet, this relative backwater of frontier forts, located as it was between the Creek and Cherokee nations, had lately been subjected to a disproportionate number of leave-takers.

Perhaps it was the very "civilized" nature of these Indians that brought about that condition. At least on the northern plains the troops had the opportunity to kill a few of the pernicious savages. Yet, how could these soldiers desert? The United States was torn asunder, the Union in danger of dissolving. While here at Fort Gibson, they played nursemaid to "civilized" Indians. And all of them, Creek, Choctaw, and Cherokee alike, were Southern sympathizers, he thought disgustedly.

A last trill of brassy music faded away and Colonel Bledsoe lowered his arm. Of late, it had been his practice to attend reveille formation at this position. A reminder, perhaps, that this was not a true fort, but an expanded outpost. If ever these heathen redskins rose up, they could stream in between the buildings without the slightest hindrance.

Another item for officers' call. Of late, larger numbers of Creek had been gathering outside the fort. They set up their brush and skin lodges and settled in as though to make a permanent home. So far it didn't constitute a threat, merely an irritant. Col. Owen Bledsoe stiffened a second at the sound of footsteps on the planks behind him.

"Begging the Colonel's pardon, sir; breakfast is laid in the Colonel's quarters."

Bledsoe turned to look kindly on his orderly. "Thank you, Private Jennings. I trust the cooks have come up with something refreshing?"

"Oh, yes, sir. Biscuits and gravy, fried ham, three eggs,

potatoes, plenty of coffee, sir."

The same every blessed day, Bledsoe thought angrily. "I pray for the day the commissary runs out of ham," he said aloud, then amended it slightly at the scandalized expression of his orderly. "Not that ham is not a delightful breakfast choice, but I would gladly exchange Excaliber for a plate of bacon."

Mentioning his own beloved horse thawed the expression of Colonel Ice. "Very well, Jennings. I'll be along shortly."

"Yes, sir. Thank you, sir." The gangly private saluted and made a smart about-face.

Left alone again, Colonel Bledsoe clasped hands behind his back and stared out across the rolling prairie toward the gold-orange ball that rose through a slight mist. "The Cherokee are traitors," he spoke aloud thoughtfully. "They have thrown in their lot with the Rebels. Perhaps my concern should be directed not at the Creek, but beyond the rising sun."

Segeeyah Oaks awakened to an unaccustomed sense of unease. Had he made the right decision in sending the under-aged Saloli Juska-jo'i along with the prisoners to Tahlequah? Yes, of course he had, his reasoning side told him. After the brief, furious fight with the wagon escort, he had no doubt they were riding into something dangerous, even deadly. The little ripper, Squirrel, had spirit aplenty, granted. No need that he be sacrificed needlessly, though.

By now, the messenger would be at headquarters in Tahlequah. He wondered what the lawgivers would make of the news. No doubt it would set them off into endless debate over what course to follow. For his own part, Segeeyah knew how to handle this. Hunt down the guerrillas and eliminate them, like rabid coyotes. He came to his moccasins and folded the light blanket that had covered him.

"We'll eat and move on. I want to close with this so-called Colonel Moritus soon," he informed the Lighthorsemen.

Early morning saw the Cherokee nation's lawgivers hurrying toward the capitol in Tahlequah. They moved with efficient energy, forewarned of the topic that had called them from their homes and comfortable offices. When they arrived, they soon found they had not been misadvised.

"Judo," the Speaker addressed them as brothers, "we are met to discuss the growing problem of Union troops who are reinforcing the ring of forts around our nation." A rumble of soft comments went through the gathered representatives. "Fort Towson, in Choctaw country has been increased in size, and three hundred additional soldiers billeted there. Fort Washita in the land of the Chickasaw has also been strengthened. This is no doubt due to Texas joining the Confederacy. Worst of all, Fort Gibson has been reinforced with troops marching brazenly through our nation from Kansas." A mutter of anger answered him.

"What can we do about it?" one man asked. "Even most of the Lighthorse are off with Col—er—General Watie."

"You're right. That's the crux of our problem," the Spraker summed up. "Nearly all of the men of fighting age, including the Lighthorse, are serving with Gen. Stand Watie, fighting with the Army of Tennessee, although the treaty expressly forbids that. It has left us with hardly the nucleus of a cadre to train new lawmen, let alone any surplus of men willing to fight if necessary."

"Colonel Drew is doing his best with the First Regiment of Mounted Rifles," another lawgiver argued.

"Where and when he can," the Speaker injected. "That

still leaves a vast area unprotected."

"What can the Confederate soldiers do to help?" a portly lawgiver from Going Snake District demanded.

"Nothing. They aren't here to police the nation," the man next to him answered.

"Those of us who came reluctantly to the consensus on a treaty with the Confederacy warned of this situation," a Ross faction representative reminded the assembly. "Since we entered this war on the United States, we have known nothing but shortage. A shortage of men for the harvest, to tend herds, even to police the nation. So much so that these Union soldiers swaggered right through the nation without so much as a by-your-leave. They ignored all protests. Why, it's a wonder they didn't simply march on Tahlequah and seize the government."

Smiling, the Speaker answered him. "I think the American government finds us a too-large bite to swallow. From the start, they expressed respect for Chief Ross, and have denied that a state of war exists. It would look foolish of them, I suspect, were they to now capture our capital and declare us vanquished. The big question that should haunt all of us is, will this military move establish a precedent? Will the whites now flood in to once more take away our land, using this war as an excuse?"

Shouts of outraged protest rose from the standing lawgivers. Several proposals came on the floor. All failed to win enough support for passage. At noon, they recessed for a meal. When they returned, the messenger sent by Lieutenant Oaks had arrived and been brought over by an officer from Lighthorse headquarters. The grizzled old captain, recalled to service by the thinning of ranks, sent in a note and was soon summoned by the doorkeeper.

He walked with purpose to the podium and brought the messenger along. "Gentlemen . . . brothers, we have received disturbing news at headquarters during the noon hour. A band of border guerrillas, estimated to number between forty and fifty desperate men, has crossed over into the nation. They have killed a family in Going Snake District and are being trailed westward by Lt. Segeeyah Oaks and his detachment.''

"Quantrill!" one lawgiver shouted.

"Bill Anderson," another suggested.

"No, no. They are not Confederates. That much we know. As for the rest, more messages are to follow. Something must be decided as to how to handle this."

"Was Colonel Hood informed?" the Speaker asked.

"Not as yet."

"Then I'll entertain a motion to send a page to summon Col. Gavin Hood so we may consult with the head of the Lighthorse and lay some basis of action."

Gavin Hood sat at the table with his wife, the former Greenleaf Sixkiller, and their four children in their home in Tahlequah. The remains of a roasted chicken lay on a platter in the center. A bowl still held a few slices of stewed turnip, while corn cobs had been piled high on another platter. Greenleaf gave her husband a fond, admiring look.

The woman must be befuddled, Gavin thought for a countless time. His was a face to frighten babies. Not that he came by it other than honorably. Missing his left earlobe, one eye, and three fingers, he had suffered the losses in service to the Lighthorse. His own children had accommodated to it well enough, he had to admit.

Gavin's eldest son worked for the *Cherokee Phoenix*, the universal newspaper in the nation. He came home every day for his noon meal. The youngest three still attended school. They, too, came home to eat. They all apparently adored their father. Even when he had been recalled to the Lighthorse, his offspring had greeted the news with good cheer. Not so, Greenleaf. Not even the news of his brevet advancement to Colonel had altered her dislike of his service.

That would change, he decided, as a knock sounded at the door. "Go see who that is, *Walela*," he said to his daughter.

At thirteen, Hummingbird Hood had already taken on the form and figure of a young woman. Her trim waist she liked to accentuate with a tight band of bright ribbon, and her long hair shone with a special gloss, born of hours of brushing. She walked with grace to the door and responded with only a slight expression of surprise to find a lad her own age, a page to the lawgivers, standing there.

"I have a message for Colonel Hood," he informed her in a formal tone.

"Do come in," Walela invited.

Obviously nervous, the boy entered and walked directly to the table. "Colonel Hood, the compliments of the Speaker, and would you report at once to the capitol?"

"Ummm, some life-or-death situation, no doubt," Gavin Hood teased.

Looking grave, the youth responded seriously, "Yes, sir. It is. White guerrillas have entered the Tsalagi nation. Your advice is needed for a decision to be made."

Startled, Gavin Hood rose at once. "I see. I'll come immediately." He excused himself and went to his room, where he put on the minimal items that comprised his uniform.

With the youngster fairly skipping to keep pace, Gavin Hood set out at a brisk pace for the capitol.

Leige Tanner was one-quarter Cherokee. He had lived the whole of his twenty-three years in the nation, although he often wondered why. The other Cherokees treated him like a white most times. Whites saw him as an Injun brat as

43

a child. Born of two worlds, he didn't fully belong in either. Except for here, on the job. The drivers, station-masters, and wranglers of the stage line saw him carrying his load and treated him like all the rest.

Being a shotgun guard carried responsibility. Leige believed that he, even more than the driver, was directly responsible for the passengers and any valuables on the run. It made him doubly alert, particularly in these long, lonesome passages with few farms and towns between relay stops and way stations. Old Plummer liked to joke about it. He had started in early this run.

"Elijah, your knuckles are going to lock permanent in place if you keep squeezing that shotgun so hard," he croaked now as they topped a rise on the road from Claremore to Tahlequah.

"It pays to be ready," Leige replied defensively. He was not about to allow as how he took his job too seriously.

It paid off this time as six heavily armed and masked men appeared suddenly on the reverse slope beyond the crest. Leige saw them at once and reckoned correctly that they intended to rob the stage. He swung down the twin-barreled Greener and triggered a load of buckshot. It instantly cleaned one highwayman from the saddle.

Immediately the others opened fire. Leige sent a second column of shot toward the holdup men before three .44 balls smacked into his torso. Heat bloomed deep in Leige's chest and belly, and he lost his grip on the shotgun. His mouth went suddenly dry, and a dizziness swept over him. He tried to cry out, but could make no sound.

More shots blazed from the robbers, and Plummer cried out in agony as a red stain spread on his left shoulder. Two of the gunmen matched speed with the lead team and slowed the six plunging horses.

"You hold them steady, hear?" a masked man commanded the wounded driver. He rode on to the side door as Plummer tied off the tight-hauled reins to the brake lever.

"All right, folks, come out of there. Time to make a little donation."

Frightened or flustered, as their natures dictated, the passengers eased their way out of the coach. "Line up along the side, folks," the leader ordered.

Two of the bandits dismounted and passed along the line of wide-eyed people, burlap bags in hand. One of them repeated to each victim, "Drop everything of value in the bag, folks. Drop it all in the bag."

One woman swept openly and muttered low protests through trembling lips. A man in a stylish suit blustered, "Now, see here, there's no call for this."

Yellowed, horsey teeth showed in a flash of smile. "Yes, there is. We want what you've got. Simple as that."

One passenger, a man darker than the others, remained quiet. He folded his arms across his chest and stared hard at the outlaws. When the robbers approached him, he spoke in a level, unfrightened tone. "I have nothing but my medicine bag. It is of no value to you or anyone else."

"We'll be the judge of that. Hand it over."

"Sorry. I cannot." So saying, the tough-minded Cherokee removed his hands from his armpits.

One hand held a push-dagger which he swiftly rammed into the chest of the nearest outlaw. Acting with equal speed, he yanked the dying man in front of himself and relieved the *yoniga* of his revolver. Before the Cherokee could bring the weapon to bear, two slugs popped loudly as they entered his skull.

He fell instantly, to lay lifeless on the ground. The other collector stepped over and fumbled through his clothing. From under the dead man's shirt he removed a small deerskin bag. This he opened and looked up with incomprehension at the leader.

"Heck, ain't nothin' here but some scraggly old feathers, a dried bird's foot, an' some rocks. Not worth dyin' for, I'd say."

"No matter," the faceless one in charge responded. "Finish off the rest of them as well."

"NO!" the woman shrieked. "Think of my children," she babbled on.

"Perhaps, madam, I am," the leader advised her, before he shot her between the eyes. A flurry of reports marked the end for the remaining passengers and the driver. "Get the strong box, and let's move out. Colonel Moritus is going to appreciate this day's work."

At the capitol, Colonel Hood went directly to the Speaker's desk, where aged Captain Seeker talked animatedly with the house leader. Several acquaintances among the lawgivers called out questions to him. When Gavin Hood reached the cluster around the table, he spoke in low, strained tones.

"What exactly is going on? The page said something about an invading force of guerrillas."

Quickly the Speaker filled in the missing information and briefly discussed the ramifications of the various courses of action suggested so far by the lawgivers. Then the Speaker restored order and addressed the assembly.

"We've asked Colonel Hood here to advise us. So I'll ask the question directly. Given the circumstances, what is there that we can do?"

Gavin Hood considered it a moment, then spoke to all of them. "About the Union forces occupying the forts, nothing. At least for the time being. It appears to me we have a major threat in these border ruffians. I will immediately dispatch units of the Lighthorse to round up and bring in for trial the white invaders."

"Objection," called an agitated lawgiver. "We are under obligation to turn white offenders over to white justice. Considering the war, exactly who is it that we surrender them to?"

"Why, the U.S. Marshals, don't you know anything?" a colleague snapped.

"Not so," a third countered. "With our treaty with the Confederates, our responsibility to the American lawmen no longer exists."

"Then to the Confederate authorities. After all, Arkansas is part of the Confederate States of America."

Hood thought it prudent to insert a little calm and careful consideration. "I think the folks in Arkansas are busy enough right now, without having to tend to our obligations. It's clear to me that we no longer owe anything to a country with which we are at war. The nearest U.S. Marshals are in Kansas, anyway. Anyone want to take a little ride up to Kansas?"

"What! Those Jayhawker killers may love the nigras, but they consider us worse than things that live under a rock," an angry lawgiver blurted.

"True thing," another agreed. "We're not only Indians, some of us own slaves, and we are allied with the Confederacy. Not a chance I'd go up there."

Colonel Hood raised his arms, palms outward. "There you have it. We needn't burden our Confederate allies with criminals from the nation. The Mounted Rifles are under military orders of the Confederacy. So we have an obligation to our own people to keep the peace. Remember, a Tsalagi family has been brutally murdered already. Who knows how many more have suffered? I'll send sufficient additional Lighthorse to see that the ones responsible will be brought to Tahlequah for trial and execution. It's become our duty, brothers."

On that somber note, the lawgivers thanked Hood, and he departed to assume this new, heavy burden. A life of service to one's country could be a swift pain, he reflected as he walked down the steps of the capitol.

Five

An old woman and two somber-eyed children came up out of the root cellar. They stared unmovingly at the Lighthorsemen reined in at the smoldering ruins of the farmhouse. Slowly, tears welled up in the eyes of the little girl. Her older brother, who couldn't be more than eight, sniffled and fought back sobs that threatened to burst out.

"You Lighthorse, you are too late," the ancient woman accused. "The *diyoniga* came and killed my son, his woman, two of their children. We are smarter than those people. We run and hide in the ground. No one see us. You come too late."

"When?" Segeeyah Oaks asked.

"Yesterday, with the sun. Many white men, many *diyoniga*, come," the woman informed him.

"We're not far behind them," Wolf Wind remarked in a growl.

"A day and a half. Not bad. They are bearing more to the south now. We'll catch up before long. When we do, I'll be honest, I'd like to have more men along."

"They worry you, Segeeyah? So far they've attacked peaceful people, or someone they way outnumbered," Wolf advised.

"Evil men like this have a way of attracting more of their

kind. I wouldn't be surprised to find they are a lot stronger now. Even for the losses they have taken."

Wolf smiled at that. "We've found plenty of their bodies. Even here. No one is giving in easily."

"That's why scum like this don't like it where the whole countryside can be armed," Segeeyah Oaks observed. "People who can protect themselves make poor victims."

"Or costly victims, from an outlaw's view," Wolf amended. "It's a good thing we kept that part from the American Constitution about the right to keep and bear arms in ours."

Segeeyah snorted. "Where do you think most of that sort of thing came from? Remember in school, what we learned about the Confederation of Onandaga? Our people have always known that safety and freedom only come from having the arms to protect them. Enough, I'm beginning to sound like a teacher."

"Maybe an *ahljadohvsgi*," Wolf jibed with a nudge of his elbow in Segeeyah's ribs.

"*Yoah* protect me from sounding like a parson," Segeeyah answered, laughing. "We have things to do here, small ones to comfort, graves to dig. We'd better get started."

Halfway through the digging of graves, a messenger charged up the rutted lane and reined in. "Lieutenant Oaks," he called out. Sgt. Friday Whittler pointed to where Segeeyah Oaks squatted beside the two children. Dismounted, the young Lighthorseman crossed the farmyard with a dispatch extended in one hand.

"Lieutenant Oaks, sir. Compliments of Colonel Hood, and would you leave immediately for the Downing Convention Ground to meet with Captain Conroy?"

"Yes. Uh—give me half an hour. These youngsters have just lost their parents to the guerrillas. I'm almost through talking with them."

"Yes, sir. I am to accompany you, sir; also, you are to bring one of your detachment sergeants."

"Sounds important," Segeeyah said.

"I believe it is, sir."

Further to the south, in a lush, green valley formed by the flood plain of Pecan Creek, Colonel Moritus and his band of brigands had made an early camp. The horses, securely hobbled, grazed contentedly on the thick grass, while many of the men made use of the warm water of the creek to wash away days of accumulated dirt, sweat, and odor. Augustus Moritus sat on a camp stool, his back against the rough bark of a blackjack pine, and waved an arm expansively at the surrounding terrain.

"This is what I have been talking about, promising to the men. Only much bigger, of course. With higher walls to conceal our presence. We could live out the rest of our days in such a bastion."

"I'd get bored to the jeeber-jabbers," one crusty, ten-year veteran of the border fighting remarked.

"Come now, Hollister," Moritus gently chided. "Wouldn't you like a secure, bountiful place from which to conduct your raids?"

"'Course. Anyone would. We had one up in Missouri. At least until them damned slaver trash under Bill Anderson runned us out."

A vertical trough formed a scowl briefly between the bushy eyebrows of Augustus Moritus, then he produced a bleak smile. "I gather you did not share the pro-slave sentiments of old Bloody Bill."

"Not by a long sight. Truth is, that's why I throwed in with you. I aim to make some of these Rebel Injun trash pay."

"A noble cause, I assure you. Now then," Moritus directed to Silas Tanner, "what is this about seeing signs of someone else encamped around here?"

"That's right, Colonel. Me an' the boys come on some fire pits, couldn't be more'n a couple of days old."

"They could be miles from here."

"Didn't look like they were in any hurry to leave. The way I figure it, they took to the trees to give us a look-over. Might be they're fellers on the dodge, too," Tanner speculated.

"Set up sentries," Moritus instructed Danvers. "Have them doubled in number after dark. Ride all around our campsite. Make sure they let no one in without being identified."

"Yep, Colonel. I wondered when you was gonna take to doin' that," Quint Danvers responded. "Seein' as we're most surely in hostile country now."

"Yes. Which reminds me. We received a windfall from that stagecoach robbery this morning. In addition to the money in the strong box. An excellent map of this Cherokee nation. Quite detailed." Augustus Moritus removed it from an inner coat pocket and unfolded it onto his knees. "I'm thinking that we should be seeking our promised land somewhere in one of these southern districts. Illinois or Canadian."

"How the devil did Injuns come to be callin' parts of their country by names like that?" Quint asked, genuinely puzzled.

Augustus Moritus returned him an expression of guileful slyness. "Haven't you been listening to those we have overtaken in our journey? We're dealing with 'civilized' Indians. They even have a written language. It's said that more Cherokees can read and write their own tongue than can white people in America."

"Now I can't believe that," Quint growled, annoyed at the prospect.

"I've had it on the best of authority that they can. For instance, can you read English or any other language?"

Danvers produced a pained expression. "That don't have a danged thing to do with it. No. No, I can't." He gave Moritus a "so there" look.

"And how many others do you suppose are just like

51

you?" the guerrilla leader probed.

"Jist about anybody what don't live in one of them big, fancy cities back East. Schools is few an' far between elsewhere."

"To conclude your illustration, there are tens, hundreds, nay millions of us who are blessed by being born white. The Cherokees teach their children to read and write in their homes, long before their formal education begins at about eight years of age. How many white parents do you believe could, or would do that?"

Danvers' brow wrinkled. "That ain't fair. They's borned different from us. An' dang it, Mr. Colonel Moritus, danged if I don't think you're sayin' they're better than us."

Augustus Moritus started to unleash a hot retort, then caught his breath to hold it in. His face took on a strangely serene expression. "You know, Mr. Danvers, you might not be far wrong. Ah, well, it is always more noble to have a superior enemy to defeat. Don't you think?"

Nonplused, Quint Danvers wandered away, muttering to himself.

Shortly after a quarter past eleven the night broke its silence with a shouted alarm and the flat report of a discharged revolver. Augustus Moritus and the camp came alive in an instant. Only the past experiences of the hard cases gathered in the confines of the encampment prevented a disastrous free-for-all shoot out. With a fire rekindled and two torches flaming, the center area around the tent occupied by Moritus gave off a soft, yellow glow by the time two sentries frog-marched a scraggly-bearded man into the ring of grim-faced guerrillas.

"Make some account for yourself," Moritus demanded.

"Sure, yer honor. I'm Rand Yates. Randolph Yates, that is. Late of the Union Army and damn glad to be shut of it. Who might you be?"

Quint Danvers delivered a backhand, his rock jaw and glittery black eyes alight with yellow highlights from the firebrands. "Watch that mouth of yours."

"Hit me hard like that again and I suppose I might be able to, what with an eyeball on my cheek. Ah, well," Yates sighed. "It was this mouth got me in trouble with the army. Floggin's not a pretty sight, especially when you're on the receiving end."

"We'll see that if you please," Augustus Moritus commanded imperiously.

Quint Danvers yanked up the deserter's shirt. Dark red weals ran in cross-hatch over his back. He had taken a good set of ten, perhaps more than once. There appeared older, white lines below the freshly healing stripes. Quint lowered the shirt, almost gently.

"They're for real, all right, Colonel."

Yates went rigid, his face blank. "Well, now, if I've run into a colonel, perhaps I've overplayed my hand."

"A title of convenience, my good fellow," Moritus assured him. "I lead a budding regiment, so I felt I should have the rank. After all, Bill Quantrill has no more men than me any more, and he's a genuine colonel, with Confederate commission papers and all."

For all his lowly station, Rand Yates' eyes narrowed, and his lip curled in disgust. "You running the border for the Rebs?"

"No. We only take care of ourselves. It is a for pure profit proposition," Augustus Moritus advised. "Are you alone, then, Mr. Yates?"

"Not exactly. I have sixteen other lads who, for one reason or another, have taken their leave of the Union blue."

"Would they be willing to join a going and prosperous expedition?" Moritus probed.

"May-hap. I'd have to ask." In fact, the men had all but begged Yates to present himself and make the best deal possible.

53

Quint Danvers shoved his face up close to the unshaven Rand Yates. "Suppose you just do that. In fact, why not take one of us back with you to explain the deal to your friends."

"Well now, they might not accept that," Yates bargained with an empty sack.

"They'll accept it, or they can just go to He—ah—go to the devil," Danvers said heatedly.

Yates picked up on it right away. "No cussin' allowed in your outfit, eh, Colonel? Tell me, what good's a man who can't swear a blue streak? He'd not keep his stripes, or his teeth, a week in any man's army."

"Profanity is a snare of the devil, Mr. Yates," Augustus Moritus stated piously.

"Oh, Christ, we're gettin' in with a bunch of Holy Joes," Yates sighed in exasperation.

"That had better have been a sincere prayer, Mr. Yates, or your back will be host to another set of those stripes of shame," Moritus warned through gritted teeth. "To blaspheme is the foulest of sins."

Yates decided right then. Of course, having his hat, not his head, shot off in the dark of night had begun to convince him already. "It was. Sweet Jesus, it surely was."

"I'm pleased. That's a good fellow, now, Mr. Yates. Go along with you, and I shall send one of my lads in company to visit your companions."

This one's missin' the roof to his outhouse, Rand Yates thought as his captors led him away.

They came in an hour after sunup. Seventeen scruffy-looking men, most of whom wore remnants of uniforms, the blue of Union soldiers. Most had retained their kepi field caps, and Augustus Moritus recognized the pale blue trousers and yellow stripes of cavalry on three men. Disconcertingly, he also saw the blood-red stripes on two pair of trouser legs that denoted artillery. If the Union had sent field guns into the nations, his grand ambition could be in jeopardy. From the group, his own men came forward with Rand Yates, who gave a jaunty half-salute.

"Mornin', Colonel," Yates drawled. "These are my boys. We done voted to jine up if you'll take us in."

"As it happens, Mr. Yates, I have need of a few good men," Moritus told him with dry sarcasm. "Only one question. When the going gets rough, do you intend to desert my cause as you did your army?"

Rand Yates blinked. "That's unfair, Colonel Moritus. What we objected to was being treated like dogs, beat like animals, and fed worse than vulture's grub. Even on the march, I've seen that your boys eat better than any company I've ever carried a rifle in."

"That's reasonable enough," Moritus observed.

"Yes, sir. You feed us decent, look out for our other needs, we'll stand by you to the end," Rand promised. He hated to grovel like this, especially to a prissy old preacher like Moritus. But he and the others had gone hungry a long time, done worse than even in the army.

"Do we get paid?" asked one of the cavalry deserters.

"In goods and services, like the rest of us, my good man," Moritus answered coldly. "At least until we are established securely and can undertake to relieve plump banks of their hard money."

"Cheap ol' fart, you ask me," the ex-cavalryman grumbled.

"You lock a lip over that kinda talk, or I'll bust your skull," Rand growled. The man quailed.

Sudden realization came to Augustus Moritus as to how Rand Yates had established, and maintained, dominance over these hard-bitten fugitives. He appreciated the judicious employment of that method. Armed, desperate men were dangerous men.

"Very well, Mr. Yates. See that your men are fed and supplied with powder and ball. We decamp in an hour,"

Augustus Moritus rapped out, as he turned on one heel to stalk back to his tent.

Both prisoners grumbled at the discomfort of being bundled onto their horses by their Lighthorse captors. Young Squirrel looked hotly at Slick Willie Hillery and tried to force his voice to a lower register.

"Keep that mouth shut, or I'll belt you with a rifle butt again," the boy warned.

"Kid, when we get shut of these chains, I'm gonna whup your butt like your pappy should have done long ago. Then I'm gonna use you like a woman."

Pete Carter stepped close to Slick Willie's horse, sunlight glinting off the seven pointed star and wreath of his badge. "Mister, we have orders to deliver you to Tahlequah. They don't say nothin' about bringing you in alive."

Hillery sneered. "Hidin' behind this green-horn, huh, kid?"

A knife flashed in Pete's hand, his face darkened with menace. "In the old days, our people used to take heads. Would you like to add yours to the collection?"

Eyes fixed on the threatening blade, Slick Willie swallowed hard. "N-No. Nothin' meant by it. Just raggin' the kid a bit, all right?"

Squirrel Three-Skulls looked up at Pete Carter. "Even if we have to turn them over to the U.S. Marshals, they'll hang, won't they?"

"I think you can count on it."

Squirrel shifted his gaze to Hillery. "That'll shut your smart mouth, won't it?"

That kid's hard as nails. The thought was shared by the two guerrillas and Pete Carter.

Six

Fierce oaths filled the air, along with dust, powder smoke, and heat. The shooting exercise went well enough, and the Downing Convention Ground on Blackbird Creek provided long enough ranges to satisfy the requirements of marksmanship, such as they were, for membership in the Lighthorse. Until recently, that is, Capt. Chad Conroy amended.

Some whizzer, whose family had remained in North Carolina and had recently come out to the Cherokee nation after service in the United States Army, had brought along the conviction of the value of the prone position. To many old-timers, lying on one's belly, ideally behind a mound of protecting dirt, seemed a cowardly way to engage one's enemy. A veteran of the most perilous campaign of the Lighthorse, Chad Conroy wasn't all that sure. Providing the smallest target for your enemy seemed a good idea.

In the fight against the mad Col. Britton Ashley and his Texas vigilantes, in which Chad had lost the lower half of his left arm, they had unwittingly invented prone firing from rifle pits, and it had worked excellently. So, when he had been recalled to active service with the Lighthorse, Chad had welcomed the innovation. He did not welcome the assignment of providing the basic knowledge of Lighthorse duties to a flock of hopelessly aged and painfully young raw recruits.

Nevertheless, that assignment had been given him by Colonel Hood. He watched now as each muzzle blast raised another cloud of dust and powder smoke. On a nearly airless day like this, it prevented the men from seeing their bullet's strike. Chad wished mightily that they had some means of marking the targets so that the goal of accuracy would at least be achievable.

Not that his forty recruits were strangers to firearms and accurate shooting, Chad reminded himself. They had all grown up hunting and participating in marksmanship contests at family and clan gatherings. It became another story, Chad knew well, when someone was shooting back at a person. All of one's cool-headed accuracy tended to go out the smoke hole.

"Don't matter which way we turn them, *Adlameha*," Lt. Everet Vann observed, using Chad's Tsalagi name, Bat. "Without a breeze, they don't see anything but dust and smoke."

"We might as well end this, Ev," Chad advised. He and Everet had been friends longer than their service in the Lighthorse, and Chad welcomed Everet's service with him in this difficult time. Vann had an instinctive ability to deal with the new men and get quick results. "We can drill them in riding and firing at targets in a line of skirmishers," Chad suggested. "Do you think they'll show any improvement, Ev?"

Lieutenant Vann snorted. "If some of those kids can keep from falling off this time, I'd say yes. Otherwise, it's gonna be a disaster."

Captain Conroy sighed. "Like yesterday, and the day before, and the day before that. Point well made. Have the sergeants end this waste of time and powder and have them get to it. I'm headed for the creek. *Jisgwogwo* took his little brothers down for a swim."

Robin Conroy had attained the ripe old age of nine and swam like a fish. Yet his father worried about him as much as his younger brothers, Stivi, six, and Wili, five. All three were enough to wear down any man with two arms. They feared nothing, and Chad encouraged them in this . . . to a point. A little overseeing of their adventures he considered definitely in order. With a casual wave he turned his horse to the east and the bank of Blackbird Creek.

There he found his boys splashing in the water, bare as the day they were born. Robin took the lead as usual in their daring-do. At present, he was jumping off an overhang some eight feet high into a backwater pool deep enough to absorb his mass when he struck the surface. To Chad's surprise, Stivi hesitantly followed his older brother's lead.

Squealing in delight, the small boy hurtled off the lip of the grassy bank and plummeted down to the water. A crystal spray rose from the impact. A loving and indulgent parent, Chad felt a moment of apprehension until Stivi's head broke clear of the reddish tint of the water, and he began to dog paddle toward the lower bank. He came out smeared with mud. Already Robin had climbed again toward the jump-off. Stivi followed.

They saw their father when they reached the summit and waved enthusiastically. Chad returned the gesture, then froze at the piping sound of his youngest son's voice. "Look at me, Poppa! *Ni! Ni-na!*" he cried. "Look here," he repeated. "I can swim all the way across."

"No! Wili, don't do it," Chad shouted hoarsely.

But it was already too late. The little boy pushed off from the shallows, in the safety of limits imposed by his father, and struck out across the creek. After half a dozen strokes of his small arms, the swift course caught him, and he struggled futilely to make headway. Quickly sapped of his strength, the small lad cried out in terror as the current grabbed him and began to sweep him downstream.

Chad came off his horse without conscious direction. His legs churned as he ran for the bank. His one hand fumbled at his waist to free him of the cartridge belt and heavy Remington revolver that hung from it. He hurtled clumsily outward and arched his back. He took the violent contact with the water on his barrel chest, his arms and legs thrashing to give him momentum.

Through the water streaming over his eyes, he dimly made out the black dot of his son's head. Hell of a thing for a one-armed man to have to do, he thought giddily. Nature had compensated for the partial missing limb by strengthening the other and his powerful torso. Gradually, the distance closed. Then sudden fear stabbed at Chad's heart.

Wili lay face-down in the water, his tiny back breaking the surface. He had stopped fighting entirely. He could drown before help reached him, Chad realized with a terrible pang. He forced renewed effort into his handicapped body. Chad gulped and sputtered on a mouthful of water and, when his eyes cleared, he saw he was within reach of his son.

His legs thrashed again, and the distance closed. Burning with desperation, he flung out his good arm and closed his fingers on Wili's limp wrist. He jerked the boy to him and nudged his slack-necked head up on his shoulder. Slowly, Chad relaxed. His legs sank, and he felt sandy bottom under his moccasins.

Gingerly, he tested his foothold and took a couple of tentative steps. Confidence growing, he strode toward the bank. Careful to see that Wili's head hung downward, he shifted the youngster higher up in his grasp until the point of his right shoulder rested under the boy's diaphragm. Wili's flaccid head wobbled from side to side.

Suddenly the boy began to gulp and choke. Sputtering, he ejected a stream of creek water from his open mouth. Gratitude to all the Spirits flooded Chad Conroy. The water came only to his knees now. He made better time the last twenty feet. Wili had begun to sob and cry pitifully, still expelling spurts of reddish water from deep inside him.

Chad came up onto the grassy bank, his other sons crowded around him, jumping with their anxiety and relief. He looked up to see two mounted, turbaned riders looking on impassively. The younger one stammered as he spoke.

"M-Message for Ca—Captain Conroy. I was told he could be found here at the creek."

"I'm Conroy," Chad said, dripping wet, the naked child still upended over his shoulder.

"You . . . are?" His amazement was clear to see.

"My sons were swimming. The littlest got carried away," Chad explained in a way that added to the messenger's consternation. "Who might you be?" he addressed the other Lighthorseman.

"Lt. Segeeyah Oaks. I have orders to report to you, Captain."

"*Sio*, Oaks. I—ah—generally don't meet young officers sopping wet," Chad began.

"No problem for me, sir. I have younger brothers who have plagued me for years."

Chad's brow wrinkled. "Oh, I remember you now, Oaks. You look a little grave."

"That's . . . because . . ." Segeeyah began to explain, interrupted by little guffaws, that grew to outright, belly-deep laughter, "I'm trying . . . to keep . . . a straight face, sir."

"I fail to see the great humor in it all, Lieutenant," Chad began, disapprovingly, his dignity wounded.

"You can let me go now, please, Poppa," young Wili implored from Chad's shoulder.

"I've a good mind never to let go of you again, boy," Chad snapped to his son, his great love for the child overriding his usual even hold on his emotions.

"Being wet isn't what I'm getting at, Cap'n Conroy. It's just that I've never before reported to a superior who had a bare butt on one shoulder."

Chad swiftly lowered Wili and gave him a gentle shake of one shoulder. "You could have died out there, son. I make you stay in the little pool for a good reason. You aren't as strong as your brothers. The water can be fun, but it is dangerous, too. You remember that and never, never go out in the current again."

"Yes, Poppa," the five-year old replied, thoroughly chastened.

"Go on, now." Chad then turned his gaze to Oaks. "Excuse me, I had to make the point while it was fresh in his mind. You know," he went on, a hint of smile lifting the corners of his full lips, "it is sort of funny. I squish when I move."

"No offense meant, Captain," Segeeyah began, then started laughing again as he went on, "only dripping wet, with that little boy hung over your shoulder, you did look awfully funny." He continued to laugh until a shrill yell from Robin Conroy cut through.

"Stivi, look out!"

Chad and Segeeyah turned as one and rushed to the edge of the bank. They made it in time to see little Stivi Conroy struck by a mostly submerged snag that came whirling down the swift channel of Blackbird Creek. Instantly, Chad took on the look of having received a powerful physical blow.

Winded, his strength sapped by the rescue of one son, he now saw another in deadly danger. A low moan escaped his lips, and he started forward. Segeeyah Oaks read his intention and spoke sharply.

"No, let me. I'll get him for you."

Without giving time for Chad to reply, Segeeyah dived into the creek and began a strong crawl stroke toward where the small boy had gone down. He reached it quickly enough and sucked in air before turning upside down in a surface dive.

A murky light passed through the water, enough to give Segeeyah a sense of direction. Although he worked more by feel than sight, he wormed his way back and forth over the bottom with desperate speed. Twice he believed he had found the boy, only to discover that his fingers grasped strands of tough water grass. Burning lungs forced him to the surface.

Segeeyah gulped quicky and dived again. This time he worked a bit farther downstream. He made wide sweeps with his arms, kicking himself along with his feet. Seconds ticked away, and he began to suspect his efforts were for nothing. Then his fingertips touched something cold and smooth.

Instantly he whirled in the water and groped for the object. It had moved away. Fighting a growing sense of defeat, Segeeyah forced himself to move with the current, again casting over a broad area. That touch came again, like frigid silk. He forced himself to keep steady in relationship to it and reached again. He felt lumps, like the knobs of vertebra.

With both hands, he explored further. An arm! Faint-headed from the used-up oxygen in tortured lungs, Segeeyah pulled the small form tight to his chest, blew out his stale air and shot upward, propelled by his powerful legs. His head broke the surface with a roaring demand for breath.

He greedily sucked in the warm air and sputtered to keep water out of his mouth. He clumsily fitted the unconscious boy on his back, held him in place by his chin clamped down on one small arm, and began to swim back to shore. Faintly he heard the voices of two men and a child yelling encouragement. He put more effort into his strokes.

The creek bed came up abruptly to grate against his chest. Quickly he stopped his struggles and got his knees under him. He raised up and then carefully came to his feet. Eager hands reached out to give aid.

"Here, hold on," Chad Conroy urged. "We'll pull you out. Give me the boy."

Giddy from his exertion and a lack of air, Segeeyah quipped, "How can I do that and hold on at the same time?"

He came squelching out of the water. Carefully he knelt and lay the injured Stivi on the grass. The boy had a bad gash behind his left ear which bled profusely. At least his heart must still be beating, Oaks thought in a rush. He helped the boy's father gently roll Stivi over.

Light pressure, applied twice, got the water gushing from the lad's open mouth. On the seventh compression he began to splutter and thrash about on the grass. Chad Conroy breathed out a heavy sigh.

"He'll live," he diagnosed. "How—how can I thank you? Without your help, he might have died."

"The help was there when you needed it, that's all that counts," Segeeyah depreciated his part in the rescue.

Suddenly the two men looked at their sodden condition and began to laugh uproariously. They pointed at each other with their chins and held their ribs while they chortled without restraint. A final heave of water came from Stivi, and he sat upright.

Bleary-eyed, he peered at his father and this stranger. "What's so funny?" he asked in a croak.

"If you . . . only knew . . . son," Chad Conroy panted out with his laughter, and embraced his puzzled boy.

Mind in a turmoil over how fate conspired against him, Col. Owen Bledsoe paced around the perimeter of the parade ground at Fort Gibson. Hands behind his back, head lowered so that the black plume in his garrison hat jutted straight upward, he ignored the presence of everyone. Several junior officers gave him startled looks as he passed, oblivious of their rigid postures of attention and crisp salutes.

He continued to prowl and protest until he literally blundered into the regimental sergeant major. Each man recoiled from the abrupt and uncomfortable contact and instinctively reached out to steady the other.

"Colonel, sir, I'm terribly sorry, sir," Eldon Carl, the RSM blurted.

"No cause for that, Sergeant Major," the colonel answered affably enough. "I seem to be sleepwalking in the daylight. I see by the morning report that desertions are increasing again."

Carl looked grim. "Yes, sir, they are. It's this do-nothing duty, sir."

"Yes. My officers and I have come to that conclusion. There's no call for this inactivity," he criticized his superiors, a decidedly unpolitic thing to do, especially to a non-com. "Our orders prohibit us from taking punative action against an enemy nation, of which we now occupy a small part."

Uncertain as to what response the colonel expected, Eldon Carl chose the safe middle ground. "Yes, sir, that's quite right, sir."

A faraway gleam came to Colonel Bledsoe's eyes. He spoke as though to himself. "How I long to send men marching and riding through these traitorous Cherokee villages, to use fire and the sword to cleanse the land."

"But, sir, the orders say we are to disregard their so-called declaration of war, that only a minority of the leaders agreed to it."

"Phaugh! What difference does that make? These Cherokees have grown too big of heads. Imagine," he launched into a favorite lament, "they have their own

65

written language. As if savages could conceive of such a notable achievement. Oh, I know all the arguments. They elected a representative government, just like our own. There are many of them who profess to be Christians. They have schools, an insane asylum, and orphanages. They even have a, by-God, newspaper. They're . . . *civilized*." Bledsoe made it sound dirty, like something that had crawled out from under a rock.

"That's all quite true, sir," RSM Carl replied, resigned to hearing the entire tirade.

"I'm convinced it doesn't mean anything. It's a clever ruse to bamboozle the idealists in Washington. The way things are, I can't say I blame these deserters all that much. At least they can't go far. They will stick out like hailstones in a mud hole." Bledsoe paused to snort derisively. "Not that the savages would make any effort to help the army."

"There's always the Lighthorse, sir. They are supposed to round up white men illegally in the Cherokee nation."

"That reminds me of one thing, Sergeant Major. I want you to make it clear to the guard detail that not a one of those Johnny Reb Cherokees is to get within two hundred yards of the fort."

"They've already been told, sir. You ordered it only last week, sir."

"Well, I want it to apply especially to those treacherous Lighthorse," the colonel snapped and stomped away.

Seven

Capt. Chad Conroy and Lt. Segeeyah Oaks relaxed in front of the temporary pole lodge that served as a headquarters for the Downing Convention Ground training camp. They had discussed the orders delivered by the messenger, which included instructions for Lieutenant Oaks to take two additional patrols from Captain Conroy's best-trained men and proceed to run down the guerrillas. Chad Conroy summed up the situation in the real world, unfamiliar to the lawgivers in Tahlequah.

"It's not like we were a standing army," he spelled it out. "Our use of ranks at all is simply to designate who makes decisions in the field. We're policemen. We're supposed to think like policemen. *Indian* policemen at that."

"I agree," Segeeyah said softly. "I've not been among many white men, but I have come to observe and believe that we essentially think in different terms than they do. Even our language, when we translate it literally into English, implies this. For example, take the simple English sentence," he said, switching to English, "'He heard nothing good.' In Tsalagi, we'd say it, *'Hla gohusdi osda yutvgane'i,'* which translated literally into English is, 'Not something good not he heard.' On which, I rest my case," Segeeyah concluded with a smile.

"You sound like a school teacher, instead of a policeman," Chad remarked.

Segeeyah chuckled ruefully. "At one time I wanted to be. Then the family tradition reared its head, and I joined the Lighthorse. But I still read everything I can get my hands on. Mind you, I'm not saying we are superior to or less than the whites. It's simply that the tracks in our heads run different ways. We see the world in a more direct and immediate way, with an intensity that requires a lot of qualifiers when expressing aloud our thoughts or feelings."

"Which still brings us to the fact the lawgivers don't see this problem the way we do. How do you propose to go about dealing with this Moritus and his border guerrillas?"

Lieutenant Oaks gave a moment's pause, then responded with a grin born of self-consciousness. "I've read the reports. So, I have been considering approaching the problem like you did with those Texicans."

"That was damn foolish," Chad exploded. "I was young and impetuous, full of dare and defiance. I could have gotten a lot more people killed. A lot of innocent ones, too." Momentary pain flashed across Chad's face as he recalled the loss of his oldest friend, Two-Hats Brand, in that fighting.

"But you didn't. It worked, and I think it will work again," Segeeyah pressed.

"I wish you luck, then. In a way, it's a good thing we're not a tightly organized outfit. At best, the way we have to turn them out of here, we're lucky to be able to know they can hit what they shoot at and will ride into the face of gunfire if ordered to. I'll select the best to send along with you, then I had better answer the nervousness of the assembly by sending two more patrols to keep an eye on the Union soldiers at Fort Gibson."

"Thank you. We'll leave first thing in the morning," Segeeyah replied, rising to join his new men.

*　　*　　*

It could have been created for exactly the purpose Augustus Moritus intended. A broad, rolling valley, contained within confines of the prairie plateau, with a wide, clean stream meandering through the center opened to the guerrilla leader's view from one rim.

Augustus Moritus gazed in wonder at the basin, which seemed to have sunk below the normal terrain at some time in the far past. It left behind steep walls that one came upon abruptly, often to the detriment of the traveler, as scattered bones at the base of the steep walls testified. A narrow, high-sided gorge, that followed the creek's course, provided the only easy access. Augustus Moritus studied everything and found it ideal. He turned to the men behind him, who had gathered with awe-struck expressions.

"Gentlemen, we have found our paradise," he declared, flinging his arm in a dramatic gesture toward the basin. "We'll circle the rim and find the mouth of that gorge. Once inside, our comforts are assured. There is ample water and grass, plenty of wood for fuel, and timber to build permanent dwellings. From here we can raid with ease and be secure when we return."

"How can we be sure someone won't come after us?" Blake Sessions asked.

Moritus gave him a bleak smile. "With that gorge secured by sentries and lookouts, we will be virtually impregnable." In an intensity of mood, he barked cheerfully, "What are you waiting for, men? This is our promised land."

Over the next three days, the guerrillas became laborers. Albeit much against their will, they bent their bare backs to hauling boulders and fallen snags out of the way, to create a road through the gorge passable to wagons and other wheeled vehicles. They cursed and grumbled under their breath at the indignity of common labor. Some among them, those with an agricultural bent, looked forward to turning the sod of the basin and planting crops that would insure their provender through the coming winter. One such man approached Augustus Moritus when less than a hundred yards separated them from their goal.

"Colonel, I've been thinkin'. Those ploughs and that McCormack drill we relieved them Injuns of will come in mighty handy. There's time to grow corn and oats, I'm figgerin'. Maybe beans. We can cut tall grass and use the side-delivery rake to windrow hay. This place could be ever' bit the paradise you said."

Moritus beamed. "A man of vision!" he exclaimed. "Mr. Bean, you see this valley as I do. Yes, that's exactly why we dragged along all of that farm machinery. Seed, too. Man, this is our future here. With the nation involved in this great conflict, it is certain that Union forces cannot be spared to do anything about us. Given how long I suspect it will last, we can be so well established here that no one can dislodge us."

"You sound mighty certain, Colonel," Terrance Bean replied.

"Of course I am. With men like you, who have an eye for the future, how can we fail?"

"There's always the Injuns. This is part of their country," Bean suggested.

"Forget them. They are as nothing to us. Outside of that one unfortunate incident, have any of the savages come bothering us?"

Terrance Bean thought of the missing men, killed or captured by someone, and of the relative peace since. "Well—no—no, I guess not."

"Then relax, mark out your fields and tend them, good

ploughman," Moritus advised eloquently, confusing the simple farmer.

While the bucolic tasks of farming and animal husbandry got under way in the basin west of Joshua's Mountain in Canadian District of the nation, Augustus Moritus did not remain at peace for long. On the third day of their entry into the lush valley, he led a large force out on a foray against several small communities of three or four extended families.

First of these was called Price, after a Cherokee settlement in North Carolina prior to the Removal. Ezra Longwalker was up as usual before dawn, tending to chores. He heard the rumble of hooves and suspected it might be the Lighthorse on a periodic cast through the area in search of border jumpers. He set aside the bucket he had used to slop the hogs and hastened to the house.

"Mother, there's riders coming. Better add more coffee to the pot," he advised.

Smiling pleasantly, his gray-haired wife responded in her musical voice. "I'll wake up Sara to help me. If it's the Lighthorse, they'll welcome some sweet cake."

"Good. We're lucky there's any Lighthorse left, what with this confounded war," Ezra grumbled. "Best make sure they're kept happy and come around often."

Hanah Longwalker frowned slightly. "Wasn't it that half-Indian, Jefferson, who said, 'They govern best who govern least'?"

"No. I think it was said by the fat *yoniga*, Franklin."

Hanah's kindly trill of laughter brightened the large comfortable lodge. "I'm sure it was Jefferson. It sounds like something an Indian person would say."

"You are probably right. I've the cows to fork hay to, so I'll be going," Ezra told his wife.

He stepped outside into the faces of seven grim-looking

71

men. "Who else is inside, old man?" one demanded in English.

"*Gado usdi jaduliha?*" Slyly, he refrained from asking, "What do you want?" in English.

"It don't matter, Heck," another voice declared. "Jist plug him."

Heck Williams, one of the Fort Gibson deserters, agreed. A shot roared out in the pale light of dawn, and Ezra Longwalker slammed back against the doorpost of his lodge. An expression of curiosity crossed his face before it slackened, and he slid down the wall to a sitting position.

At once, gunfire erupted throughout the small community. Shouting guerrillas kicked their way into the houses of the residents and blasted some in their beds. Others died as they leaped to grab weapons. A fire broke out in one pole lodge and quickly engulfed a wall.

Women screamed and children shrieked in alarm. Laughing, the raiders helped themselves to any valuables and all of the firearms around. Augustus Moritus set the stage for his followers by cornering a little girl in one lodge.

He loomed over her a long minute, savoring the fright in her big, dark eyes, then reached out with both hands. He closed long fingers around her neck and began to squeeze. Slowly, he choked the life from her slender body. At last he gave a convulsive shudder, much like someone achieving an orgasm, and turned to the onlookers.

"Put what you've taken in a good wagon, men. Then mount up; there's more places to be visited."

More of the Creek had arrived outside Fort Gibson. A shabby-looking lot, Col. Owen Bledsoe considered. Accustomed as he was to highly polished boots, shiny brass buttons, and neatly pressed uniforms, they would naturally appear so. They also created a problem. He had sent a dispatch to the government agent responsible for their well-being but as yet had received no reply.

"Why are they coming here?" he asked sharply of his adjutant.

Major Mueller blinked and gazed at the brush and hide lodges. "There is considerable unrest, as you know. Word of the White Chiefs War, that's what they call the War of the Rebellion, sir, has reached nearly every savage on the frontier, I dare say. The Creek nation is allied with the Confederates, too. I'd imagine these folks feel insecure, knowing that their leaders are siding with the Cherokee and the Rebs."

"I'm not so sure these savages think things through like that," Bledsoe snapped. "I'm more inclined to believe they are looking for a handout. Beggers and thieves, the lot of them."

"Then it's we who have made them so, Owen."

Colonel Bledsoe refrained from a sharp reply. Major Mueller's sympathy for the Indians' plight was well known. Bledsoe had other things on his mind. "This deserter, Randolph Yates? He was awaiting transportation for a general court-martial?"

"Yes, sir."

"On what charges?"

"Attempted murder of a non-commissioned officer, Owen. Also assault on the same, and attempted escape. A bad case all around."

Owen Bledsoe paused and stroked his receding chin. "Small wonder he preferred taking his chances with the heathens. This desertion situation has gotten entirely out of hand. I'm considering sending out patrols to hunt them down."

"It's in the jurisdiction of the Lighthorse to hunt men illegally in the Cherokee nation, Owen."

"Be damned with that. The Army takes care of its own. And that includes the trash, as well as the good. Besides,

73

what if these deserters are behind this sudden move of nervous savages to the environs of this fort?"

"You mean if they went west, in a body, to prey on the Indians?"

"Exactly, Hans. That might account for a lot. Why don't we have one of the scouts who speaks their language question some of the Creek?"

"That's a sound idea, Owen. I'll get someone right on it. Meanwhile, shouldn't we notify the Lighthorse of possible armed men roving through the nation?"

Owen Bledsoe's face darkened and furrowed. "Bugger the Lighthorse. They couldn't do anything effective anyway."

They called their little community in Illinois District Sawmill, because that was the principal industry there. The sawmill was located on one bank of swift-moving Big Viga Creek and attracted a lot of business. It also attracted the attention of Augustus Moritus. He wanted that sawmill equipment in his valley paradise. At the head of twenty-five fierce border ruffians, he rode into *Asvgwa-losgi'i* in mid-morning. They scattered chickens, which gave squawking protest, and raised dust as they trotted along the rutted road toward the tall tower of the mill.

From it came the buzz and whine of saw teeth cutting into fresh pine. A heady aroma perfumed the air around the building, a mixture of raw wood, heated pitch, and sawdust. Blood lust glowed in the cold, blank gray eyes of Augustus Moritus. Avarice shined there, too, as he envisioned the mill equipment operating at his behest. He signaled a halt outside the busy sawmill. His small frame turned from side to side in the saddle, as he appraised the situation.

"We gonna shoot up the town?" Silas Tanner asked.

"No. Not this time," Moritus told him. "We'll commandeer wagons sufficient to haul the machinery, then disassemble the mill and take it with us. Anyone who opposes us will be eliminated."

"Haw! That sounds like the whole town, you ask me," Tanner said.

Augustus Moritus turned the fierce gaze of his icy eyes on Tanner. He didn't like being contradicted. Tanner swallowed hard and nervously looked away. Moritus smiled. "I'm feeling in a generous mood. Leave the town untouched except for this mill."

Half a dozen guerrillas headed for the portion of the building that housed the gears and shafts that drove the saws, powered by the huge water wheel that turned with a musical splash on the side of the structure. The rest, with Moritus in the lead, entered the cutting floor. Cherokee workmen looked up at their sudden appearance.

"We've come to dismantle your mill," Moritus announced.

"Impossible," a burly man in white shirt and dark trousers snapped. "Who are you?"

"I am the man who wants a sawmill. Get to work," he commanded Boston Harry Plummer.

"I still don't know who you are, mister, but I'm going to throw you the hell out of here," the owner, with sawdust on his black trousers, announced.

Augustus Moritus smiled nastily and drew a big Greenriver knife from a sheath at his waist. He advanced and drove it into the miller's belly. With a vicious yank, Moritus cut upward, disemboweling the unarmed Cherokee. Pain so intense it blanked out all sensation filled the man's body as he went slack and dropped to the floor.

Revolvers at the ready, the Leatherlegs began shooting the workers. One Cherokee expertly threw an axe that buried the blade to the handle in the chest of a guerrilla who had just gunned down the man's younger brother. The Leatherleg didn't make a sound as he died with his victim. The brief fight ended as quickly as it had begun. The coppery smell of blood and the acrid scent of powder smoke filled the air, mingled with the fresh aroma of sawed wood. Boston Harry Plummer looked around him with hands braced on hips. Each of the Leatherlegs held a smoking Colt.

"This is gonna take more than a couple of days to take apart," he said.

"We'll keep the local residents off your backs," Augustus Moritus assured him. "Do your work quickly."

"Less than half a day to Tahlequah," Corporal Tallcorn announced to his small detail as they settled around the fire to cook the evening meal for themselves and their prisoners.

Slick Willie Hillery and Grant Hollister exchanged worried glances. Hillery's ribs still throbbed and ached, the broken edges grating against each other. The only word they recognized was the name of the capital, but they could figure out the rest. This came as the least desired news. If they were to do anything about getting away, it would have to be tonight.

"We'll have to ride hard to catch up with Lieutenant Oaks," Squirrel remarked.

"If we're able to at all," Johnny Walksaround amended. "Any idea where they went?"

Tallcorn shrugged. "South, is all I know. We'll just backtrack and find the trail."

"I'm hungry," Squirrel declared.

"Ready in no time," Tallcorn assured the youth.

Half an hour after the prisoners had been fed and their bonds resecured, the tired Lighthorsemen settled down in blankets for the night. Out of consideration for his age, Squirrel had been made first to watch over the prisoners. Easier than waking him later on, Corporal Tallcorn reasoned. Also better chance he would stay awake.

An hour into his watch, Squirrel's eyelids began to droop. He yawned prodigiously and rubbed a small fist into his eyes. Slick Willie was quick to take note of it. He nudged Grant in the ribs with an elbow.

"The kid's droppin' off. We'd best get busy shuckin' these ropes."

"Any bright ideas for starters, Willie?" Hollister grumbled.

"This loop around the tree is loose enough we can turn sideways. I can undo your hands that way. Then we can get shut of this whole mess. Kill them damned Injun policemen while we're at it," Slick Willie added.

Slick Willie kept his eyes on Squirrel as the boy dropped into a light doze. He and Hollister forced their bodies to turn by bracing their feet on the ground and shoving. Suddenly, Hollister's feet broke loose, and a loud scraping sound followed. Squirrel's head snapped up, and he blinked owlishly in the direction of the prisoners.

His mind numbed by fatigue, the boy seemed satisfied that nothing untoward had occurred, and he settled down with his back against a wagon wheel. They had brought along the wagons as evidence and to see that the contents got to the proper destination. It slowed their progress to a crawl and wearied all five Lighthorsemen. Squirrel could be excused his slumberous state in light of the daylong effort to make miles.

When Squirrel's head bent until his chin touched his chest, Hillery and Hollister again fought their bonds to turn outward from one another. Slowly Slick Willie became aware of Grant's fingers. He eased his efforts and blindly sought the knots that held the cord tight around Grant's wrists.

He found them, then fumbled uselessly as his sweat-dampened hands refused to contain the knots in his grasp. He wiped them as best he could and resumed the attempt.

77

Slowly the thin cord slid as a knot gave. Slick Willie sweated and bit his lower lip to keep from gasping aloud at his exertion. The second knot yielded to his insistent prodding. Then the third.

Freed of his confinement, Grant Hollister slipped the rope over his head and turned to release his companion. Once he had accomplished that, they sat in the darkness and rubbed life into their numbed extremities.

"There's an axe over by that fire pit," Slick Willie whispered into Grant's ear. "I'll go get it and fix that smart-mouthed brat first. Then we'll have his guns."

Slick Willie Hillery raised to a low crouch and waddled over to the fire. Carefully he raised the axe and examined the edge by moonlight. The newly risen moon cast a silver coating over everything in camp. Slick Willie smiled in anticipation of burying the hatchet in that kid's head. Slowly he started in that direction.

He had made it halfway when the loud clicks of a hammer being drawn back froze him in place. He looked up to see the small boy, fully awake now, looking at him over the largest revolver he had ever seen. With escape so close at hand, Slick Willie did not let its menace interfere. He launched himself at the young Lighthorseman, his mouth open in a silent scream of defiance.

Squirrel shot Slick Willie in the chest. The first .44 ball from the Colt Dragoon slammed into the sternum, staggering the hulking killer. Squirrel's second ball ripped between two ribs on the left side and tore a hole in Slick Willie's heart. The third one had every Lighthorseman in camp on his feet. It also gave Slick Willie a third eye centered half an inch below his original two. Slick Willie Hillery fell like a stone, twitched feebly a few seconds, and lay still.

On his feet, Squirrel Three-Skulls aimed the heavy Dragoon at Grant Hollister and spoke for the first time since awakening. "There's two more in here. Do you want them?"

"Good work, *Sololi*," Corporal Tallcorn praised when he came up on the thoroughly unnerved prisoner and the boy. "Where's the other one?"

"Over there. He came at me with a hatchet. He's dead." Squirrel looked up and smiled at the older non-com. He wanted very much to go over behind a big sage bush and be sick, but fought the urge. He'd proven himself. That much he knew and was proud.

Eight

He would have looked forlorn and pathetic, if he hadn't been so huge. He stood on the side of the road, a lost, hurt expression on his large, wide face. Segeeyah Oaks and the replacements riding with him observed the slump-shouldered figure from a long way off as they rode south. Across the road from the man stood a neatly constructed pole lodge with a cheery stream of smoke rising above the roof. When Segeeyah Oaks trotted closer, a big arm raised in greeting.

"Lighthorse, Lighthorse, I need help," came a plaintive cry.

Oaks reined in and the others did the same. "What's your problem?" the Lighthorse lieutenant asked.

"I'm *Dihltadegi* Bendbow. That's my house over there. I want you to help me get back inside it."

Lieutenant Oaks looked from the lodge to the giant who stood beside his horse. Even mounted on Bashful, Segeeyah noted that the man's head came level with his chest. Nearly seven feet tall and two axe handles broad. And *he* needed help?

"Segeeyah Oaks," he introduced himself. "What is keeping you from walking over there and going right in, Jumper?" Segeeyah inquired.

"Ulalie," Jumper Bendbow answered in a sorrowful tone.

"Who is Ulalie?" Segeeyah pressed, impatient with this delay.

"My wife."

Segeeyah Oaks raised his eyes to the heavens, as though seeking the support of *Yoah*. "If she's your woman, just go over and tell her you want in the house," he suggested, as though explaining to a child.

"I can't. She's the one who threw me out."

"Why?"

"I'm not even sure," Jumper responded. "I—I only want you Lighthorse to talk sense to Ulalie and make her let me back in the house. I haven't had anything to eat since last night, and I'm getting hungry."

Segeeyah looked the gargantuan Dihltadegi up and down. "I imagine you would," he said softly. "I can't figure what we can do that you couldn't do even better."

"It's just . . . that she gets so mad at the littlest things," Jumper pleaded. "All right," he relented and offered an explanation. "I tracked mud into the lodge. What's so bad about that? And I set down the basket hard enough it cracked two eggs. That could happen to anyone, right? Then I got to readin' the *Phoenix* and let the ham burn up I was fryin' for supper. Now that's no cause to throw the skillet at me, is it?" Bendbow ended in a troubled wail.

For all their inexperience as policemen, the new Lighthorsemen recognized this domestic turmoil as a less than life-threatening situation. Several smiled and two chuckled indulgently. Segeeyah Oaks had to fight to keep his own laughter from bubbling up. He swallowed it with effort and spoke to the map of distress on Jumper Bendbow's face.

"She threw the skillet at you last night?" Jumper nodded affirmatively. "When did the other things happen?"

"Last night," Jumper admitted softly.

81

"Then I'd say it is small wonder she got a little tetchy with you."

"Yesterday was a bad day for me," Jumper offered hopefully. "I saw a white owl in my sleep the night before. Then our milk cow had a breech birth, and I had to get the tackle and pull the little one out. My oldest boy got in a fight with the neighbor boy and came home with a bloody nose. He has eleven years and should know better than to get himself hurt like that. Then I shot a fox, and some of the pellets killed our rooster."

Segeeyah could hold back no longer. His laugh began as a low rumble, that burbled up his throat and out into the clear air. He shook with the force of it, and moisture blurred his eyes.

"My friend," he chortled, "some spirit must have walked across your grave right enough. A day like that could put a man in a terrible mood. All right, I'll try and see what I can do to help."

"*Wado, wado,*" Bendbow thanked him profusely as Segeeyah dismounted and walked across the road.

Indulgent chuckles followed him from the too young and too old recruits as he approached the tight little lodge. Segeeyah Oaks stopped short of the entrance and called out tentatively.

"Miz Bendbow? Uh—Ulalie? This is Segeeyah Oaks of the Lighthorse."

All of the laughter ended abruptly as a cast iron trivet sailed out the doorway and missed Segeeyah's head by only inches. The Lighthorse officer looked disbelievingly at the door and then back at Jumper Bendbow. The huge Tsalagi made urgent shooing motions with his large hands, as though to scatter chickens. Segeeyah shrugged and called again.

"Ulalie, Jumper says he's right sorry about the mud and the eggs and the burned ham. He says he's mightily hungry and would crave to come back inside and eat."

"Let him eat dirt," a hot retort came from inside.

"Awh, now, Ulalie, he is beside himself with sorrow for makin' your day so hard yesterday. He—he's picked some wildflowers," Segeeyah added in sudden inspiration.

Looking stunned, Jumper Bendbow silently mouthed the word, "Flowers?"

Over his shoulder, half turned from the door, Segeeyah Oaks nodded agreeably and pointed to a patch of white petaled, yellow centered wild blooms that spread along the road. His agreeing nods became more pronounced. Jumper looked at his hands, at the door, and at the flowers. Sighing, he went to snap the stems of a large number of blossoms.

At Segeeyah's urging, he brought them toward his lodge. He stood, awkwardly, in front of the door. "Ulalie? Ulalie, my sweet one. I—I'm sorry," he forced from his wide, deep chest. Then he thrust the bouquet forward. "I brought you flowers."

Initially, Segeeyah Oaks thought a small child had bolted out the door to jump on Bendbow and hug him fiercely. Little Ulalie could not be more than four foot eight, a miniature dynamo that squeaked with girlish delight over the peace offering. She kissed him loudly and wetly on both cheeks. When their affection for one another subsided to less breathless terms, she addressed him with a twinkle in her eye.

"I have rabbit stew cooking," she advised.

"I know, I smelled it," Jumper responded. Then he remembered his manners. "This is my friend, Segeeyah Oaks, of the Lighthorse."

"*Sio*, Mr. Oaks," Ulalie greeted in her musical, youthful voice. "Will you take the evening meal with us?"

"I—uh—I have a whole lot of hungry young men along. I'm afraid they would eat up everything in the house. Thank you all the same."

"You'll take some honey and cornbread along to share

with them in your camp tonight?" Ulalie offered.

"Gladly. There's not a one of them knows enough about cooking," Segeeyah said with a light laugh. "You two are lucky to have each other," he went on, teasing. "It isn't everyone whose little misunderstanding can call out twenty-four Lighthorsemen."

Husband and wife looked contrite. "I'm so sorry," Ulalie apologized for them both. "But he can be—be so . . . thick-headed some times. Don't you know that I love you, you old wooly bear?" she addressed her huge husband.

"Yes, I do. Now fetch that cornbread so these nice men can ride on."

Ten minutes later, Lieutenant Oaks and his new patrols rode away from the Bendbow farm with light hearts. "It's too bad that not all of our problems can be so easily solved," Segeeyah Oaks tossed off to Charlie Singer.

Col. Owen Bledsoe looked at the reply to his dispatches to the War Department with a growing scowl. Not only had they again denied his request for a transfer to the command of a regiment actively fighting the Rebels, they had also laid the problem of desertions squarely back on him. Angrily, he called to his adjutant.

"Hans, come in here a moment, please."

Maj. Hans Mueller entered the CO's office at Fort Gibson with little expectation that the news from Washington had been good. He gave his commander and friend an inquiring nod. "Do I detect something about to happen around here?"

"Yes," Bledsoe snapped, barely in control of his temper. "And nothing pleasant. Who is next up on the duty roster for patrol actions?"

Mueller consulted his memory. "Lieutenant Prentiss, I believe."

"No—no, he's too valuable to waste on this sort of nonsense. Assign Lieutenant Funston. We are directed by the War Department to conduct searches for our deserters. Also to apprehend any other deserters rounded up in our sweeps. Funston will do just fine for that."

"Parker Funston is a green troop commander, Owen. Why, he only has the Cavalry School between him and West Point."

"Well, Hans, he'll just have to get out and question these 'civilized' Indians of yours and run down our deserters."

"I doubt that an inexperienced second lieutenant will command much respect from the Cherokees and Creek, Owen."

Owen Bledsoe snorted and reached for the coffee pot. "I suggest he'll command what respect he must. We have also received a communication from the Cherokee government alleging that a gang of border ruffians is running rampant in their nation. If that is true, we'll need Prentiss and the more experienced commanders to deal with any Confederate threat."

"Are you sure they are Confederates?" Mueller asked, a worried frown creasing his brow.

"There are Confederate military posts inside the Cherokee nation. What else would they be?"

"My point, exactly, Owen. The Cherokees, or at least part of them, are on the side of the Confederates. What sense would it make for them to warn us of the presence of their allies?"

Colonel Bledsoe considered that a minute. "Who knows what Indians will do? And to make matters worse, they claim some of our deserters are in league with this band of border villains, supposedly led by one Augustus Moritus."

"If that's the case, shouldn't we send someone with more experience in command of the search party?"

"Not necessary," Bledsoe dismissed the suggestion. "I

suspect this is only a ploy on the part of the Cherokees to get us to do their work for them. Lieutenant Funston will be quite adequate to the task.''

Augustus Moritus looked up at the much taller men gathered around outside the variety of structures that were fast becoming a village in the center of the basin in which they had settled. He drew himself up to the full extent of his five feet four inch height and addressed them in a serious tone.

"Because of other obligations, I will not be going with you on this adventure into Texas. I trust you will conduct yourselves with the usual bravery and ferocity as when I am leading you. The way should be open to you without restraint. There is only one condition upon which that depends."

Hand thrust inside the wide velvet lapels of his swallowtail coat, Augustus Moritus began to pace in a measured stride. His knee-high, brightly polished black boots stirred the dust as he clomped along in front of the waiting men. All he needed was the cocked hat to be a mirror image of his model, Napoleon Bonaparte.

"You must, at all costs," he continued his harangue, "stay well clear of the Union forts along the way. Avoid contact with the Army. If they learn of us, it will spell disaster. Once in Texas, you should have no difficulty. What with the 'brave boys' off fighting for Southern rights, the only resistance you will probably encounter will be old men and wet-nosed boys. Much the same as we have seen among the Cherokees. Prey on the banks, the stage-coaches, the saddlers.''

"Why saddle makers?" Heck Williams asked.

"They do fine silver work down there in Texas. Saddlers have a lot on hand. Our concern is not where the wealth comes from, only that you garner a lot of it."

86

"We're gonna move slow, weighted down with all this stuff you said we should take," Butch Tucker complained.

"Believe me, you will need all of the ammunition you carry, Mr. Tucker, provided you do the job the way I want. You are to spend two weeks at this enterprise, then return here with your treasure. I would be pleased to find every man outfitted with a silver-chased saddle and bridle. That goes for everyone in this great band of ours." He turned away, went to his horse, and swung into the saddle. "Now, I'm trusting a lot in you men. I'm positive you won't let me down. Good luck and good fortune."

Squirrel Three-Skulls felt like he did when he had just eaten a big bowl of juicy, sweet blackberries and spoon cream. To think, Colonel Hood had shaken his hand and praised his victory over the white enemy. Even the Speaker of the lawgivers had paraded him in front of the assembled body and said glowing words about him. If only his father could see him now. But he was off with Gen. Stand Watie.

Runt of the litter, his older brothers had scornfully called him before they, too, went off to fight the Union Army. He would show them. He had known only fourteen summers, yet he was in the Lighthorse and already a—a hero.

"You'll be staying with my family," Corporal Tallcorn advised him. "And I want you in bed an hour after sundown, same as my boys," the NCO added.

What a crushing blow for a hero! "Do I have—" Squirrel started in protest, then cut it off, conscious of his responsibilities as a Lighthorseman. "Yes, Corporal Tallcorn. As you say."

"We leave at dawn to rejoin Lieutenant Oaks," Tallcorn explained.

"So soon?" Squirrel asked, disappointment evident on his face.

Tallcorn snorted. "What do you have to hang around here for?"

Unable to stop himself, Squirrel let it spill out. "There was this girl today at the assembly. She looked like she wanted to talk to me so bad she was about to bust."

Soft laughter came from the six foot Lighthorse corporal. "Breaking killer horses, knocking a border ruffian out of the saddle, then shooting him when he tries to escape, now taking a fancy to the ladies. You're a Lighthorseman, right enough."

That made Squirrel feel as good, almost, as to have gotten to talk to the girl. He glowed at the praise all the way to the Tallcorn house and even after, in the darkness of the loft where he and the corporal's three boys lay down to sleep.

"We lost them," Wolf Wind reported to Segeeyah Oaks when the latter rejoined his command.

"How did it happen?" a tired Lieutenant Oaks asked his second in command.

"We trailed them easily all the way down into Illinois District, to a spot some twenty miles north of Mackey's Salt Works. The tracks led into the Illinois River there. Only they didn't come out. I sent scouts up and down stream but ne'r a sign of them coming out. We stuck to the river bank all the way to *Ah-tah-lah-tees*. Then we turned back up here. Didn't want to get too far separated from you. Don't know how they managed it with those wagons."

"Rafts," Segeeyah snapped. "They got ahold of, or built, river rafts and floated right away from you."

Wolf looked chagrined. "I should have thought of that. Why they could be clear down to Arkansas and plum out of the nation by now."

Segeeyan considered that for a moment. "I somehow

doubt that. Moritus and his murdering scum would get a warm welcome in Arkansas. I think we need to do some looking down the way of Canadian District."

Wolf lost his glum expression. "Then we still have a chance of catching them?"

"Yes. And with these reinforcements, we should easily round up the whole rotten crew."

"When do we leave?" Wolf prompted.

"First thing tomorrow. Hopefully by then the detail I sent to Tahlequah will have caught up."

Segeeyah's early worry over the safety of little Squirrel had been assuaged somewhat. Five more rode with the recruits from Captain Conroy of about an age with the boy. He had reconciled himself to making sure they remained out of the heavy fighting, without making it appear he was favoring them. Only one thing commanded his full attention now: locating Augustus Moritus and his brigands.

Nine

Smoke still rose from the smoldering haystack. The large pole lodge had collapsed in on itself, and a thick pile of coals still radiated heat. Five corpses littered the ground, one partway inside the ruins of the burned-out barn. What sent pain to the heart of Segeeyah Oaks was the lost, blank expressions on the faces of the three orphaned children who stood amid the devastation of their farmstead.

"Mother and Father are gone," the middle-sized one announced mournfully as he stared at the fallen figure of a woman.

"Do you know who did this?" Segeeyah asked, certain he knew the answer.

"Diyoniga."

"How many?"

"Sgiga'du," the small boy answered, lifting one hand, to open and close it three times.

"How long ago?" Segeeyah asked tenderly.

"Svhi sunale'i."

Yesterday morning. Not all of Moritus' marauders had disappeared into the southern corner of the nation, Segeeyah thought angrily. Fifteen of them had been here only a day ago. And why? he questioned angrily. "What possible good could it have done them?" he demanded of no one.

"They like to kill," Wolf Wind opined. "Or they like to kill *Jayvwiya'i.*"

"It appears they took nothing, only burned and murdered."

"Someone could have come and run them off," Charlie Singer suggested.

Segeeyah asked the children. "No. They come, hurt, set fires, and go away," the little spokesman responded.

Face set in grim lines, Segeeyah looked up at the sergeants. "You could be right, Wolf, they like killing Indians." He put a hand on the boy's shoulder and guided the youngsters away from the scenes of slaughter. Charlie and Wolf escorted the other two. "We have to do something about these three," Segeeyah broke a long silence.

"But what? Do you have any family?" he asked the children.

Heads shook negatively. "Only an old aunt. She lives way up by Oseuma," the middle boy informed them.

"Where near Oseuma?" Segeeyah pressed.

The boy shrugged. "Oh, up there." He nodded vaguely to the north.

Segeeyah Oaks considered his predicament. At least he had a few men to spare. The prospect of finding a woman in the far northern portion of the nation could become a fox chase. Much closer, and easy to find, was the orphan asylum on the Grand River in Saline District. That could be rough on these youngsters, so recently orphaned. It was said that Carleton Rushes, the director, had grown crustier as the years went by. It still offered the best solution for the time being.

"Friday," he summoned Sergeant Whittler, "detail two of the new men to escort these children to the orphan asylum. It will be a good two day's journey, so have them take plenty of supplies. Then they are to report to Park Hill when they finish."

"Too bad the little ones don't have family close at

91

hand," Friday observed.

"*Sgidv*—yes, that's it," Segeeyah agreed. "All right, we'll take time to bury these folks, then move on. We've a long way to go to reach Canadian District."

Four men crouched around the low fire, gnawing ravenously on the roasted quarters of a jackrabbit. They had not eaten all day. Their light blue trousers gave them away as deserters from the Union forces. Desperation had driven them together. They stiffened at the crackle of fallen limbs beyond the light of the blaze.

"Who's out there?" one questioned uneasily.

"A friend. Mind if I come in?"

"Come, but keep your hands in sight."

Rand Yates walked his horse into the firelight, hands held before him, conspicuously empty save for the reins. "You Army?" another of the fugitives demanded of him.

"Was," Rand corrected. "I'm with a wild bunch now; we live off the riches of this country."

"What riches?" a tall, lean deserter asked scornfully.

"Oh, there's plenty. If you go at it right."

"Who might you be?"

"Name's Rand Yates. Late of Fort Gibson. I seen you there, too."

"Right you are. Wilber Loftus. This be Harvey Decker, Vincent Butoni, Zack North. They hail from Fort Towson, down in Choctaw land. Injuns hunted them right out of the country."

"Well, now, that's too bad. How'd you like to throw in with some border raiders who for sure eat a lot better than you all have of late?" Rand offered.

"Any cash money in it?" Loftus inquired.

"Might be," Rand said sparely. "There's some of the boys settin' off to raid in Texas. Their targets are banks."

Brightening, Loftus rubbed his palms together. "Well, now, that sweetens the deal somewhat." He looked at the

92

others. "I for one am tired of jaw-wrestlin' stringy jackrabbit for a meal. What d'you say?"

"Count me in," Decker agreed.

"*Cui bono*," Vincent Butoni accepted the offer.

"I make it all of us," North summed up. "Where do we go?"

"For now, you ride along with me. I hear there's some more runners around here-abouts. I'm to round them up and then take you to where we're holed up."

Loftus cast a gimlet eye. "Mighty secret about that place, ain'tcha?"

"That, Brother Loftus, is how it's gotta be. You'll ride the last twenty miles blindfolded. Once inside, you'll be watched until it's sure you can be trusted. Orders of Mr. Moritus."

"What if we don't go for that kind of monkeyshines?" Loftus growled truculently.

In a lightning move, Rand Yates closed on Wilber Loftus. His big ham-fist slammed into the tough deserter's jaw and spilled him backward off his heels. Loftus yelled a curse and started to get up. Yates kicked him in the belly. Whooping, Loftus doubled over and vomited up the rabbit he had consumed.

Yates leaned down and grabbed a handful of shirtfront. He jerked Loftus upright and backhanded him twice, puffing full, pouting lips.

"Then you'll get the crap kicked out of you," Rand Yates informed him levelly.

Platoon Sgt. Sam Gresham rubbed a square chin and peered slantwise at Second Lt. Parker Funston. Green as grass, Gresham considered. Well suited to the task at hand, he admitted. Round up deserters, his mind scoffed. A waste of time. Especially in this country. A feller couldn't tell by looking at one of these Cherokees if he sided with the Rebs or not. Those who didn't might point out the illegals in their country. Or they might not, just because it was their nature to be contrary.

"Sergeant Gresham," Lieutenant Funston announced suddenly, "I think it's time to dismount and walk the horses a while."

"Yes, sir, right you are, sir," Gresham answered with a half-salute.

Parker Funston had not the slightest appearance of the career soldier. At twenty-two years of age, he still had the soft, round lines to his face of a callow youth. Full, generous lips, and longish blond locks, added to the boyish image. Having once served at the U.S. Military Academy as a weapons instructor, Sergeant Gresham wondered how so delicate-looking a young man could have made it through the years of harassment and near-savage discipline. Gresham shrugged off the impressions that whirled in his mind and raised his right arm to signal.

"Platoon . . . halt! Prepare to dismount. Dis—mount! All right," he went on after swinging gratefully out of the saddle, "walk your mounts. No chatter in the ranks." Then, to Funston, "Sir, just how do you propose to go about finding these deserters?"

Funston gave him a warm, gleaming white smile and rested his gauntleted left hand on the cover flap of his holster. "I suppose we should question some of the local inhabitants. Provided we can find any of them. They do seem to melt away into the prairie whenever we show up."

"Beggin' yer pardon, sir, but it's been my experience that though they are friendly enough, the Cherokees consider our presence an invasion of their country. They were taken from their homeland by American troops and marched out here at gunpoint. The way I got it, that happened in the dead of winter. It wasn't an easy journey. The treaty with our people gave them this land forever. It said nothing about forts or troops ridin' through their nation."

"Where did you learn all of this about the Indians,

Sergeant?" Funston asked, genuine interest coloring his question.

Gresham smiled self-consciously. "I've been at Fort Gibson for eight years. There ain't no place to go from there, except some of the Cherokee villages. I got to talkin' to some of them, sir. That is, once they saw that I didn't look on them as savages. Most all of them speak English good as you or I. The old ones are bitter toward us for what happened. The young ones have learned distrust from their elders. It takes a while, but when they get to know you, they open up. And they sure enjoy a good jest. Some of the funnin'est folk I ever met. Like dances, too. Oh, not just their own style, that they do at what they call a stomp ground. They do the 'Ginny reel, waltz, and shoddosh, reg'lar way, with fiddles and a piano."

"I'll have to consider you my Indian expert, Sergeant," Lieutenant Funston said warmly.

Gresham glanced away. "I talk too much, sir."

"Not at all. I'm intrigued. With you to show the way, we may even come up with some of these scoundrels to take back to Colonel Bledsoe."

Gresham produced a grim, fleeting smile. "I know for sure I would like to get my hands on that Rand Yates."

"The one due for a general court?" Funston asked.

"That's him. About kicked the cod-stones off Corporal Plunkett when he made his escape."

"That's what laid him up," Lieutenant Funston mused. "I—I didn't have the platoon then, you recall."

"Yes, sir. You were just assigned to the post then and didn't have a command. Not meaning to criticize, sir, but if Lieutenant Boyle had of taken an interest in the men like you do, sir, maybe that wouldn't have happened to Plunkett. I mean, sir, that Yates is a mean one. Should have kept him in chains at all times."

"Experience speaking, Sergeant Gresham?" Funston probed.

"Sort of, yes, sir. I've come across ones like Yates before.

Plain brutes, bullies, but yellow to the core when you get down to it. Got to make people fear them because they're so God-awful afraid of everything themselves."

"Not only an Indian expert, a philosopher as well," Lieutenant Funston joked in a kindly manner.

"A total of fifteen years frontier service, sir, gives a man a lot of time to think," Gresham responded somewhat defensively. "I come to see that things ain't sometimes what they seem."

"A useful ability for a lead non-com, I'd say," Funston complimented. "Well, Sergeant Gresham, time to mount up the men. We'll trot for twenty minutes."

"By the book, sir. Yes, sir," Gresham indulged in his own humor.

Long Tom Longdon had not seen the likes of it since he'd ridden with Bloody Bill Anderson. Full thirty men, hard and mean as wildcats, armed to the teeth, and riding out to empty the banks of North Texas. And himself in charge. In dusters and leather britches, they looked like a regular military unit. At least they had reminded him of the Confederate guerrillas he had sided with until they hit this stand of slender blackjack pine.

They had spread out to make passage easier and quicker. Even then, several men had to dismount to lead their horses around deadfalls. The soft, moist ground muffled the thud of their animals' hooves. Long Tom had sent two men ahead to scout out what lay beyond the small forest. One of them came pounding back along the narrow, rutted trace that meandered through the pines.

"What's the hurry?" Long Tom asked when the rider spotted him and rode in close.

"Clear as can be ahead. There's hilly country as far south as a man can see. No sign of Injuns. Billy White said to tell you to hurry."

"You two took the trail. We're havin' one hell of a

96

time," Longdon replied. "I figger it's gettin' close to noonin'. We'll get out of this mess and stop for grub."

"Fine with me. I'm hungry."

"You're always hungry. Stay with us now, and maybe you can point out the best way."

"Ain't no 'best way,' Mr. Longdon. 'Cept by the track. I don't reckon you want to go single file."

"Nope. Not in case we meet any Injuns. 'Plenty of firepower on the line,' that's what ol' Bloody Bill used to say. Me, I'm hopin' we don't meet up with nothin', until we come across a Texas bank."

That brought laughter from the men within hearing. Longdon continued along the little-used trail for another half hour before he saw ahead the signs of a clearing. Beyond the last trees, tall prairie grass waved in a gentle breeze. When the last of his men left the trees, Long Tom called a halt to fill their bellies.

"Ain't nothin' out here but us an' the birds, boys," Long Tom declared with satisfaction.

Long Tom Longdon's satisfaction proved short-lived. After the noon meal they had ridden on southward into the rolling land that stretched to the border with the Creek nation and beyond. Fifteen minutes after starting out, the column crested one swell in the prairie and came face to face with the patrol led by Lt. Parker Funston.

"It's the gaw-damn army!" Billy White brayed.

"Open up, boys, give 'em hell!" Long Tom shouted above the alarmed cries of surprise from both sides.

Clearly they outnumbered the soldiers. They also fought desperately for their lives. The guerrillas' first hurried shots went wide of the mark. By then Lieutenant Funston had recovered from his shock and ordered the troops to draw arms and return fire.

He didn't know if these were deserters, and he didn't care. The sons of bitches were shooting at soldiers of the

Union Army, at *him*, and he intended to do something about it. Left hand filled with his Remington, Lieutenant Funston fired rapidly at the man he figured to be the leader.

Only the hard-bitten men didn't stand and fight as expected. They charged forward, to close rapidly. Lieutenant Funston heard the bullets crack past his head, and then came a scream of anguish from a baby-faced, tow-headed soldier who reminded Parker Funston of his younger brother. Drops of blood splattered on the young officer's face.

Gagging at the experience, Funston triggered his .44 Remington dry. All around he saw the swirl of individual actions. Another trooper fell from his saddle, scarlet spraying from a bullet gash that had ripped through the side of his neck. Dust rose, along with the copper-tart odor of blood. Confusion and indecision clouded Funston's mind. Horrified, he counted seven of his platoon down with wounds or dead. He tried to shout for the men to rally, but nothing came out.

In desperation he sought to locate Sergeant Gresham. A ferret-faced guerrilla rushed directly at Lieutenant Funston, and the young officer reacted instinctively. He smashed the man across the bridge of his nose with the barrel of his empty revolver. The impact brought forth a scarlet flow from the broken appendage, though the impact numbed Funston's fingers and wrenched the firearm from his grip. Thinking fast, he drew his saber.

The keen edge glowed blue-white in the afternoon sunlight as he brought it down in a sweeping arc and decapitated his attacker. Gagging at the sight that produced, Lieutenant Funston lost control. All he wanted was to get away from this terrible carnage.

A fat rifle ball moaned past him and took the guidon bearer in the chest. With a soft grunt, the young corporal fell from his saddle, shot through the heart. His horse whinnied in dread and sprinted away. Without thinking,

Parker Funston drubbed dull-round cavalry spurs into his animal's flanks and started after. Suddenly a big, burly form appeared at Funston's side. A gauntleted hand took his reins.

"Steady now, sir. Steady. We've got to rally the men. I'll go on this way and turn them to flank the enemy, sir. You turn back and grab a few to hold the middle."

"Yes, Sergeant, yes, of course," Funston babbled. "That's what I had in mind."

"Naturally, sir. It's what they teach you at the Cavalry School, is it not?"

"Why, yes, Gresham, I do believe it is," Lieutenant Funston responded in a tone of bewilderment.

He turned about and galloped briskly up to the four troopers who had displayed the presence of mind to dismount and use their saddles as support to fire their carbines into the mass of marauders. "Keep at it, men, steady now," Funston shouted over the crackle of small arms.

Was battle always like this? If so, for the first time, Parker Funston felt sincere gratitude that he *had not* been assigned to the Army of the Potomac. Only, what could he do? He had lost hold of his revolver. He looked down at his hand, which held the saber—an anachronism at best even now—and sheepishly sheathed it. The stubby carbine in its spyder seemed alien in his grip.

He opened the breech and inserted a paper cartridge, his hand shaking wildly all the while. Lieutenant Funston dropped the first cap, managed to seat the second, and ear back the hammer all the way. When he raised the Sharps to his shoulder, the rear sight filled with the distorted, yelling face of a scruffy-bearded man at extreme close range. Funston didn't even bother with a steadying deep breath like they taught at the Point and Fort Riley.

Rapidly tightening his finger on the trigger, Lieutenant Funston discharged the .56 caliber carbine and blew that hideous face to bloody ruin. From the east, the direction he had been running when Sergeant Gresham had caught him, he heard a wild yell and an increase in the volume of fire. Gresham had managed to rally enough troops to mount a counterattack. Good for him, Funston thought dazedly. He would write up Gresham for a commendation when they got out of this. *If* they got out, the frightened side of his mind prodded.

With a suddenness equal to that with which the skirmish had begun, the strangers who had attacked them broke through the ill-disposed line of soldiers and galloped off to the south. Slowly, following fire dwindled.

"Cease firing . . . cease fire!" Sergeant Gresham bellowed.

A minute later, he trotted up to where Funston stood with a bowed head and confused expression. The rattled young officer looked up with urgency. "We had better mount up and pursue, eh, Sergeant Gresham?"

"Well, sir, beggin' the lieutenant's pardon, sir, but I think not. We took nine killed and seven wounded, sir. That's half the command, sir. I'd say we would be wise to turn about and head for the fort, sir. We need to be reinforced before takin' on that bunch again. Uh—by the way, sir, you done good holdin' the center. It let me get enough together to force the enemy to break contact."

"Why, thank you, Sergeant Gresham. Your counterattack was most timely." Oh, God, Lt. Funston thought in wretchedness, what if they had been trained, professional troops? We would have been slaughtered, the mocking reply echoed in his head.

Ten

A thin, wiry boy of about thirteen caught up to Lt. Segeeyah Oaks' detachment at mid-morning the next day. They had once more crossed over into Illinois District, headed southward toward the suspected location of the guerrilla band of Augustus Moritus. The youngster had not expected to find so many Lighthorse, nor have them so close, but it gave him confidence, considering the message he carried.

"There has been a big fight between white people. The soldiers from Fort Gibson and other men, the Leatherlegs," he announced breathlessly to Lieutenant Oaks.

"Where did this happen?"

"South of here, across the Arkansas River. In the big grass prairie south of George's Fork of Dardeene Creek. It was told to me that many soldiers died. A big battle," he ended, wide-eyed, arms swung wide to illustrate his meaning.

"Were you sent to find us?" Segeeyan asked, doubtful.

"No. My father said to ride to the Lighthorse on this side of the river. At Illinois Courthouse."

"I see. We are hunting the Leatherlegs. It might be well if you go on and tell the others at the courthouse."

Disappointment showed on the lad's face. "Could I

ride with you?"

"No. I've got some with me already who are near enough your age to make me uncomfortable."

Eagerness spilled from the boy. "But you are going to arrest the Leatherlegs, right?"

Lieutenant Oaks pulled a face. "I have a feeling that since they've shot up the soldiers, not many of them are going to give up peacefully and let us take them in."

"Then you will fight them. I want to see that."

In order to enforce his authority over the youngster, Segeeyah closed with the boy's sweating pony and patted him on one shoulder, then ruffled his hair, something good manners dictated could be done only to a child. "No. You go on to Illinois Courthouse; they need to know what is happening. Some of those in the encounter will likely come this way, and the patrol needs to know what to expect. It is important, *achuja*."

Clearly he didn't like being called 'boy,' but he swallowed his hurt pride and considered the other words the Lighthorse chief had spoken. A quick upturn of his full lips and squaring of his shoulders conveyed his acceptance of the importance of his mission.

"I will ride with the speed of a whirlwind."

Segeeyah could not hold back all his amusement. "Your horse might have something to say about that. Go fast, though. We don't know what we will get into down south, and it would be good to have someone behind us."

After the lad sprinted off, Wolf Wind spoke in low, earnest tones. "We're going down to where the fight took place. I can feel it."

A smile lifted the corners of Segeeyah's mouth. "Much as I dislike doing it, we're going to do more than that. We need to find out from the soldiers what happened, how many of the Leatherlegs there were."

* * *

After an hour's rapid ride southward following the encounter with the army, Long Tom Longdon slowed the pace and took stock of their situation. Meeting up with the army had been the worst sort of bad luck. Telegraph wires would take word of it to every army outpost and fort for miles around. He wouldn't be surprised if somehow the Confederates got wind of it. If they did, some of the Home Guard that Hood left behind in Texas would be waiting for them. He'd lost seven dead, with three so badly wounded they might die if he continued to Texas. Half a dozen more carried minor wounds. And those soldier boys would hightail it back to Gibson and get the whole regiment turned out to hunt them.

That last decided Longdon. He signaled for a halt and gathered the men around him. "I say we're too shot-up to go on. We have to get back to Colonel Moritus and let him know what's happened. I say we ride for the basin right now."

To his surprise he received no argument. They set off toward the northwest at a fast lope. Long Tom brought his men to the mouth of the gorge late that night. He identified himself to the men guarding the entrance and rode on while the watchers passed the news down the line.

Augustus Moritus was awake and waiting when Long Tom brought his command back to the broad valley. He dismissed the men and directed Longdon to enter the small, stout log dwelling with him. It still lacked a roof, Long Tom noted, and a canvas had been spread over the rafters to keep out the night's chill and dampness. A brass kerosene lamp glowed on a small table set to a wall opposite the doorway. Moritus gestured to coffee on a low, two plate Acme wood stove.

Longdon would have preferred a good shot of bourbon, but he accepted the coffee. Silent, both men took chairs. "So you ran into the army and not a day's ride from here," Moritus mused aloud.

"They're out looking for deserters, that's all I can figure," Longdon offered.

"They tore into you, right enough?"

"Oh, sure. We had some of those runners of Rand Yates in with us. They saw blue uniforms and opened fire before I could handle it any other way."

"Considering where you were, I can't see any other alternative," Moritus framed his thoughts aloud. "Even had you convinced the officer in charge that you were not deserters, they would still have tried to take you in for being inside the Cherokee nation. No, a quick fight was the only answer. It's too bad you lost seven men."

"Another died on the ride here," Longdon regretfully told him.

Augustus Moritus scowled. "I'm deeply disturbed by this clash with Union troops. Although inevitable, and handled the only way it could have been, it could not have come at a worse time. We'll discuss it in detail with the others in the morning, especially our Mr. Randolph Yates."

Lt. Segeeyah Oaks had remained in two minds on the long ride south. He had halted the long column of Lighthorsemen when he saw the small approaching figure of Squirrel on his huge mount, Blasting Powder. He had allowed the boy to accompany the point men with some reservation. Stop babying him! Wasn't that the advice he had given to Cloud when she wanted to take care of the boy's aches and bruises?

"Soldiers up ahead," Squirrel announced with a note of anticipation.

He had to decide now. With some hard effort, Segeeyah Oaks overcame his prejudice toward the interloping Federal troops enough to reach a conclusion. "Wolf," he told his second-in-command, "keep the rest of the detachment behind that rise ahead. Jali, you and Squirrel will come with me. We're going to talk to the officer in charge."

Due to the condition of the wounded, Lieutenant Funston had ordered an early halt. His platoon went about their tasks of setting up camp, preparing to cook, and tending to the livestock and wounded. The dead were removed from the backs of their horses and placed in a row, under covering canvas. Funston was about to order pickets out when a low snort of equine greeting froze him in the act of opening his mouth.

"Do you think they could have doubled back on us, Sergeant?" he asked Gresham.

"I doubt it, sir. They seemed eager enough to break off contact."

"Then who?" Lieutenant Funston inquired in confusion.

"Hello, the soldier camp!" came a clear hail in English. "We're friendly. May we ride in?"

"Who are you?" Sergeant Gresham inquired.

"Lt. Segeeyah Oaks, Cherokee Lighthorse."

Second Lieutenant Funston frowned. He recalled only too well Colonel Bledsoe describing the Lighthorse as the most treacherous of all the Cherokees. What could the man want? He asked that of Sergeant Gresham.

"I'm sure I don't know, sir. Why don't we ask them in and find out?"

"An idea, Sergeant." Funston raised his voice. "How many are there of you?"

"Three," came the answer.

"You may advance." By then, their mutual dislike and suspicion, combined in either one, could have ignited a tragic shooting spree.

The heads of three horses rose above the lip of a draw.

The mounted figures came next. Surprise adjusted the features of Lieutenant Funston. One of them appeared to be a small boy. Not much danger there, he assured himself. They halted with about twenty feet separating them from the soldiers.

"Lieutenant—ah—Oaks?" Funston asked.

"I am he," a youngish man, not much older than Funston, responded. Seated in the saddle next to him was a man of equal age, and to his left, the boy.

"Lt. Parker Funston at your service."

"I am sure you are aware we are effectively the police for the Cherokee nation," Oaks began. "It is my understanding that yesterday you had a run-in with elements of a guerrilla band operating illegally inside the nation."

Unplanned, Parker Funston's lower lip slid out to protrude in a pink pout. Knows a hell of a lot for not being involved. "We are outside the environs of the fort looking for deserters, nothing more. As to the engagement, I'd say 'element,' rather than the plural. You understand what I mean?"

Lieutenant Oaks bristled for a moment, as though interpreting that as an insult. Then he chuckled. "If you mean, do I speak English, I believe we've been doing so for the entire conversation."

"I meant no offense, believe me," Funston went on with stiff formality. "I'm new out here and not accustomed to hearing my language from the lips of—ah—Indian people."

"I would gather from the number of bodies over there that you are also new to the tactics of these border scum," Segeeyah returned with matching rigidity.

Crimson suffused the face of Lieutenant Funston, and he opened his mouth to blurt a hot rejoinder. Sergeant Gresham's calm, affable voice caught him up short.

"They've yet to teach that subject to the young gentlemen at West Point and the Cavalry School,

106

Lieutenant. From both of which Lieutenant Funston has recently been graduated."

"I can understand that," Oaks responded, his demeanor relaxed somewhat. "Slow to make changes, to adapt, these policymakers, eh?"

"Right you are. Tell me, Lieutenant. Did you happen to come up through the ranks, sir?"

"Yes, I did. My father and grandfather were Lighthorse."

Gresham beamed, delighted to have his intuition proven right. "I thought I sensed the presence of a good, steady sergeant under that title, sir."

Segeeyah Oaks smiled. "We only use the American system of ranks so that everyone knows who it is they should blame if anything goes wrong."

"B'god, that makes a whole lot of sense. As the lieutenant here can tell you, sir, we surely did knock heads with about thirty of some sort of border trash yesterday afternoon. One might suspect they were Confederate guerrillas, but the sergeant major told us at senior sergeants' call about some feller name of Moritus who is supposed to be marauding inside yer nation here."

"And I suspect one and the same with those you fought against yesterday," Segeeyah advised. "He's believed to have attracted a large number of Union and Confederate deserters to his ranks. We've come looking for them."

After a hard glance from Sergeant Gresham, Lieutenant Funston reentered the conversation. "Surely you three, two men and a boy, are not the only Lighthorse sent to search them out."

"Oh, no. I have forty men not half a mile from here. We would have all come, but we didn't want to startle you after your encounter with the Leatherlegs."

Lieutenant Funston blinked. "What was it you said? Leatherlegs? Come to think of it, they all did wear long dusters and leather trousers. Almost a uniform."

"Augustus Moritus styles himself as a colonel. Estimates number his force upward of eighty fighting men. Although testimony from frightened survivors is not always that reliable."

Funston could not understand the apparent lack of anxiety on the part of this Indian policeman. His ingrained dislike for the savages, as Colonel Bledsoe termed them, began to wane. "Yet you seem to be intent on rounding them up with only half that number?"

"It's a job that has to be done, Lieutenant. Truth to tell, between you and me, although I haven't the authority to request it, I could certainly use some help from the Army."

That news disconcerted Parker Funston. "I understood that we were at war, enemies?"

Segeeyah Oaks sighed. "That's what our treaty with the Confederates says. But I've been advised that your government does not take it seriously. More to the point, though, what do you say? We're both out here, close to the enemy, one it appears from what the sergeant has said, your army is under orders to apprehend also. It also appears from my count of boots as we rode in that you must have lost almost half of your command."

He'd touched a raw nerve, Segeeyah saw when Funston bristled. "Sir, I resent the implication of mismanagement. It was a surprise attack, fiercely fought and quickly over."

"I don't doubt you. If I had any reservations, I would hardly ask for your help."

Lt. Parker Funston saw the light of sincerity glowing in the oddly green-flecked brown eyes of Lt. Segeeyah Oaks. Something inside of him gave a sort of lurch, and he drew a deep, swift breath. How brave they are, he thought wonderingly. And how straightforward. Perhaps he had misjudged, been misled by the prejudices of others?

"My twenty and your forty would make a formidable force," Lieutenant Funston remarked at last.

"There's another eleven up in Illinois District who can

join us if needed. That makes enough, I think, to swing the balance. Especially if they don't suspect we are anywhere near."

"Yes," Funston contributed, growing more involved, "take them by surprise."

"That could be easier than you think. We suspect they are hiding somewhere. Holed up in a canyon or some remote valley, removed from everyday doings."

"Any idea where?" Funston asked, completely taken up with the prospects.

"You had this run-in some twenty-five miles from here, south of George's Fork?" At Funston's nod, Segeeyah went on, "Our information indicated they were in Canadian District. I would judge not far from where we're now located."

"And I picked this place to make camp," Funston declared disgustedly.

"If you hadn't, we might not have come across you," Segeeyah assured him.

"All right," Funston stated, a smile coming with his decision. "We'll work together on this. I'll detail men to escort the bodies and wounded to Fort Gibson, along with a report on why we're remaining in the field."

"Might I suggest that you do not mention our cooperation in that dispatch?" Segeeyah offered.

Funston saw it at once. "Yes, that would be impolitic of me."

"Good," Segeeyah accepted. He extended his hand, white man style, to be shaken. "We can start at first light tomorrow. My men and I will ride over, and we'll head westward, toward Joshua's Mountain. That will give you and the good sergeant here time to prepare your troops for our arrival."

"Done. And—ah—thank you for the chance to rescue something out of this disaster, Lieutenant Oaks."

"Your name is Parker, right? Mine is Segeeyah. My

friends call me Bat," he added, not certain why. "Until tomorrow."

Augustus Moritus glowered at his gathered subordinates. He had given the better part of a day to a study of the problem handed him by Tom Longdon. He had little liking for any of the alternatives he devised. That decided him on his present course of action.

"Gentlemen, I would be interested in hearing any suggestions you may have to correct this situation," he announced after a brief summary of the potential danger of arousing the Federal troops at Fort Gibson. "Please don't hesitate to put forward anything you believe will help."

For two long minutes, the lesser leaders muttered among themselves. The consensus came out that they ought to lay low for a while. That was distasteful to Augustus Moritus, also dangerous, he acknowledged. Men of the caliber of his followers, if left idle, would eventually explode into violence among themselves. Before he could reject it out of hand, to his surprise, Rand Yates rose from his campstool.

"The way I see it, we need to get on the good side of the Federals. Maybe this will help. Colonel Bledsoe, who commands at Fort Gibson, absolutely hates Injuns. He gets downright frothing-mouthed over the Cherokees. Calls them Rebel scum, for sidin' with the Johnny Rebs. Now if those boys was out lookin' for us who walked away, it's my thinkin' that they don't know about this outfit at all, or don't care, because we're plunderin' the Cherokees."

"That's very interesting, I'm sure, Mr. Yates," Augustus Moritus observed dryly. "Do you happen to have some way it can be used to our advantage?"

Yates nodded. "Yep. Matter of fact, I do, Colonel.

Bledsoe's higher-ups have refused his request to take—ah—what was that word, Butch?" he asked Butch Tucker.

"Punitive," Tucker responded.

"Yeah, punitive action against the Cherokees. So what I figger, we can get on the good side of Bledsoe by making a big, bloody raid against a fair-sized Cherokee village."

This idea appealed at once to Augustus Moritus. His face brightened and the scowl disappeared. "No. Not a 'village,' Mr. Yates . . . a large town." Face wreathed in a smile, he reached for the map on the low folding table before him. "Yes, I can see how such an action might win the good colonel's approval. For maximum effect—" Moritus went on, eyes fixed on the map, "I think the community of Park Hill would be ideal. It is not far to the south from Tahlequah, their capital. I can also see how it might gain a kinder attitude toward you and your associates."

Augustus Moritus had some other ideas about such an enterprise. Those he chose to keep private. Clearly, he believed, if all the dead left behind turned out to be deserters, this Colonel Bledsoe would probably stay out of Cherokee country for quite a while. And, it would rid his own command of a dangerous man like Rand Yates.

Eleven

Collaborating with the enemy, deep within the Cherokee nation, which was how Segeeyah Oaks saw this present enterprise, might be misunderstood by many Tsalagi. Particularly, he reminded himself, the Knights of the Golden Circle. Even though Stand Watie was outside the nation, his followers were numerous. For ten years there had been no killings attributed to the feud over the Treaty of New Echota. Segeeyah Oaks did not want to be the one to change that status.

Particularly, he ruminated as he rode along beside the young *yoniga* officer, since this most recent division among the people over the War for Southern Independence. Even the factions of the Echota debate had split within themselves over that. Chief Ross had wanted the nation to remain neutral, although the other civilized tribes that had been removed from the South had early on sided with the Confederacy. For that reason, among many others, he tried hard to break down the barrier he sensed between himself and the obviously inexperienced American officer.

"Parker, I've not known many Americans," Segeeyah tried his latest gambit.

Parker Funston glanced at him with surprise. "Why,

you are an American," he stated with renewing stiffness.

"No. I am a Tsalagi, a citizen of my own nation. We were *once* Americans; farmers, townsmen, plantation owners, slave holders as some of us still are. Until the Removal. Perhaps that is what has kept us apart for the past twenty-five years. The older people among us feel it intensely. I was only a year old at the time. My only impressions of Americans have come from my association with the U.S. Marshals during my time as a Lighthorseman. I've found most of them to be tough, but fair, men. Honorable, as we would say. Actually, I've sort of liked the people I met in Fort Smith."

"Then how could you go along with the Confederacy?" Parker Funston found he could not fathom this big, powerful man. He conversed in English like a native, an educated man, yet he looked somewhat like a barbarian. And this so-called nation of his throwing in with the Rebels . . . well, that only made it worse.

"Who said I had gone along with the Confederacy? Me, Segeeyah Oaks? That decision was made by a consensus among our people, urged by Stand Watie. I am required to go along, like everyone in the nation. But I chose to remain at home and enforce the law, not go off to war with the Mounted Volunteers. We have a hell of a problem on our hands now. I hope that together we can work it out."

That brought a smile and a relaxation of the formality. "Well, Bat, after that defeat at the hands of these guerrillas, I can only suspect that you've picked a rather weak vessel in which to put your hopes."

Segeeyah considered that. "An honest response," he said plainly. "Not necessarily accurate, though. From what I gained from Sergeant Gresham, you were out looking for deserters, men on the run, frightened and in hiding. You met up with an armed band of guerrillas. Our leaders in the Lighthorse have always told us that surprise is the major element that contributes to a victory."

113

"You are being kind, for which I am appreciative," Funston responded, then his deep-seated mistrust of Indians in general reasserted itself. "Or is it condescending?"

Segeeyah Oaks read the uncertainty in the other man's eyes and tone and chose to laugh softly. "Hardly that. So far, we've run into only a small number of them, seven, and it cost us the life of one man and three wounded. Only two of them came out of it alive, by the way."

Funston frowned. "They fight with desperation, like men with their backs to a wall."

"Figuratively, they are. I don't imagine you heard much about these border guerrillas at West Point," Segeeyah explained, eager to breech the gap in their mutual understanding. "It wasn't called 'Bloody Kansas' frivolously. Both sides acted with a ruthlessness that frightened everyone in that state. It spilled over into Missouri, and gave considerable worry to those of us in the nation. Men, women, children, all died at the hands of one band of freebooters or another. But, I'm going on like a school teacher, which my sergeant, Wolf, constantly reminds me."

"Not at all. I'm interested." And Parker Funston found he meant it.

"Both sides in the current dispute, the—ah—war, have denounced actions of these border ruffians, and disowned the deeds of some of their own. Remember, although it was Robert E. Lee who hanged John Brown, he was in your army at the time."

Parker Funston considered that, and his attitude toward the men he had lost, and made his decision. "Perhaps we have a lot more in common than we think. I gather we have crossed over into this Canadian District now? If so, where do you suggest we go to further our campaign against the brigands?"

"Find them first," Segeeyah said with a straight face.

114

"Until we know where they are, how many, and how well-armed, anything we consider is only speculation."

"And when we find them?" Funston pressed. "Isn't it in the Marshals' jurisdiction to apprehend white men?"

"The nearest are in Kansas at this time. Arkansas is a part of the Confederacy," Segeeyah reminded him.

"Then what do you suggest?"

Segeeyah eyed him levelly. The moment that counted most had been reached. "We send for reinforcements from Fort Gibson, if necessary. If we can handle it ourselves, we destroy them as an effective force, and take the survivors to Tahlequah for trial and execution."

A more positive opportunity presented itself to cement the new-found spirit of cooperation between Segeeyah Oaks and Parker Funston slightly more than an hour later. One of the point scouts sent forward by the Union officer returned at a quick gallop and reined in to report.

"Sir, Corporal Hansen's compliments, sir, and I wish to report that we have made contact with a body of white men, sir."

"Oh? What sort of white men, Private Williams?" Lieutenant Funston asked.

"They look to be ratty specimens, sir. They are apparently running some sort of saloon."

"A road ranch," Lieutenant Oaks provided. Quickly he evaluated the situation. "We're here and they are here. We might as well do something about it."

"Such as what, Bat?" Funston asked easily.

"Selling whiskey in the nation is illegal. Whites running a road ranch are also breaking the law. I suggest we ride up there and tear the place down."

Funston frowned and narrowed his eyes. "We are supposed to be hunting a band of guerrillas, Bat. What has this to do with it?"

Segeeyah smiled and spoke in a relaxed manner. "They're right on our way, breaking the law, and I for one don't want to leave them behind to carry word to Moritus of our passing."

Lieutenant Funston chided himself silently for overlooking this obvious complication. "You're right. Very well, Williams, return and tell Corporal Hansen to remain out of sight and wait for the column to arrive."

"Yes, sir." Quickly he reversed his horse and galloped off to the south.

"They can't be far off. Hansen was not to precede us by more than two miles," Funston surmised. "You know, it might restore the men's confidence to take on these ruffians."

"That thought had crossed my mind, too. My Lighthorsemen are spoiling for a crack at someone. What better ones to take on for now?"

Stretched out to a fast canter, the column came upon Corporal Hansen a mile and a half further south. He pointed out a thin column of smoke rising from behind a low hill. "We saw 'em, sir, but I don't think they saw us. From their looks, they could be with those guerrillas the— ah—other officer told us about."

"Lieutenant Oaks speaks English, Corporal. So do his men," Funston reminded the non-com tightly. He turned to his troops. "Men, Corporal Hansen has located a number of white men, illegally inside the Cherokee nation. How many, Hansen?"

"I'd say fifteen, twenty, sir. Least that's what we saw at a glance, sir."

"How many horses?" Segeeyah Oaks asked.

"A lot, uh—sir. More than thirty I'd say."

"Then we can figure on more than thirty men down there," Oaks responded. "This kind can hardly afford one horse, let alone remounts."

It became Funston's turn again. "Lieutenant Oaks

116

has advised me that it is our duty, lacking the presence of U.S. Marshals, to break up this saloon and destroy the liquor."

From far back in the ranks came a couple of groans. Segeeyah and Wolf exchanged glances and chuckled. "It would be nice to keep some for evidence, Parker," Segeeyah suggested.

"Yes, of course. Could I confer with you aside for a moment?" Funston asked Oaks.

"Sure."

With their lead NCOs, the two officers walked their mounts a distance from the troops. Funston looked thoughtfully at the column of smoke. "How do you think we should do this?"

"The idea is not to let any of them get away. There's not often much resistance when a road ranch is raided. Maybe a little hand-fighting. So, the larger part of the detail should screen the place closely to prevent escapes."

"Since this is your country and your laws that are being broken, do you want to lead the way?"

"They are the laws of the United States, too, Parker. But, yes, I'd like to be in on the arrest. I'll take Charlie Singer's patrol, and Dami Adalala's. The rest can join with your troops in closing off any way out. Give us ten minutes to get in place."

"Fine with me."

"Wolf, you stick with Lieutenant Funston and see that our men understand what is expected. Especially those new ones."

"Sure, Bat. Have a snort for me," Wolf teased.

Segeeyah made a face. "It smells like medicine and tastes worse. I'll get Charlie and Tom."

In less than two minutes, Lieutenant Oaks and the two patrols trotted away around the base of the hill. A ramshackle structure that looked as though a strong wind would blow it away came into view. Smoke rose from a tall tin stove pipe that extended above the slant of a brush and sod roof. A dozen men lazed under brush arbors in front of the building, most of them sprawled in chairs in a state of drunkenness. Segeeyah Oaks studied the scene carefully as they approached.

"What the hell you want here?" a truculent voice challenged them when the Lighthorsemen came within seventy-five feet of the road ranch.

"Tsalagi Lighthorse. You men are under arrest for illegal sale of whiskey and trespass," Segeeyah called out.

"You got no authority over us, Injun."

Segeeyah located the source of the voice. A large, dark-complexioned man stood in the doorway of the rude shelter. He wore no shirt and his long, woolen underwear showed signs of extensive wear since the last washing. He held a long-barreled percussion rifle with curly maple stock and brass furnishings. The hammer, Segeeyah noted, had been drawn back to full-cock.

"Since we are at war with the United States, all those old agreements are out," Oaks stretched the point. "We're policing everything for ourselves. Now, put aside that rifle and step out here where we can talk reasonably. No one need be harmed. We only want to destroy this place and place you under arrest."

"You will like hell," the man shouted, sudden anger burring his voice as he swung the rifle forward and started it to his shoulder.

Segeeyah Oaks drew his .44 Colt in a smooth, steady motion, web of his right hand over the hammer so that it eased back to the ready by the time the muzzle settled on the middle of the belligerent whiskey peddler. With the same casual-seeming motion, Lieutenant Oaks triggered a round that smoked toward the man menacing him.

"Gawdamn, I'm shot," the saloonkeeper gasped out. His rifle clattered to the ground.

Immediately, the inebriates in the yard spilled from

their chairs to hug the ground. Several, white men of disreputable appearance, went for their weapons. A shotgun in the hands of Robert Runningdeer made a flat crack as one barrel discharged a load of buckshot. One border smuggler cried in pain and dropped his .36 Navy Colt.

With the guns of the Lighthorse menacing them, the rest of those outside became reasonably peaceful. Colt still aimed at the doorway to the road ranch, and Segeeyah Oaks dismounted. Charlie Singer joined him as he walked toward the man Segeeyah had shot. The Lighthorse lieutenant looked down at him.

"Just your shoulder. You'll be all right," Segeeyah advised.

"Like hell. You're gonna ruin me."

"I'm not the one breaking the law," Lieutenant Oaks reminded him.

Together he and Charlie entered the low-ceilinged saloon. Instantly they had to duck low to escape being brained by a chair swung by a huge, bearded, totally bald man. Off balance, he stumbled sideways past Segeeyah, carried by the chair.

Lieutenant Oaks shot an arm forward and laid the hot barrel of his .44 alongside the head of the bear-like white man. It made a meaty smack, yet only served to further antagonize the giant. With a loud roar, he let go of the chair and charged Segeeyah Oaks with arms open to encompass the Lighthorseman. Shouts of encouragement came from the six other men ranged around the bar.

Not a small man by any lights, Segeeyah Oaks looked like a boy compared to the raging hulk that menaced him. He holstered his revolver, stepped back, and set his feet. Balled fists came close-in and tight. He snapped a hard right to the open mouth and two quick lefts under the heart. Nothing changed.

"Damn Injuns. We got a right to do's we please," he

grunted as Segeeyah's punches went home in a layer of protective fat.

Segeeyah said nothing. He saved every bit of air for the fight. Those big, bulging arms closed in on him, and he dropped low to avoid them. Fast for all his bulk, the mountainous man locked his grasp around Segeeyah's shoulders. A quick raise of his elbows slipped the Lighthorseman free, and he staggered back. Charlie Singer closed in to wallop their opponent with the butt of his rifle.

With more of the same suddenness, the bull of a man swung his left arm and batted Charlie away without so much as a grunt of effort. "Finish them both, Gunnison," a voice called from behind the bar.

That gave Segeeyah an opening, which he quickly used. A solid kick to the swollen gut of his attacker doubled Gunnison over. Segeeyah kicked him again in the head and slammed his open palms against large, hairy ears.

Yowling, Gunnison dropped his efforts to ensnare Oaks and brought both ham hands to his aching head. He massaged his offended ears while his bellow of pain changed to small squeals. Segeeyah Oaks danced in lightly and kicked Gunnison in the mouth. Those big hands came away from Gunnison's head and lashed out blindly at his tormentor.

Lieutenant Oaks dodged and spun to one side. His heel made a sharp, snapping contact with the ribs on Gunnison's right side. Staggered, the huge man swayed and pawed the air fruitlessly. Already Segeeyah came at him. His fists pummeled Gunnison and hurt his injured ribs even more. From the corner of his eye, Oaks saw the man at the bar snatch up a revolver.

One final punch, already launched, and Segeeyah Oaks gave his full attention to the would-be back-shooter. His Colt .44 came clear of leather and leveled on the bartender's middle. A light twitch of his trigger finger, and

120

Segeeyah's Model 60 bucked in his hand. A cumulo-nimbus of powder smoke rose in the center of the room, lanced through with a lightning stroke of burning gases.

Beyond them, the imprudent barkeep lost interest in the revolver he had yanked from under the bar. He stared down in disbelief at a raspberry stain that spread an inch below his diaphragm and the small black hole at its center. Slowly his hand opened, and the six-gun dropped from unfeeling fingers. The cheering patrons went instantly silent.

Then bright lights erupted inside Segeeyah's head as Gunnison slammed over-large knuckles into the juncture of neck and skull. Oaks fought to drive away darkness as he catapulted forward. Dimly he heard the yelling of Gunnison's companions. Bright anger exploded behind the concussive effect. Segeeyah forced it to keep apart from his dazed concentration on the fight. He still held his Colt and turned now to face his attacker with it leveled on the brute's chest.

"Never punch a man with a gun in his hand," Segeeyah spoke for the first time.

Groping for the .60 caliber single-shot pistol he usually kept in his waistband, Gunnison sneered at him. "Think you're gonna shoot me with that?"

Segeeyah took a step toward Gunnison and produced a crazed expression. "I figure to do just that."

In the same moment, Gunnison discovered he had dropped his hide-out gun in the course of the fight. His face went slate gray, and he nervously eyed the barrel of Segeeyah's Colt. Slowly he dropped to his knees. The Lighthorseman approached rapidly then and slammed the barrel of the revolver against Gunnison's forehead. It made a wet sound. Gunnison's eyes rolled up, and he toppled over backward without a further sound. Segeeyah Oaks turned to see Charlie Singer covering the other occupants.

"Everyone outside," Segeeyah forced himself to say calmly. "This place is closed."

A shout of alarm came from outside. Angry yells answered and then the ragged crackle of gunfire. Charlie Singer nearly beat Segeeyah Oaks to the door. What they saw put them into immediate action.

Some twenty hard-bitten men poured from a low, rambling shed behind the road ranch. They fired weapons as they came. One Lighthorseman lay on the ground, writhing from the wound in his shoulder. Segeeyah emptied his revolver and holstered it. He ran to his horse, Bashful, and yanked the 10 gauge Purdy from the saddle horn. He had half-turned to use it when a thunderous fusillade erupted from the brush beyond the clearing.

Nine men went down in a twinkling. Two more threw up their hands and fell a moment later. Then the blue uniforms of Union troops appeared among the sage and greasewood bushes, firing as they came. One determined ruffian stormed directly at Segeeyah Oaks, and Oaks cut him down with a load of buckshot from the Purdy.

Suddenly the surviving white men had enough and, bleating for mercy, gave up. It took the soldiers only minutes to round up the remainder of the intruders. Segeeyah Oaks walked among them and asked questions of the glazed-eyed prisoners. He received only curses for answers until he reached a youth with a smooth, baby face.

"What are you doing here?"

"We—we come to join up with a man named Moritus. You—you ain't heard of him, I bet."

"Oh, I know of Augustus Moritus, all right," Segeeyah responded. "He's blood-thirsty scum like the rest of you border trash. Looks to me like he's going to be missing out on quite a few reinforcements."

"Wh-what are you gonna do to us?" the frightened youth asked, aware at last he was in the hands of a number of hard-faced Indians.

122

Lieutenant Funston walked up then, leading his mount. Segeeyah glanced from the boy to him. "I think I'll let Lieutenant Funston tell you that. Parker, I'm turning these men over to you for proper punishment under United States law. Trespass in the Tsalagi nation, selling whiskey to Indians, armed rebellion, and a few more we can think up later on."

Funston grinned like a kid with his hand in the licorice jar. "Why, thank you, Bat. I appreciate it."

Later, while the cavalry patrol formed around their prisoners, Funston sought out Sergeant Gresham. He paused beside the non-com and removed his hat. His gaze cut to where Dlayhga Mooney dabbed at the cuts and bloodied nose of Segeeyah Oaks.

"You know, Sergeant, I'm beginning to suspect that perhaps I have misjudged this Indian lawman."

Twelve

Dr. Ambrose Reardon stood in the large bow window of his office in the Cherokee Insane Asylum, some ten miles west of Park Hill, in Tahlequah District. Hands clasped behind his back, he gazed out on the grounds of the institution with a pensive expression. A gentle, kind man, a Quaker by up-bringing, Dr. Reardon was deeply troubled.

The presence of Confederate troops in the Cherokee nation made a constant reminder to him of the terrible war that raged to the east. More disturbing, his discovery upon assuming the directorship of the asylum six years earlier that the Cherokees kept slaves caused him to make some serious readjustment of his outlook. Not that his patients could be condemned for being pro-slavery. Hardly. For them he felt nothing but compassion.

Few of his patients were confined for the recognized mental aberrations. Most of them were in for alcoholic treatment. They had become inebriates for the usual variety of reasons offered by whites in Dr. Reardon's experience. Some had been harmed by contaminated liquor made and sold illegally by whites to the Indians.

Dr. Reardon, over the years working with the Cherokees, had developed another theory. For some reason, alcohol seemed to poison the brains of Indian people.

They had no tolerance for it, and it rapidly established what the good doctor called an addiction, a craving like that of the Chinese for opium. It also affected their reasoning and promoted hostility. He had written papers on the subject, which received universal ridicule from his colleagues. "A drunk is a drunk because he is weak," they thundered. "A man becomes a drunk because he wants to," shouted his detractors.

For all of that, the tall, spare man with the long, delicate fingers of a surgeon, remained steadfast in his belief. In regard to his other patients, Dr. Reardon saw them as victims of complications brought on by the distresses of having their way of life and culture ripped up and strange, new ones imposed on them. Put simply, they could not cope with the harsh conditions of Indian Territory.

He saw them as seeking to withdraw from the unreality of their new lives. Not that he could blame them. Dr. Reardon genuinely liked Indian people. He had grown up in western Pennsylvania, on his father's farm. That gentle Quaker soul had given freely of his largess to hungry, homeless, wandering Indians who happened upon his acres. Young Ambrose had grown up playing with Indian children. Many of their parents had been led into the Society of Friends and accepted Jesus Christ as their savior.

In later years, Dr. Reardon had remembered the plight of those peaceful folk. After he had obtained his medical degree, he had decided to dedicate his life to helping the first Americans, as he saw them, wherever and whenever he could. His early practice had led him into the field of the mind and its puzzling aberrations. In his early forties, that guided him into accepting the position of director for the insane asylum of the Cherokee nation.

Until recently that had been a richly rewarding experience. Now the dark clouds of war threatened to split him asunder. His family had also participated in what became known as the Underground Railroad. Harriet

Tubman had hidden escaped slaves in the Reardon barn on more than one occasion, before she went on to become the leading spokeswoman for the abolitionist movement. Thus, recent events in the Cherokee nation put his scruples in conflict with his sense of obligation to his patients. Where would it all end?

A knock on the door prevented the kindly doctor from answering his own question. "Come in," he invited in Tsalagi, as he turned from the window.

Travis, one of his Cherokee staff, entered, his face alive with agitation. "Dr. Reardon, there is a young boy in the lobby. He says he has an important message for you, most urgent."

"*Wado*, Travis. Is it about one of our patients?"

"I'm not sure, sir. He said he was to speak to you personally."

"I'll see him then." Dr. Reardon gave a final glance over the clusters of patients taking in the early morning sun on the grounds of the asylum as the staffer exited. He sighed heavily. No doubt this would be more bad news.

Two minutes later, Travis ushered a youth of about sixteen into the doctor's office. He looked tired and excited. His agitation projected itself to the knowledge-able physician as clearly as though he had spoken it. Dr. Reardon stepped behind his desk and wet his thin lips.

"Now, young man, what can I do for you?"

"You're Dr. Reardon?"

"That's correct. Who might you be?"

"Dami Sixkiller. My father sent me to warn you."

"Of what?" Dr. Reardon inquired in carefully modulated tones.

"There is a large number of *diyoniga* headed this way. They carry many guns and look to be out for no good."

"Confederate soldiers?" the doctor asked, unease spearing his heart.

"No, sir. They have no flag and don't wear the gray. My paw said to tell you they all wore leather trousers."

"I can't for the life of me attach any significance to that," Dr. Reardon responded in a calming tone. "Is it certain they are white men?"

"Oh, yes, sir. And they're coming on fast. It looks as though they will be here by late afternoon."

Dr. Reardon frowned. Other than those admitted under various treaties, whites were prohibited in the nation. A large band of heavily armed ones was a worse situation. Committed to non-violence, the kindly physician felt confident that a medical facility would not be the target of any group of border ruffians, which the report indicated these men to surely be.

"Well, Tom, you've done well by your father. I appreciate the information."

"Paw said to tell you they were shootin' folks and burning everything in their path."

An icy fist clutched Dr. Reardon's heart. How could he protect his patients from such a threat? His staff would be as helpless against the marauders as would the inmates, he'd reasoned. If these brigands chose to take action against the institution, the poor, frightened, defenseless folk would surely perish. There had to be some answer.

"What is being done about these intruders?" Dr. Reardon asked the Sixkiller boy.

"I took time to warn everyone between home and here, Dr. Reardon. Some folks are makin' up to fight."

Talk of fighting upset the man nearly as much as news of the threat. Yet, if these patients of his were to have a chance, he would have to put aside his convictions, at least a little bit.

"Are you able to carry another message?" Dr. Reardon asked, thinking through his intentions as he spoke.

"Yes, sir. I ain't near winded as yet. Nor is my horse."

"Good lad. What I want you to do is contact every farmer and town council for ten miles around. Ask the people who want to resist these border ruffians to gather here. Out patients need protection, and it is a good, central place to take a stand. Perhaps," the doctor went on, more to himself, "a show of force and determination will convince them to leave the asylum unharmed."

From his position in the vanguard, Augustus Moritus watched a distant figure grow larger as the horse it rode drew closer. Sprinting up to the column on a lathered mount, one of the advance scouts sent out by Moritus sought out the self-made colonel and reported excitedly.

"Colonel, there's a small village of heathens not five miles from here. They're right peaceful and quiet this early in the morning. Thought you'd like to know. It's only two miles off our route, but looks to be a right prosperous town."

Avarice glowed in Augustus Moritus' eyes. He considered the implications and decided quickly. "Very well. Lead us to it, Mr. Walsh."

A mile and a half down the road they followed, Ed Walsh guided the column onto a narrow side lane. Half a mile along this trace, Augustus Moritus observed the other scouts, standing beside their horses, near the top of a rise. He halted his band of brigands and consulted with them.

"It's a right peaceable place, Colonel," one observer repeated Walsh's earlier comment. "Figgers to be forty or fifty people in all."

"What is the name of the town? I don't see anything indicated on this map," Augustus Moritus demanded.

"I dunno. They had a little sign tacked up on a fence post. It was in their lingo, so I copied it down for you." He handed Moritus a grimy scrap of paper on which he had written:

$$z\text{ꝺ}z\text{b}$$

Moritus could make no more of it than his henchman. He shrugged and shoved the paper in a vest pocket. "I want to go forward and study the place," he declared. "It might be we can ride right in."

With Walsh and the other two scouts to lead him, Augustus Moritus advanced up the slope to where the town came into view. It was small indeed, he noticed first. A dozen typical pole lodges, arranged with no noticeable pattern, two three frame, clapboarded structures and a larger pole building. People walked about their business with no sense of impending danger.

Women carried net bags or baskets on their arms with the products of their shopping. A couple of dogs lounged in the shade of walls; three horses had been tied off outside the largest of the frame buildings. A heavy man sat, cocked back on a low stool under a slanting wooden awning. All of the dwellings sat apart far enough that Moritus didn't want to risk anyone getting away to carry word of the raid. He drafted a plan and returned to the column.

"Mr. Longdon, Mr. Sessions, I want you to take twenty men each and circle the town to the south. Stay well out of sight. Block off the road east and the southern side. Mr. Tanner, take twenty men and block the north. No one is to get out alive. The rest of us will attack from this direction. I'll give you half an hour to get in position. When you hear us firing, that is the signal to close in."

Business went on as usual in Star for the next half hour. Augustus Moritus sensed the tension that built in his loins at the prospect of killing and revenge against these slave-owning Indians. He could hardly contain himself for the allotted time. At last, he eyed his big Hamilton pocket watch with relief as the minute hand closed on the appointed moment.

"Let's go forward, Mr. Danvers," he told his second-in-command.

Puzzled at the sound of a plethora of clopping hooves, the man loafing in front of the community bathhouse in

Star raised his head and tilted back the brim of his hat to peer curiously at the large band of men who progressed along the street. They appeared to be heavily armed and, oddly enough, *diyoniga*. In the space between heartbeats, the strangers opened fire.

At the sound of the loud reports, Mr. Drew went over sideways off his stool and crouched low. He sincerely hoped that they had not seen him, or thought he had been shot. Shouting now, the white men charged lodges and fired into open doorways. Women hoisted their skirts and ran for whatever shelter they could find. Some dropped their parcels and bolted away from the menace of the blazing guns. Others screamed in helpless terror, frozen in place. Then Mr. Drew heard the sound of gunshots from behind him, to the south. Still others answered from the east.

By then the raiders had nearly reached the spot where Mr. Drew lay flat on the porch. He tried to think of himself as dead and not move the least little bit. He bit at his lip to keep it from trembling. Then, above his head, he heard a thin tearing sound. The muzzle of a rifle poked out, and flame spurted from it. Deafened by the loud report, Mr. Drew did not hear the shouts of alarm from the street.

"Over there! He shot Ben. Get him," a guerrilla shouted.

Again the rifle spoke. The bullet knocked the cockaded hat from the head of Augustus Moritus. Alarmed by the close call, Moritus turned in the direction of the shot. He saw the rifle protruding from one side of the thinly scraped, oiled hide that formed the window pane. He flung his arm toward the bathhouse, index finger pointing out the target.

"No!" he bellowed. "Over here. In that window."

Realizing he held a revolver in his hand, Augustus Moritus took aim and fired. His pistol ball went low and tore a trough in the back of Mr. Drew's head. Pain erupted only to be smothered in a wall of darkness for the Tsalagi

130

man who had hoped to remain invisible to the invaders.

More shots came from the north as some of the helpless citizens attempted to escape. A torrent of lead slammed into the bathhouse window, shredding it. Still the hidden shooter continued to return fire. His third and fourth bullets downed two more guerrillas. Augustus Moritus adjusted his aim and fired into the wall to the right of the casement. A softly audible grunt followed the crack of the revolver, and then a thud sounded the end of resistance.

But not from everywhere. From the roof of a lodge behind the main force, a thin, foot-long sliver, tufted with a ball of goose down, sped from the blowpipe in the hands of a teen-aged boy. His target felt a stinging sensation in the back of his neck and slapped at it, thinking he had been struck by a wasp. The dart broke off, leaving a quarter-inch under the skin. He came away with it between two fingers and looked at it stupidly. While he did, fire erupted in his neck. A burning, tingling sensation spread rapidly toward his brain.

His vision blurred, and he had only seconds to wonder what had caused him to wet his britches. The powerful substance, made from a thick syrup of boiled down tobacco leaves and the venom of the copperhead, diffused swiftly through his brain. A nerve poison, it left the hapless man paralyzed in seven seconds. He could not even speak or cry a warning during the last fifty-three seconds of his life.

By then, the lad had launched nine more deadly missiles. One struck a horse, which gave a shudder, then relaxed for a while before it took an unsteady leap into the air and gave off a squeal of dimly perceived distress and fell over on its rider stone dead. Two more of the invaders died like the first. Another was spared by the thick leather vest that covered his back and shoulders. The boy had fired hurriedly, and his aim had not always been true. Still, it managed to create panic among the marauders, before the approaching gunmen with Long Tom Longdon spotted the youngster and blasted him into the spirit world.

Rifle fire continued to come from several lodges. Augustus Moritus constantly shifted position to avoid the clouds of powder smoke and dust that rose in profusion. He saw two of his men rush a small lodge and enter, revolvers blazing. A moment later he heard from inside the screams of a young woman, a girl really, he decided. His face twisted in disgust. Lust in a man showed weakness. Yet he was wise enough to realize he could not deny his followers their indulgence. An older woman came from the lodge beside that one in an attempt to surrender.

Augustus Moritus turned his cold eyes on her. His thin, purple lips spread in what passed as a smile, and he shot her in the face. She went down without a groan. He looked up from his victim in time to see a man strike a flint wheel and light a sputtering fuse on a stick of Giant powder. This he hurled into the bathhouse, from which stiff resistance had resumed.

A flat explosion followed which raised the roof of the establishment. Smoke and debris flew through the single window and hurled the unhinged door into the street. In the wake of the blast, shots and the screams of women being violated came from the fringes of town. Two men rode into the blacksmithy and overturned the cooling tub. Water splashed across the hard-pounded dirt floor. At once the blacksmith appeared and buried a large hammerhead in the the skull of one guerrilla. The other shot the smith with cool indifference.

Abruptly, the shooting ceased. Silence filled the street, except for the wails and sobs of ravaged women or those being ravaged. Unmoving, Augustus Moritus surveyed their conquest. A pink tip of tongue flicked out and moistened his lips. He tasted the tang of dust and powder residue. It pleased him mightily.

"Round up wagons, and load everything of value," he commanded.

132

His men set to work at once. They stormed into lodges and came out with every imaginable item of worth, from oil lamps to cook stoves. These they piled in the streets, while others located wagons and hitched teams to them.

These went slowly along the street, where the booty began to fill the wagon beds. Billy White and another guerrilla came out of the general mercantile with wide grins. They approached Augustus Moritus to share their good news.

"Th' feller who kept that store musta run a sort of bank for the folks here-about," Billy crowed in delight. "We found a whole lot of Yankee gold coin and some Confederate paper money."

"Excellent. You've done quite well for yourselves here today," Moritus praised. "See that all of the cash money in town is gathered up. We'll share it out equally among the men." He consulted his Hamilton watch again and sighed heavily. "We've wasted a good deal of time here. It appears we shall not reach Park Hill until tomorrow afternoon. Ah, well, we at least have the satisfaction of this being a lucrative interlude."

Rand Yates approached Augustus Moritus from between two of the lodges that now held only dead Cherokees. He whipped off his hat as he came near and spoke with an obsequious voice. "We're gettin' everything loaded up, Colonel. Some of the boys was askin', could we maybe burn this place to the ground when we leave?"

Augustus Moritus thought that one over a moment, examined what might be gained and nodded his head. "I don't see why not. It would certainly give your Colonel Bledsoe a clear indication that we hold no fondness for these slaving heathens. By all means, burn it down."

Thirteen

Tall black columns of smoke made fine beacons to lead the Lighthorse and cavalry to the ruins of the small village. Segeeyah Oaks clearly read shock on the faces of Lt. Parker Funston, his sergeant, and many of the white soldiers. The wanton slaughter had left not a person or creature alive. Men, women, and children lay sprawled in death. Even the dogs of the town had been shot and lay in the streets.

A choking, gagging sound came from the ranks of the soldiers more than once as they took in the carnage. Angry curses and mutters of outrage reached Segeeyah's ears when the men discovered the victims of the marauders' lust. Unaware of it being bad manners, Lieutenant Funston grabbed ahold of the arm of Oaks, overcome with emotion.

"What sort of animals would do a thing like this?" the young American officer blurted, voice shaky with feeling.

His own grief for his slaughtered people prompted an impolitic reply from an infuriated Segeeyah Oaks. "We call them *diyoniga*—white men."

"Not . . . not all white men, my friend," Parker Funston denied fervently. "I—my men—are outraged by this." He cast his gaze over the smoldering ruins and huddled corpses. "I'll admit I had some reservations about this alliance of ours. But not now. Now I only want to get my hands on the barbarian scum who did this and squeeze until their eyes pop out like grapes."

Segeeyah read Parker as being more truthful than the officer had been at any time so far. It touched him. "I, too, want to see them pay. Excuse my hot words of a moment ago. But, Augustus Moritus *is* a white man, one illegally in the nation, like the prisoners you already have in custody. They are of the same ilk. Believe me, I want nothing more than to avenge these, my brothers and sisters, unknown to me, but—" his voice faltered. "But grieved for nevertheless."

Lt. Parker Funston swallowed with difficulty. "My sorrow is joined with yours. If you would permit us, I think my men would like to join yours in tending to burial, or however you care for your dead."

"Burial is fine. Most of these folks were Christian. See the unburned cross over on the ashes of that large lodge? I—ah—I follow our traditional beliefs. Perhaps someone in the detachment, or one of your people, knows the words for Christian services?"

"I have my field Bible with me," Parker Funston offered. "It has the service for the dead in it. I would be honored."

Tears filled Segeeyah Oaks' eyes, but failed to flow. "Thank you, my friend, *wado*."

"And after that?" Parker Funston asked, clearing his throat.

"The arrangements will have to be done quickly. The ones who did this aren't far away. I am eager to find them."

Since the coming of dawn, Dr. Ambrose Reardon stood in the protruding bow window of his office looking on in amazement and gratitude. Tsalagi men and youths had streamed into the asylum grounds, summoned by the message carried by the young Sixkiller boy. Dr. Reardon felt a pang of conscience as he noted the arrival of five more, all heavily armed like the rest. If they meant to fight these white marauders, how could he condone it?

Yet, he had to admit, they had come as much to protect his patients and himself, as to defy the border ruffians. For that he was grateful. Some of them brought news of the approach of the invaders. One such stood before the doctor's desk at the moment. Reminded of that, he turned away.

"You say there are nearly a hundred of them?"

"Yes, Doctor," the young Tsalagi man told him. "They will be here by some time in the afternoon if they keep coming at the speed they were making when I saw them. They have wagons piled high with what appears to be . . . other people's belongings. It is a terrible thing."

"What is it you intend to do?"

The man shrugged. It was simple to him. "We will fight them."

"I must speak with your leaders. There are considerations for the patients."

"We have no leaders," came the reply.

"Oh, certainly . . . someone has to be in charge," the kindly doctor protested.

"We had—had sort of hoped that you would organize us and lead the fight."

"That is impossible. I am a man of peace. A healer and physician. I have taken an oath to preserve life, not to take it."

Deep appeal glowed in the face of the Tsalagi. "We are simple people: farmers, woodsmen, tradesmen. We had hope that you would show us what to do."

Deeply moved by this appeal, Dr. Reardon considered it in silence. At last he sighed and his shoulders sagged. "I cannot bear arms against my fellow man."

"But you know how it should be done? You can show us what it is we must do to make this hospital into a fortress? You are a learned man, Dr. Reardon. We appeal to you to help. *We* can do the fighting. That we know about. But we must be clever to defeat such a large number."

Dr. Reardon considered all the mental arguments again. He paced back to the window and saw men turning wagons on their sides in the center of the yard. They formed a crude, but effective, barricade, he realized. It would be better if erected at the outer fence, he also understood. Even modestly accomplished horsemen could jump the fence and come on at a rush. With the wagon beds against the split rails of the outer fence, that would prevent this. Shocked at the course his mind had set upon, Dr. Reardon looked at the unskilled preparations with a new eye. He turned back.

"Go and get your leading men. Have them come to me. I will help you to prepare defenses. Perhaps these white men will see we are ready and pass us by."

Although many years junior to the good doctor, the young man doubted that enough to shake his head and make a short response. "I fear not, Doctor. But I will give the good news to those outside and have the three clan chiefs present come to you."

Left alone, Dr. Reardon at last gave in to his frantic anxiety over the impending danger. He directed his attention outside once more and tried to arrange his thoughts on what might be done to defend the asylum from the deadly, determined men riding toward it.

It sat on a flat-topped hill, surrounded by aged trees. Augustus Moritus studied the three-story structure and its outbuildings through field glasses. What surprised him most was the barrier, obviously hastily erected, around the outermost fence line. Wagons, carts, and any sort of movable objects had been strung out behind the split rails to form a defensive wall.

"It appears we are expected," Quint Danvers remarked dryly. "What is that place, anyway?"

"The insane asylum," Augustus Moritus answered him. "Which makes this—ah—display even more surprising. I wouldn't expect Indians, let alone crazy ones, to be capable of organizing a defense. Building fortifications of any sort should be completely beyond them."

"They look to have not known that," said Danvers in an effort at humor.

"Very amusing," Moritus snapped. "So much for that," he went on, planning aloud. "We will divide the men in half. You will lead on the north, and I will command the western advance. Two attacking forces, each supporting the other, is something I'm sure they will not be able to handle. Take that distasteful fellow, Yates, and his deserters with you." Moritus consulted his Hamilton watch.

"We'll attack in . . . twenty minutes," he declared.

"How do you propose to deal with that barricade?" Danvers asked.

"Not so difficult as you might think," Moritus answered confidently. "Locate among the men you take those who can handle a lariat with skill. You only need a small opening, so a pair of them on each of two wagons should do. They will drop a loop over the exposed wheels and pull the wagons over the fence. Once the breach has been created the men can get inside the defenses easily. What I don't understand is why they would choose to fight here."

Quint Danvers considered that a moment. "It does occupy a commanding position. For all that they are savages, I think it is a mistake to discount the abilities of these Cherokees. I would say that someone with military knowledge is directing all of this. After all, the Cherokees fought beside Andy Jackson in the Creek War. It's said some served in the Continental Army during the Revolution and even in the Mexican War a decade ago. Some of them must have learned something from all that."

Abruptly, Moritus smiled, a rictus-like spreading of his purple lips. "I'm fortunate to have you with me, Quinten. Sometimes I don't show my appreciation, but I am grateful for your insight. You help put things in their right perspective. There appears to be some forty men manning that outer defense. I wonder how many are kept in reserve?"

"If these were plains Indians, I'd be inclined to say none. With the Cherokee, it's hard telling. It wouldn't do to get caught with our backs to those wagons and a wall of rifles in front of us."

"Precisely why I'm changing my plan, Quinten. We'll split into thirds, with one portion to remain in place in the event we need a relieving force. That way, these stubborn Cherokees won't have a chance."

George Waters stood on a low stool behind a wagon facing west. That allowed him, at six foot three inches, a clear field of fire. His brother, John, was with the slightly larger force of Tsalagi who had deployed around the inner fence on the grounds of the asylum. He turned now to speak calmly to those hunkered down with their backs against the upended wagon beds.

"They're coming at us, sure enough," George stated. "There looks to be close to a hundred."

"All headed right for us?" a startled younger man asked.

"Hope. About half are coming from the north," George advised. "I think they are going to make it rough for us."

Men came to their feet as the word of the assault passed among them. Each checked the bright copper cap on the nipple of his weapon and made ready to fire. George

Waters had been elected to lead by the men on the west side of the barricade. Although an honor, he cared little for the responsibility. Some of these men, he knew, would be dead within the next five minutes.

"Why are they bothering with a place like this?" the nervous young man asked George Waters.

"They are *diyoniga*," George stated simply.

Waters distrusted white men. He had never known any except for the brutal soldiers who had harried him, a frightened and confused six-year-old, along the Trail of Tears. It had seemed a reasonable and proper thing now to join with his neighbors to fight off the invaders who threatened their homes. Being in charge, however, had not been in his reckoning. The Lighthorse should be here doing the leading, he thought with a silent curse for the war that raged so few miles away in Arkansas. The charging whites looked to be about a good rifle shot away.

"Take aim," Waters called out to the eighteen men along the western barricade. "Make every shot count." Then, his heart pounding ever faster, "Open fire!"

"They turned back onto the main road about a mile from here," one of the point men reported to Segeeyah Oaks after the Lighthorse lieutenant had crossed a shallow creek.

A troubled frown creased Segeeyah's forehead. "They must be headed for Park Hill. And the asylum is between them and the town."

"Even these white men wouldn't attack a hospital?" Dlayhga Mooney questioned.

"I wouldn't bet on it," Lieutenant Oaks responded. "We'll pick up the pace from here on. I'd like to catch them looking one way and being shot at from another."

*   *   *

140

Augustus Moritus had the attack well under way. After the first ragged volley from behind the wagons, which had taken eleven men out of their saddles, the lead riders had recoiled momentarily. Pressed by those behind, they soon started forward. The short, waspish Moritus had counted eighteen rifles in the second fusillade that erupted when less than sixty feet separated his followers from the barricade.

This time the guerrillas returned fire. From his left, Augustus Moritus could hear the sounds of Quint Danvers' men enaging the northern side. Already the picked men in his command had spun loops and roped wagon wheels. Together, one pair turned their mounts and spurred them away. The ropes snapped taut, and the wagon they had hooked began to cant toward the attackers.

Then one of the riders threw up his hands and pitched forward onto the neck of his horse. The panicked animal faltered in stride and put all the weight of the vehicle on a single rope. Plunging powerfully forward, the other man gave out a pain-filled cry when the line between his saddle horn and the wagon's axle snapped and whiplashed around him. The buckboard settled back in place.

A loud crash came as the carriage next to it toppled forward and splintered the rails of the fence. Ed Walsh and Blake Sessions dismounted and grabbed up the abandoned ropes. They scrambles to their saddles as a Cherokee fired wildly at them with an aged Colt Dragoon.

"Well done!" Moritus actually gave a shout of praise when Walsh and Sessions succeeded in pulling down the buckboard. From beyond the wall of vehicles, he heard a voice shouting in the alien speech of the Cherokees. No doubt, Moritus reasoned, a call to retreat.

By then his own mount had carried him to the opening. He quickly saw that the oddly dressed men on the other side had not broken to flee in disorder. They walked backward, firing their weapons as they retreated. Then, to his consternation, Augustus Moritus saw the windows of the asylum bristle with rifle and shotgun barrels, and twice the number of men as at the barricade appeared in the tree-shaded yard.

Turning quickly to a young guerrilla beside him, Moritus snapped, "Have Mr. Tanner bring up the reserve."

"Right away, Colonel," the boyish-faced ruffian replied.

Before the youth had disappeared, a sustained crackle of gunfire came from beyond the asylum grounds in the direction where the reserves waited.

"What the—" Augustus Moritus blurted and cut himself short, coming the closest to using profane speech since he was thirteen years old.

Sgt. Wolf Wind looked grinning at Lt. Segeeyah Oaks. "You got your wish, Bat. There they are, watching the attack on the asylum and blind to our being right behind them."

"Time to bloody these border scum a little, Wolf," Segeeyah said tautly. To the detachment sergeants, he added loudly, "Spread out in a skirmish line. We'll hit them all at once. I know we're in range now, but don't fire until I give the command."

Over on the north side of the asylum, Segeeyah Oaks knew, Lt. Parker Funston would be giving the same command. They had split up immediately upon hearing the sounds of battle. Lieutenant Funston had suggested that Moritus would be likely to have kept some of his force in reserve. He offered the privilege of hitting those guerrillas to the Lighthorse. Oaks had accepted eagerly. Now he eased Bashful out of the line of trees, and the forty Lighthorsemen with him did the same.

They set off at a fast walk that increased to a trot and sped on to a gallop. Weapons at the ready, each man picked a target among the unsuspecting border ruffians. At a distance of fifty yards, the pounding of hooves could not be heard over the din of battle. Closer in, at thirty yards, Segeeyah Oaks let go a shrill whistle and fired one barrel of his Parker shotgun. The column of buckshot spread enough to wound two of the white marauders.

With a jarring crash, the guns of the Lighthorse fired in near unison. Twenty-one men went down. Several thrashed in their death throes. The Lighthorse collided with the stationary guerrillas and smashed through their position with ease. Whirling their horses, they confronted the enemy again.

Revolvers came into play as the Lighthorsemen closed on the stunned, uncomprehending marauders. The crackle of fire rose in volume. Segeeyah Oaks saw two of his men fall from the saddle, and then he emptied the second barrel of the Parker into the face of a screaming guerrilla.

He clubbed down another with the butt stock and then slid the sling over his head and shoulder. Releasing the shotgun, he went for his sidearm. The Colt bucked in his hand and sent a .44 ball buzzing past the arm of a cursing marauder. Adjusting his aim, Segeeyah put the second ball dead center in the florid-faced killer's chest.

Quickly he expended the remaining four. Reholstering his revolver, Segeeyah drew his pride and joy from a saddle holster a Confederate LeMatt .44 revolver. The huge, heavy weapon carried a cylinder of nine rounds, and he used the big gun to good effect now. Three desperados quickly left their saddles as Segeeyah triggered and recocked the LeMatt. He had fired three more when a more collected guerrilla decided the time to be right to jump this ferocious Indian.

Grinning, he rode directly at Segeeyah, slowly raising

143

his Remington into firing position. The Indian cocked his empty six-gun and took aim in turn. Fleetingly, the white border trash wondered what the Injum would think when his hammer fell on an empty chamber. Surprise! Flame and smoke spurted at the overconfident guerrilla behind a .44 ball that turned his brain to porridge.

A sudden lull came in the brief battle. Only the groaning of the wounded could be heard. Segeeyah looked around and saw that the enemy reserve had been eliminated. Still the fighting raged around the asylum.

"Form up!" he commanded. "Reload on the move!"

Working furiously to rearm themselves, the Lighthorse set off to where the main struggle continued. Segeeyah Oaks knew only too well that all could still be lost. A new worry assailed him. He had not as yet heard any indication of Lieutenant Funston and the soldiers joining the attack.

Fourteen

Sergeant Gresham paused and pointed between two wind-twisted tree trunks. "If we cut through here, sir, we can swing right in behind the guerrillas. I'd say we could spread out in line of skirmishers right away, and every man have his carbine ready to open fire on command. That way we save time and can catch them by complete surprise."

"Do we charge them, Sergeant?"

Lieutenant Funston had learned since his disastrous first encounter with the Leatherlegs. He came to trust the experience of his platoon sergeant and asked more often for advice. This was no idle question. With only twenty men fit for duty, a charge might be another invitation to failure.

Gresham produced a grin. "Ordinarily, sir, that would be the textbook solution. But in this instance, I think we should let them run into us."

A twinkle came to the young officer's eyes. "I see your point. I was thinking it might be prudent not to give up the element of surprise. How do we go about getting them to run into us?"

Sergeant Gresham relaxed into an easy smile. "I have a feeling those Cherokees will have them running soon enough."

"Very well, Sergeant, move 'em out. We'll halt on the edge of the cleared fields."

Lieutenant Oaks and the Lighthorsemen had crossed half the distance from the dead of the reserve. The volume of fire increased sharply as they closed on the breached barricade. Spent balls thudded into the ground, and a few cracked past them. Then from closer to the tall structure of the asylum came a growing shout. A constant roar of gunfire swelled to drown out the whoops and war cries of the aroused Tsalagi defenders.

"Get ready," Segeeyah called out. "I think the Leatherlegs are about to be pushed back. Spread out and take aim."

They came in a rush, pursued by the yelling defenders. Knives and war clubs flashed in the sunlight. Some of the guerrillas turned from confronting the aroused swarm closing on them to stare in horror at the waiting Lighthorsemen.

"Fire!" Segeeyah Oaks commanded and discharged his reloaded Parker. Both barrels banged off in close order. Two Leatherlegs lost their faces in crimson smears. All along the line, the Lighthorse blazed away at the fleeing marauders. A voice called out over the tumult.

"To the north! Head out that way!"

Unaccustomed to being routed, Augustus Moritus experienced a moment of blind panic as what remained of his army of brigands swarmed around him. He thought back to the only other time he had known ignominious defeat. That had been with John Brown and his Jayhawkers. They had been raiding across the border in Missouri and had been attacked in turn by the men who followed William Clark Quantrill.

Disaster had resulted, and Moritus saw the likelihood of

it happening again. He had to regain control of the swiftly changing situation. To that end he put spurs to the flanks of Excaliber and jostled into the clear.

"Turn and fight your way out. Make them pay dearly," he shouted to his disorganized men. "Hold at the fence."

Slowly, his words had effect. Men on the verge of fleeing moments before reloaded and faced back toward the menace of the impromptu militia and the Lighthorse. They began to walk backward, reloading and firing as they withdrew in a more orderly fashion. Encouraged, Augustus Moritus pushed through them again and made for the opening in the northern barricade. Beyond it, he exhorted the Leatherlegs to make an organized resistance.

"Form up! Close the gaps," he commanded. "Return their fire, blast you."

Quint Danvers appeared out of the throng and came to his side. "We should go north a ways. There seems to be Cherokees all around us any other direction."

"Yes, good idea, let's get them moving," Moritus decided.

In only seconds it appeared as though the way had been found to break off contact. Augustus Moritus took heart from the return of discipline to his followers. Only one bitter truth taunted the small figure of Moritus.

He had lost nearly a third of his effective force. Going on to Park Hill was out of the question. If only he could break out of this trap, all would go well.

And it did. Until their northern retreat ran into Lieutenant Funston and his solders.

"Here they come, Lieutenant," Sergeant Gresham announced jauntily.

"Thoughtful of our Cherokee friends to chase them this way," Funston quipped back. "Steady, men, fire on my command. Take aim . . . Fire!"

A wall of smoke appeared at the tree line. Dismay and

fright ran through the ranks of the Leatherlegs. Their spirits badly trampled by the ferocious encounter with the Cherokees at the asylum, they had little fight in them. Most thought only of escape.

Yelling to release the terrible tensions within, they set off blindly to the west. Another volley slashed into them. Seven men went down, along with four killed horses. Over the thunder of controlled fire, Augustus Moritus heard a voice giving commands he could understand, and it chilled him.

"One more volley. Aim . . . Fire!" came the English words.

It could only mean the army. Every man among the Leatherlegs knew that as well, and it added urgency to their efforts at flight.

"Third and fourth ranks, prepare to mount . . . mount!" came a different voice.

"First and second ranks, prepare to mount . . . mount!" answered it. "Wheel right and form line of skirmishers. Forward at the gallop . . . Ho!"

Augustus didn't stay to hear more. Spurs punishing the flanks of Excaliber, he bolted to the front of the fleeing Leatherlegs. Some of those in the rear retained presence of mind enough to turn in their saddles and fire a parting volley at the soldiers.

Lt. Parker Funston, in the lead, felt a solid blow to the top of his shoulder and a hot explosion of pain. A quick look revealed his left epaulet blown away and a deep gouge in the meat below, which freely ran with blood. Uncomfortable, he evaluated, but not incapacitating. Further to his left he saw the Lighthorsemen streaming at an angle to intercept the fleeing Leatherlegs.

Pounding hooves sent clots of turf sailing high; powder smoke and dust obscured the rapidly departing enemy. Lieutenant Funston had settled in at the center of the charging formation. He drew his sidearm to signal the others to do the same. They would have little effect, he

148

admitted, but it might lift the morale of the men to see those who had humbled them running for their lives.

Taking their lead from their officer, the cavalrymen opened fire on the guerrillas. Few of their rounds struck men or horses. They shot their cylinders dry and sought to replace them with ready loaded ones. Inevitably, percussion caps went flying, and one man dropped his replacement cylinder. Within a minute, better than half had at least four ready loads in reassembled revolvers.

Those were expended quickly. Gradually, the terrain began to rise before them. It put a strain on already tired horses. The gap between the Leatherlegs and the cavalry widened. Lieutenant Funston noted that the Lighthorse had begun to lag also. The prairie seemed to swallow the men they pursued, and Funston recalled a creek they had forded on the way to the asylum. Time to make a decision, he realized. He raised his right arm to indicate his intention.

"At the trot . . . ho!" Funston commanded.

"We lettin' them get away, sir?" Sergeant Gresham asked, his tone formal.

"No. We'll keep pressing, but the horses are about run out. Look, the Lighthorse are dropping back, too."

"You're right, sir. Way we're goin', we'll join up with them in a quarter mile."

"None too soon. We need to lay a plan on how to deal with what's left of the Leatherlegs," Funston suggested.

Augustus Moritus and his Leatherlegs barely slowed as they splashed through the creek. For the moment they had lost sight of the troops pursuing them. It did little to ease the anxiety of the badly demoralized men. Up until today they had had it easy, most realized. Now they had gotten a taste of what real resistance could be. Few had any liking for it.

By nature, men who shunned organization and responsibility, the border trash, bandits and petty criminals who made up Augustus Moritus' command, had little beyond their bravado upon which to rely. The presence of federal troops had badly shaken them. Their headlong flight had not given rise to any discussion. That would come later. All they knew was that friends and acquaintances had died at the hands of Indian farmers, the professionals of the Lighthorse, and Union soldiers, obviously from Fort Gibson. It left them fearful and uncertain.

Such debilitating thoughts had settled on Augustus Moritus as well. He had taken a disastrous loss. Had he been a man given to cursing he could turn the air blue now. Had the Cherokees switched sides all unknown to him? That would account for the presence of Union troops. What else could it be? Back on the prairie, Moritus banished such thoughts. He looked back toward the creek to see the cavalry and Lighthorse halted together near the lip of the opposite bank. It appeared as though they had broken off the chase.

That heartened him. Yet, it left him with another imponderable. What if the two units worked together? How could that be? From what he had heard from Rand Yates of Colonel Bledsoe, it was doubtful at best that such an alliance had been worked out. Still, he couldn't deny what his eyes revealed to him. A shrug eased the gnawing concern. With a light touch of spurs, he struck out on Excaliber to take the lead. When he reached Quint Danvers he spoke up with forced cheerfulness.

"We'll put some distance between us and them. Then we can take a rest and work out what to do next."

"I can tell you that now. I say we head straight back to the valley. We can hold off an army there."

Augustus Moritus mulled that over a moment, adjusting his horse's gait to that of his second-in-command. "As usual, you've come up with the right answer, Quint. That is precisely what we shall do. We fortify the place, put sharpshooters in the gap."

"If them soldiers and the Injun police are working together, they'll come after us."

"Oh, yes, I'm counting on that," Moritus stated brightly. "And we'll have a nice little surprise waiting for them."

Chasing the retreating Leatherlegs had taken the Lighthorse and cavalry some twelve miles distant from the asylum. Although he wanted to ride back and make certain everything was secure at the hospital, Segeeyah Oaks knew that his duty demanded he remain to hunt down the white invaders and take the survivors in for trial. Provided, of course, he could convince Lt. Parker Funston to let him have custody.

"We might as well camp here," Funston had suggested at the east bank of the creek. "I could use some patching up."

Segeeyah Oaks disagreed. "Camping by moving water dulls the senses. A man cannot hear someone sneaking up on him. Have someone bandage your wound, or I can do it, then we can make a few more miles before nightfall."

"Thank you for the offer. My Sergeant Gresham is a handy man with things medical. Besides," he added for the sergeant's benefit, "I think he might have some painkiller along that would be most welcome about now."

Blushing furiously, Sergeant Gresham unconsciously patted one saddlebag. "Yes, sir, Lieutenant, sir. As it happens I do have some medicinal alcohol along."

"Fine, then. I'll start with three fingers. Join me, Bat?" he asked of Segeeyah.

"Thank you, but I have never taken a drink."

"Oh. That's right, it is illegal here in your country," Funston offered to cover his own embarrassment. Then, to Gresham, "Pour it in a tin cup, Sergeant. I'll down a little and use the rest on my wound."

"Yes, sir. I've already made arrangements for our other wounded."

"You're a gem, Sergeant Gresham," Funston praised sincerely. He seated himself on a rock and waited for the whiskey, his attention back on Segeeyah. "Do you really expect those Leatherlegs to sneak back during the night?"

"No. I imagine they are making all speed back to their hideout. It's simply that incorrect actions become bad habits quite easily. Back in our mountains, we had a natural alarm system in fallen limbs, leaves, and such. Out on this prairie, there's not a lot of that. You need to hear the swish of the tall grass against a man's legs."

"I've a lot to learn, I suppose," Funston admitted. "Ouch! Damn, that stings, Sergeant," he yelped, caught by surprise by the bite of the raw liquor in his wound.

"You'd prefer horse liniment, sir?" Gresham asked straightfaced.

"No-no, that's all right, Gresham."

Segeeyah Oaks hid his amusement behind a big, square hand. He admired the deftness of the sergeant in cleaning and binding Funston's wound and noted that others with minor scrapes or punctures had theirs treated with equal skill. The soreness along his ribs prickled Segeeyah. The ministrations of Wolf Wind to his hurts seemed crude by comparison. Within twenty minutes, the joined forces were ready to ride out.

Low fires ringed the campsite. Soldiers and Lighthorsemen moved about freely, sharing their differing rations with the eagerness of boys at a picnic. A low prairie breeze stirred the grass in a prolonged sigh. Segeeyah Oaks and Parker Funston sat with their backs against blanket-draped sage bushes, tin cups of coffee in hand. They had been talking easily about the day's engagement with the Leatherlegs of Augustus Moritus. Now, in the mellowing

152

hours after supper, the conversation turned to personal matters.

"Do you have a family, Parker?" Segeeyah asked.

"Parents, yes. But not a wife. A young officer, just starting out, is hardly in a position to afford a family. That comes with promotions and maturity. What about you?"

"I'm married, her name is Cloud. We have two children, a girl who is seven, and a boy five. And I have three younger brothers, the oldest just fourteen. The same age, I suspect, as our young Squirrel Three-Skulls."

"Where do you call home?"

"I'm assigned to an outpost in this district. My wife is there."

"My home is in New Hampshire."

"Then you are a genuine Yankee," Segeeyah quipped.

"You're familiar with New England?"

"We study geography as well as history, Parker. You know, truth to tell, I think you'd fit in easily as a Cherokee. At least in one of the larger towns."

"I take that as a compliment. You, your men, too, could be any troops I've encountered in the Union Army, for that matter. I'll admit I'm impressed. Now, what should we be planning for Augustus Moritus and his scum?" Funston added, changing the course of their revealing conversation.

"I'm visualizing a gallows and a rope. But first we have to catch them. As it stands we don't know where they are holed up. I want to put out advanced scouts, at first light tomorrow, after everyone has rested. We come on behind. I think it wiser to trail at a distance until we track these guerrillas to their lair."

"My impression, too. It will give the men and animals a chance to recover, too," Lieutenant Funston surmised.

"Yes. And a good thing," Segeeyah Oaks expanded. "Because when we find them we have to hit hard and fast."

Fifteen

Col. Owen Bledsoe looked at his adjutant in astonishment. "Not so much as a message?" he demanded.

"No, Owen. It is as though Lieutenant Funston and his platoon had ridden off the edge of the world. No communication with them at all. You don't think . . . ?"

Colonel Bledsoe made a gesture of impatience. "The idea of desertion would never occur to him. Though his men may have risen up against him."

"He has Gresham for platoon sergeant. A good, steady NCO. He'd see something like that coming and put a stop to it fast. Although outside of foul play, I'm at a loss to suggest what could have kept him from reporting in," Major Mueller added.

Colonel Bledsoe drove one fist into the palm of his other hand. "It's not bad enough we have a lieutenant and a whole platoon gone missing, we are being surrounded by Indians. They grow in number daily. And I'm not unmindful that these Chickasaw, Creek, and Choctaw have all aligned themselves with the Confederates. Damn this rebellion and the men behind it."

"Politicians, Owen."

"Yes, Hans. Men in satin-striped pants, morning coats, and top hats. They howl and bluster like a blizzard, and all that comes out of it is more misery for the likes of you and I. I wish by all that's holy that the constitution required that all these politicians who drum up wars had to lead troops into the first engagement. You'd see a world at peace damned fast that way. But that doesn't take care of our Rebel Indians. Do you suspect that they are getting up to an attack on the fort?"

Mueller shook his head. "Not likely. I've had some of the reliables, the half-breeds who scout for us, out among them. They listen to the talk in the lodges at night. So far not a thing has been said about turning to war. All they seem to expect is to get their rations earlier."

"Sometimes I feel like a man on an island that is slowly sinking into the sea."

A chuckle came from the adjutant. "One strip of sand left, eh?"

"Something of that sort. Well, I'm not going to merely sit here and stew over it. I want three companies assembled after the noon meal. They are to go among the savages and disburse them. Get them moving back to where they belong."

"That might be a risky undertaking, considering we are undermanned," Mueller suggested.

"If we do nothing, there will be more here tomorrow, and the day after, more still. The way I see it, Hans, it is better to take immediate action than wait around."

"Very well, Owen," Mueller said, rising with a sigh. "I'll advise the company commanders."

A finger's width after the sun's high point, a line of soldiers showed up outside the lodge of the Choctaw chief. With a lot of shouting and gesturing, they made it clear that they expected everyone to break down their lodges and leave the ground outside the fort. Chief Warbow came out to face them, arms crossed over his chest, obsidian eyes glittering with suppressed anger.

"Why do you do this?" he asked.

Through a Delaware interpreter, a man the whites called a halfbreed, the soldier with three stripes answered him. "Colonel's orders, Chief. There are too many of you gathering around the fort. After all, you are sidin' with the Johnny Rebs."

"We may agree with them, but we are not at war with you. We came here to be at peace. So long as there is no fighting, what reason is there for you to run us off?" Warbow demanded.

"Because the colonel says so."

"Is he the White Chief in Wah-sing-ton?"

"No. But he is our chief. What he says, we do. So, it's pack up the women and children, Chief, and move back into your nation."

"We will not move."

"Then we'll move you," the sergeant snapped, his patience wearing thin.

Elsewhere in the growing encampment, the troops met similar opposition. Severely outnumbered, they wisely decided to take this turn of events back to their officers and let them figure out what to do. Observing from the uncompleted parapet over the gate, Col. Owen Bledsoe watched in white-lipped fury as only a handful of families struck their shelters and made to depart. With an hour all of the troops had returned to the garrison. They had accomplished little, Bledsoe noted sourly.

With hard, jerky steps, he climbed down and crossed the parade ground. Inside the headquarters, he snapped testily at the regimental sergeant major. "I want the company commanders of those troops in my office in fifteen minutes with an explanation of that fiasco."

Near mid-afternoon two Lighthorsemen, accompanied

by one of Lieutenant Funston's troopers, returned to the main column. They quickly detailed their information. The news encouraged Segeeyah Oaks.

"They kept moving fast, didn't spend five hours in camp, I'd say," one of the Lighthorse informed the two officers. "We trailed them all the way to the Arkansas. Once across, they struck southwest into Canadian District. West of Joshua's Mountain, we came across a large, deep valley cut well down below ground level. They have buildings and broken ground down there. It looks like they plan to stay a good while. We, and Henry here," he pointed to the soldier, "scouted the rim all around. There's no easy way down. At the far end, where the river that runs through the valley has cut a gorge, we got a look at the only sure way in."

"Which is no doubt heavily guarded," Lieutenant Funston suggested.

"Yes, sir," Henry contributed. "We saw sharpshooters stationed along the walls, high up and right beside the narrow path that runs along the stream."

"Would it be possible to approach from that direction undetected? Say at night?" Funston pressed.

"I'm not sure, sir. I'd say not. One shot fired would alert everyone all the way into the valley."

"Nevertheless, it seems to be the only way in. What do you think?" Funston asked Oaks.

"My men are fairly good rough country riders. Unless the valley walls are straight up and down, I'm certain we can get in somewhere."

Funston considered that for a long moment. "Now then, I propose that I take my platoon along the road to the nearest point to the gorge. We'll force entry and proceed at all possible speed toward the enemy encampment."

"Meanwhile, we'll find that right spot on the rim and be in position to support you. If these men say there is only one way in, they mean it. At least, I'm willing to wager

Augustus Moritus believes so, too."

"How long for us to do this?" Sergeant Gresham asked.

"I'd say a day and a half, if we move cautiously and avoid any discovery by the Leatherlegs," Segeeyah Oaks said. "That's wide open country down there. We crippled him some yesterday, but Moritus has enough men that if we are caught in the open, they can still wipe us out," he concluded.

Grim faces filled the committee room in the capitol at Tahlequah. Word had come of the bold raid conducted less than thirty miles south of the city. The Speaker raised a hand for attention and spoke slowly, thoughtfully.

"We need a consensus on this. Our people need something more than what they read in the newspaper. We should call a convention at once."

"What have our Confederate friends said or done about this invasion?" asked a portly lawgiver.

"So far, nothing. There hasn't been time to inform them fully of the situation," the Speaker responded. "From what we have learned, these guerrillas—Leatherlegs they call themselves—have been repulsed at the insane asylum. They suffered heavy losses. The Lighthorse are in pursuit."

"Yes, the Lighthorse," the rotund man caught up. "We should send more of them."

"We don't have that many more," the Speaker offered.

"What about Colonel Drew's men?" another lawgiver inquired.

"The former commander at Fort Gibson gave them parole, provided they do not bear arms. They are doing what they can, where they can. We cannot arm them and risk a confrontation with the Union Army," the Speaker insisted.

"Our people are not going to be shooting at one another," the heavy-set lawgiver responded. "We should have Drew's men take over all police duties, and send the Lighthorse to deal with these—ah—Leatherlegs."

Mutters of agreement went among the gathered Tsalagi legislators. The idea grew support as it went around the room. The Speaker considered it, found it had appeal. Perhaps this offered a solution without the cost in lost time calling a convention to decide. At last he signaled for silence again.

"We should vote on this. If someone can put the proposal into sensible order, we can reach a conclusion and put it in operation."

When the discussion ended and the motion framed, the vote went for it unanamously. A delegation left the capitol to take their decision to Colonel Hood for activation.

Puffball clouds cast dappled shadows across the tall, lush grass of the basin as Augustus Moritus stood surveying the activities of his disgruntled band. They smarted from their defeat and rout. He had encountered resistance that bordered on mutiny when he outlined his plans for defending the valley.

When he pointed out how easily they would entrap the Lighthorse and any soldiers who came after them, open disbelief registered on the faces of the men. He had promised an immediate distribution of the hard money they had obtained, which raised spirits some. Two days had gone by after that with visible evidence of their improved outlook. Now, he decided, was the time to unveil his final trump card.

"Gather up the men," Augustus Moritus advised Quint Danvers.

While the Leatherlegs streamed in from their efforts to erect defensive bastions, Moritus walked to a small tent beside his own. There he loosened the sidewall facing the assembled men. He let it drop away to reveal two shrouded objects that sat squat and indefinable in the center of the shelter. When all except those on lookout in the gorge had arrived, Moritus stepped forward slightly and grasped the edge of the canvas cover.

"Some of you have asked how I can remain so confident of victory over any force sent against me. Many of those are new and unaware of recent developments. Under here is the answer to your doubts. They were taken a short time ago from some Confederate troops in Arkansas." With that he yanked away the tarpaulin to reveal the dark barrel of a six-pound field piece.

He took short, measured steps to the second cover and pulled it away, revealing a second light cannon. "That's the way, Colonel!" a bearded guerrilla shouted. "I done served in the artillery. If you want someone to shoot those babies, I'm willin'."

"Good man," Moritus barked cheerily. "Now you see why we are all but invulnerable in this sheltering basin," he went on. "I say, let them come! We shall defeat them with shot and shell."

A ragged cheer broke out. Augustus Moritus smiled to himself. His ploy had worked. Secretly he wished that the enemy would not find them, yet he realized that to be beyond any likelihood.

Deep and somber, war drums throbbed in the southwest corner of Indian Territory. Hundreds of warriors of the fierce Kiowa had heard of the unrest to the north. They gathered now to talk of it and decided what to do. Chief spokesman among them was a firebrand known as Two Moons. Only a few years past forty, he was in prime condition as a war leader. He had ridden up out of north Texas to carry the call to battle to others of his people.

A squat, powerfully built man with thick, muscular arms and legs, he was known to whites as Iron Shirt. The name had come from the ancient, rust-scabbed Spanish *curias* he wore into battle. In earlier days it had saved his life and the lives of his predecessors who had possessed it. That had been in the time of lower chamber pressures and exclusively round ball ammunition. Wise in the ways of such things, Two Moons wore the armor now for the symbolic medicine it possessed.

Two Moons brought with him his life-long friend and companion on the war path, Bullhide. Bullhide had been born the summer Two Moons reached his eighth year. The older boy had befriended the younger when Bullhide turned four. They had been inseparable since. In adulthood, Bullhide's youthful vigor added a fine counterpoint to the mature reserve of Two Moons, so that they planned raids that were invariably successful. Equally stocky, yet taller than Two Moons, Bullhide stood now beside his friend near the large sacred drum.

Together they surveyed the swarm of warriors who had answered their call to a war council. Each felt satisfaction for his own reasons. Two Moons noted the older, more settled men among the Kiowa who had turned out. Bullhide took pleasure in seeing so many young men, even stripling youths, apprentices who would tend the horses, care for broken equipment and serve as eyes for the war party when it went out to engage the white men.

"We are fortunate, brother," Bullhide expressed his enthusiasm.

"Yes. If they agree, we can punish the whites who invade our home and return with many songs to sing," Two Moons observed.

"Once," Bullhide declared, his arm extended in a wide, sweeping gesture, "this was all our home. Then the whites took it and gave it to other people. I think we should take it all back."

Two Moons frowned, and he made a show of pondering the point. "It would not be wise to fight one tribe against the other at this time, Bullhide. Visitors have told of how the people of the Creek and Chickasaw look with kind faces on the whites of the Southern side. If we come among them in a friendly manner, many might join with us. If we show an angry face, they can stand in the way of our victory over the whites."

Bullhide smiled at his old friend. "You are the wise one between us, Two Moons. I had not thought of that."

"Be sure you remember it when we talk in council," Two Moons admonished.

North and east of Joshua's Mountain, Lt. Segeeyah Oaks listened to an excited report from young Sololi Three-Skulls. It appeared that a large band of Creeks had entered the nations.

"Slow down and tell me again," Segeeyah urged the boy.

"There must be fifty of them. They are headed north, toward Fort Gibson it looks like."

"How far from us?"

"A short ride," Squirrel measured mentally. "Over two ridges. Corporal Bauxman is keeping track of them."

"This is interesting. Take the drag and cool out your mount. We'll head that way at a trot."

Lieutenant Oaks and the Lighthorse came upon the large war party within fifteen minutes. The head count had been fairly accurate, Segeeyah acknowledged. He figured it to be around fifty-six or -seven. When the Lighthorsemen showed themselves, a deputation of three Creeks, painted for war, trotted away from the column to meet with the policemen. At a distance of sixty feet they slowed, made friendly sign, and came on.

"You are a ways from your homeland," Segeeyah

prompted when the courtesies had been exchanged.

"We go to punish the white soldiers at the fort," the spokesman stated flatly.

"Why is that?"

Eyes narrowed, the Creek explained. "Some of our people have been badly treated by the soldiers. They went to the fort to be sure to get their rations. The chief of the whites forced them to leave. It is a bad thing."

"Yes," Segeeyah agreed. "From what we know, that is not like the soldiers."

The Creek cocked his head to one side, his full lips downturned. "They have done this thing to other people. The new chief is not like the one before. He sees us as dirt. He must learn differently."

Segeeyah made a negating gesture. "This cannot be done from inside the Tsalagi nation. Our leaders do not want to excite trouble."

"You have the gray-coat soldiers in your nation. There will be trouble anyway," the Creek stated scornfully.

"So far there has not been. We intend to keep it that way," Segeeyah said more forcefully.

"We will fight them."

"My men and I will prevent you."

"You would spill the blood of the *Augusa,*" he demanded, using the Tsalagi word for Creek, "for the sake of white men?"

"I would spill no man's blood. But, I can't let you go on to do something that would draw us into the fight."

Sizing up the number of Lighthorse, the Creek warrior stated flatly, "You are not enough to stop us."

"Yes, we are," Segeeyah countered. Hedging the details somewhat, he added, "Only two days ago, we defeated a party of white men twice your size."

Eyes widened and brows arched, the Creek offered mockingly, "You are fierce warriors indeed. Here me, Lighthorse. Not the white men, not any of you are Creek."

163

Segeeyah had been doing some quick thinking. "Listen to me. I believe we can defeat you. I believe one of my Lighthorse can beat the best single man of your war party."

A cold smile creased the face of the Creek. "I do not agree."

"Can you agree on this? Let us choose our best and let them fight, not to the death, but until one gives up. If our man wins, you will return to your country, do no harm to the soldiers. If your man wins, we will do nothing to stop you in your attack."

Light flickered in the Creek's eyes. "If we win, you will join us in our fight against the soldiers."

Segeeyah gave that a thought for a long, silent moment. "I have your word that we will abide by this saying?"

"You have the word of a war leader of the Creek and the son of a chief."

"Then I agree. Pick your man."

In ten minutes the Creeks came back to the neutral position between the two forces. They brought with them a veritable giant of a man. He reminded Segeeyah Oaks of Jumper Bendbow, without the thick middle. At least three axe-handles wide at the shoulders, his arms bulged and rippled with muscle.

At once, Segeeyah accepted the inevitable. It had been his idea. Which was why he had made no effort to select a champion. He would face this huge threat himself.

Sixteen

Stripped to the waist, Segeeyah Oaks made ready to engage the giant who towered over his six-foot-two by nearly a head. He cast an uncertain glance at Wolf Wind. "Remember, if I lose, we join them."

"We can't fight the soldiers," Wolf protested.

"I've given my word." Segeeyah turned to the war leader of the Creeks. "I am ready."

"No knives. No guns. When one man cannot get up, the fight is over." His broad, dark features took on a smirk of confidence.

"Agreed." Fire flashed and the green flecks stood out in Segeeyah's eyes.

Without warning, the huge Creek launched himself at Segeeyah. The Tsalagi jumped to one side and smacked the Creek on one side of his head with an open palm. Snorting his irritation, the Creek spun back to face his opponent. He came in again, slower, chin lowered, arms wide. Segeeyah feinted to the same side, reversed himself, and kicked the huge Creek in the ribs.

Grunting, the Creek grabbed Segeeyah's ankle and spun him around. "Good, Touches-Sky," the war leader encouraged.

Touches-Sky released Segeeyah when momentum had

built. Staggered, on one foot, the Tsalagi tottered toward his silent, watchful men. He recovered and turned on Touches-Sky in time to duck a vicious swing with a war club. It swished over his head, and he drove a fist into the Creek's arm pit.

His arm numbed, Touches-Sky released his grip on the club. It thudded to the hard turf. Segeeyah followed up with two fast kicks to the exposed belly of Touches-Sky. Gagging through a roar of anger, the Creek left his head vulnerable to a two-handed clap over both ears.

Pain and a strident ring erupted in the head of Touches-Sky. He pawed the air in search of his enemy. Segeeyah danced around, working on his opponent's legs with low, flickering kicks. Touches-Sky began to sag. With a bellow of outrage, he flung himself at Segeeyah when the Lighthorse lieutenant stepped injudiciously close.

Burly arms encircled Segeeyah's middle. The floating rib on his right side cracked and agony enveloped him for a flash before he gained control over it. Slowly the pressure drove the air from Segeeyah's lungs. He fought for a foothold, while his hands plucked uselessly at the bulging forearms that confined him.

Black circles danced behind Segeeyah's eyes. With fading vision, he looked down at the wicked grin on the face of his tormentor. A desperate thought speared him. With both thumbs, in a pinching action against closed fingers, Segeeyah spread that grin unbearably wider.

Mentally Segeeyah visualized ripping off the cheeks of Touches-Sky. His arms quivered with the effort he applied to achieving that. Slowly the head bent backward. A bear-like growl came from Touches-Sky's throat. Oily beads of sweat broke out on his forehead. At last Segeeyah felt the pressure on his body slacken. He poured more of his waning strength into his effort.

"Aaah-yaaah!" Touches-Sky bellowed as the pain became overwhelming and forced him to release his grip on the wily Cherokee.

Segeeyah took a half-step backward out of that deadly grasp and kneed Touches-Sky under the chin. Large, white teeth clopped together, and the big Creek flipped over backward to flop loudly on the ground. Panting to recover his loss of breath, Segeeyah stood over him. Satisfied that the fight had gone out of his opponent, Segeeyah turned to accept capitulation from the war leader.

Touches-Sky moved like lightning, raising his legs to scissor them around Segeeyah's middle. He threw the Lighthorseman solidly to the thick turf and began to pommel him with fists and elbows. Momentarily stunned, Segeeyah suffered the blows for what seemed the longest ten seconds in his life. Then his fingers groped at his sash.

They closed over the haft of his war club, and he yanked it free. In a blur, his arm rose in a wide arc, then descended. Stars and pinwheels of colored light fountained inside the head of Touches-Sky. He rocked unsteadily to one side, pawed at his throbbing skull, and fell heavily on one shoulder. Aching, Segeeyah slowly pulled himself free. He did not trust to chance this time. Instead, he bent low over his adversary and rolled him onto his back.

In the process, Segeeyah caught a fist full in the mouth. It snapped him upright, and he rocked back on his moccasins. Lumbering like a wolf-harried bull bison, Touches-Sky came to his feet.

"Not again." Segeeyah said under his breath.

Dripping blood from nose and lips, Touches-Sky ignored his opponent for the moment. Bent double, he searched the ground for his war club through bleary eyes. He soon found it and pounced. With a grunt of effort, he came upright and faced Segeeyah Oaks.

Segeeyah had recovered his own, and with it the fingers of his left hand had scratched up a fair pinch of dirt and pebbles. Bleeding from his own share of cuts, he faced off with the giant Creek and shuffled from left to right, eyes set on those of his opponent.

Instinct told Segeeyah when the huge Touches-Sky intended to launch his attack. The shafts of their war clubs met with a loud crack above Segeeyah's head. The superior weight of Touches-Sky bore him backward and down. Without considering the worst consequence, Segeeyah let himself be driven further over.

At the last instant, he let himself go, drew his knees up against his belly and relaxed as best he could to take the contact with the ground. When his shoulders struck, he flexed his legs and powered them upward. Touches-Sky had been caught totally unaware.

He uttered a startled cry as he went flying, launched by a human catapult. He landed heavily, the air driven from his lungs. Stifling a groan of sheer pain, Segeeyah sprang to his feet and advanced on his adversary, war club raised for a terrible blow. The Creek war leader stepped between him and the fallen Touches-Sky.

"Enough. You have won. We will return to our homes."

Segeeyah Oaks gave him a faint smile. "Or at least attack from the Creek side of the border," he remarked through his discomfort. They clasped forearms in a sign of peaceful intent and, with the Lighthorse watching uncertainly, the two parties went their separate ways.

Steve Medicine Pipe turned from the small fire with a cloth dripping warm water. "You look a mess," he said to Segeeyah Oaks.

"I don't feel a whole lot better," Segeeyah agreed. "We can't waste much time here cleaning me up. We have to get on the move."

"We're going to be late in reaching the basin," Wolf Wind agreed.

"And no way of letting the *Amayehli* lieutenant know it," Segeeyah observed with irritation. "We'll make the best time we can."

Squirrel came up, eyes big. "That was some fight, Lieutenant Oaks," the boy offered, bursting with pride in his officer. "You are indeed a clever fighter."

Segeeyah sighed. "There should have been no reason for that to happen. We should be at peace with those around us. Now, everyone get something to eat and get mounted."

Two Moons and Bullhide rode at the front of their war parties. The feasting, dancing, and council had gone well. More than 120 warriors followed the two southern Kiowas, along with three of their own war chiefs directing their own societies as was proper. They had allowed three days to cover the distance to the least secure of the forts in the nation, Fort Gibson. In high spirits, all of the leaders curvetted in front of their bands, joining together to exchange jests and encourage high feelings among their followers.

"The sun is warm as the blood that will flow from the white soldiers," called Hungry Wolf to Bullhide.

"Grass will grow taller and richer as their bones rot," Bullhide shouted back.

Off to their right a meadowlark trilled sweetly. Grasshoppers sprang away in alarm from the churning shoulders of the horses. All of nature seemed to be celebrating the anticipated battles to come. Even Father Wind pushed at their backs, cooling them and urging the Kiowa on.

Friends and relatives among the warriors took up the banter. They felt strong again, truly free and in command of their own lives. The bitter taste of white subjugation fled from their mouths. Two Moons decided to reveal the news that friendly travelers had brought to him on the last night of the council.

"It is said," he called loudly, and the chatter lessened,

"it is said that the Mountain People, called Creeks, want to go to war against the white soldiers at Fort Gibson. We will talk in friendship with them. They may join us. The soldiers are lost, the soldiers are lost!" he whooped at the end of his announcement.

And, raising an ululating cry, the massed warriors believed him fervently.

Three detachments, hastily assembled, rode away from the Downing Convention Ground, following a brief summary of events by Capt. Chad Conroy. Youths and old men, for the most part, with a few of Colonel Drew's Mounted Rifles willing to violate their parole, they lacked the high spirits of the Kiowa warriors surging northward.

"It's like being asked to stop the flow of the Arkansas River," one Tsalagi observed. "We know nothing about the size of the force down there. Or even for sure where they are. We're to look for the detachments of Lieutenant Oaks. Where are they? How do we do this?"

An older man riding beside him gave him a long look and screwed up his mouth. "That's simple. Just stop complaining, listen to your sergeant, and do what you're told."

"We've been camped here overnight, Lieutenant, sir," Sergeant Gresham stated the obvious to Lieutenant Funston.

"I'm aware of that, Sergeant," Funston said dryly. "I am also aware we cannot afford to delay any longer. Even a band of drunken rabble would find us sooner or later, being no further than we are from the entrance to the gorge. Tonight we have to make our advance into the gorge, secure it, and proceed according to the plan. We made it this far early. We have to give Lieutenant Oaks time to get into position."

"Yes, sir." Gresham covered a smile with his hand. "Forty miles a day on beans and hay, sir."

His lieutenant was indeed learning. He didn't feel comfortable with reaching this point with the aid of Pvt. Henry Echols so early and easily. It increased the chance of discovery. A cold camp the previous night had not been the best for troops accustomed to their coffee, fried fatback, and beans. Nothing for it but to do it.

Dusk found the troops gathered and nervous. Their clashes with the Leatherlegs had steadied them when it came to the actual fighting, but they had yet to learn that absolutely nothing could conquer the anxiety that developed while waiting to go into action. That knowledge came only with long experience. Sergeant Gresham shared it with his fellow sergeants. Unfortunately, the platoon leader, Lieutenant Funston, lacked that saving grace. "We'd better move out, Sergeant," he suggested to Gresham, tight-lipped.

"Sir, there's plenty of time. These fellers have some military knowledge, I reckon. Chances are they'll change sentries at sundown, sir. We should wait until those new pickets get bored and lose the edge."

Lieutenant Funston considered that a moment. "What are we to do in the meanwhile?" he asked, his voice nearly plaintive.

"I'm sure you know what's best, sir," Sergeant Gresham encouraged. "We want to make our approach quiet as possible, right? Should oughta check to see the troops have anything that'll jingle or make noise tied down or taken off, don't you think, sir?"

His lessons on "Stealthful Approach" at Fort Riley recalled themselves to Lieutenant Funston. "Right you are, Sergeant. 'A stealthful approach,'" he quoted, "'to an enemy position can be enhanced by draping snaffle chains with cloths, removing sabres, and securing all loose equipment.' We need to attend to that at once."

Smiling in the darkness, Sergeant Gresham responded quietly. "Right away, sir. I'll also pass the word for no talking once we begin the advance."

"Yes, of course."

"Do you think we should pad the horses' hooves, sir?" Gresham prompted.

Lieutenant Funston considered that a moment. It would make tactical maneuvers difficult once they made contact. "Perhaps initially. When we near the basin, we need the mounts unfettered for quick response."

"Yes, sir. That's good thinking. I'll see to it, sir."

"Thank you, Sergeant." With that underway, and the need to inspect the results later on, Lieutenant Funston found he could relax somewhat. Still, the prospect of making an unobserved approach on a proven deadly enemy plagued his thoughts.

At a few minutes after ten o'clock, Lieutenant Funston led out with the platoon guideon bearer, Corporal Plunkett, as point. As they neared the entrance to the gorge, a quiet suggestion from Sergeant Gresham placed Lieutenant Funston behind the first file. It was, as the sergeant pointed out, a better position from which to control the remainder of the platoon, while maintaining contact with the forward element. The moon had not yet risen as the walls of the gorge confined them.

Whispered admonitions went along the line to avoid rocks and fallen limbs. The latter caution proved unnecessary. Few trees lined the cutback that had thoughtfully been converted into a roadway by the guerrillas. The constant gurgle of the stream further helped to mask the sounds of their approach. Even so, a sudden shout froze the uneasy troopers in place.

"Whu—!"

"Cravin, what's goin' on?" an unseen Leatherleg sentry called out.

"S'all right," Corporal Plunkett answered for the dead lookout, as he withdrew his knife from the man's chest. "Walked into a tree."

"Yeah. It's damned dark, ain't it?"

By that time, the private with Corporal Plunkett had located the speaker and moved silently into position. He bit at his lower lip as anxiety and doubt built inside him. Would he do it right? Tightly gripping the knife, he took the final, fateful step forward.

His arm snaked around the unknown guerrilla's throat to cut off his wind as he plunged the point of his knife between two of the man's ribs. His victim stiffened and arched his back, then thrashed wildly in Private Anderson's grip, completing the work of the blade. Shaken, Anderson lowered the corpse to the ground.

Back on the trail, Anderson made a useless signal to advance and whispered urgently, "All clear."

Lieutenant Funston muffled a sigh of relief and started out when the file ahead resumed their advance. According to his man, and the Lighthorse scouts, there remained only a dozen more sentries to get past safely. If their luck held . . . he mentally brushed away wishful thinking.

Better to consider, yet again, how he would handle it when they were discovered. He felt certain he would find out soon enough. No room to spread out and no light to help them. Simply have to bull their way through. Oh, yes, *after* taking out the sentries.

Lieutenant Funston saw the bright flash before he heard the sharp crack of the bullet against rock and the moan of the ricochet. Any hope of maintaining the element of surprise sped away with it. Yet, his growing understanding of command and tactical control cautioned Funston not to immediately order return fire. He eased over to Sergeant Rollins and whispered close to his ear.

"Get ready and fire when you see the next flash."

"Yes, sir," Rollins breathed softly from the corner of his mouth. "Got my carbine cocked and primed."

Rollins remained stationary when the column walked on. Less than a minute passed when a bright muzzle flash registered high up the opposite wall of the gorge. Right on top of it, Rollins fired.

It seemed an eternity before Lieutenant Funston heard a soft human cry and the rattle of rocks knocked loose by a falling body. He smiled to himself. He had picked the right man for the job. He reminded himself to compliment Rollins at the first opportunity. Meantime he had something else to tend to.

"Move out, men, quick time," Funston raised his voice to command. "They know we're here."

Seventeen

"Someone sneakin' in the gorge!" The shout echoed along the high walls.

Lieutenant Funston winced and mentally urged more speed out of his troops. A pale, yellowish glow showed ahead, the rising moon. A steady, muffled thud could be heard all around him.

"Sergeant Gresham, halt the platoon and have the men remove the sacking from the horses' hooves."

"Yes, sir. Plato—oon . . . halt! Strip them hooves."

To achieve maximum quiet, the soldiers had been leading their horses along the trail. Now, Lieutenant Funston considered the advisability of that. Given the good condition of the pathway they followed, it only slowed them down, made better targets. Especially in the rapidly growing light of the rising moon.

"Have the men mount up. We'll move off at a slow trot," Funston decided.

Sergeant Gresham complied, and within three minutes the platoon set out to close with the enemy. Sniper fire began to harass them. Although relatively invisible, the troopers provided a tempting target to men eager to keep anyone out of their haven in the valley. At Lieutenant Funston's direction, Sergeant Gresham designated sharpshooters to keep on the ready to answer the enemy.

Lieutenant Funston shivered in the cooler air of the gorge. He counted four more sentries taken out of action and surmised they had passed by three others. Could he afford to have those men at his back? He decided yes. At least for the time being. When daylight came, he could send half a file back to deal with them. Another flash drew his attention.

A bullet cracked close over his head a second before the report. Cringing instinctively, Lieutenant Funston realized that the three-quarter moon had risen enough to outline his troops as visible, moving silhouettes.

"Pick up the pace," he commanded. "We have to get past these pickets."

Once more the distant rifle put out a muzzle bloom. At once a Sharps carbine barked in reply. Then another, from farther back in the column. Horses neighed in nervousness. Lieutenant Funston could see the powder smoke as lazy gray balls rising through the shafts of yellow light. It could not be much farther.

"Pass the word, point says they've reached the mouth of the valley," came down the line.

Lieutenant Funston breathed a sigh of relief. Without a command, the column increased its pace in the growing brightness. Three enemy rifles spoke from behind a low ridge of sand and rock across the stream from the column. One trooper threw up his hands and uttered a bleating cry. He fell before anyone could react to the attack.

"First file, return fire!" Lieutenant Funston ordered.

Eleven carbines blazed to life in an irregular volley. One shot answered them. To Lieutenant Funston it sounded like a revolver. Again the first file illuminated the gorge with a fusillade. A bearded figure reared up beyond the natural breastwork and discharged a round into the dirt before falling to drape across the flood ridge. His light-colored gauntlet visible now, Lieutenant Funston signaled for the advance to continue.

A wide wedge of yellow-edged silver light spread before him some sixty feet further along. In a minute, Lieutenant Funston found himself standing beside the roadway inside the valley. He summoned Sergeant Gresham with a raised hand.

"Deploy the men in lines of skirmishers. We'll attack on my command."

"Yes, sir. What about the Lighthorse?"

"We have to assume they are in position. Since this is no longer a surprise, we have to seize what advantage we can. A sudden charge should unsettle those brigands."

Augustus Moritus could not at first believe it when awakened by Quint Danvers. Danvers urgently tried to assure the older man that it was true.

"Lookouts were shootin' at someone in the gorge. Don't know who it is, but they're on their way."

"Rouse everyone," Moritus snapped as his mind lost the fog of sleep. "Get them to the defensive positions."

"Already started, Colonel."

"Good man, Quint. I'd say it's those misbegotten Lighthorse. If so, we will scatter them quickly. Savages can't stand up against disciplined troops."

Danvers had his own ideas about that, but kept them to himself. He decided to give the really bad news last. "Not a one of the lookouts got out of the gorge."

"Confound those heathen devils," Moritus railed, coming close to a profane oath.

"Will we use the cannons?" Quint inquired.

"Waste of time in the dark."

"It's bright as day out there, Augustus," Quint urged. "Near a full moon."

Moritus considered it. "No. Save the rounds and powder we have for a real threat."

Then, thin and thready from the distance came a high-pitched voice. "As skirmishers . . . forward at the trot . . . ho!"

"What the hell?" Danvers blurted, forgetting himself.

"What, indeed. It couldn't be the Army?"

A heavy rumble of pounding hooves answered him, along with the command, "At the gallop . . . ho!"

"Ah—Augustus, that doesn't sound like Cherokees to me."

"It *is* the Army. Oh, thunderation, what brought them into this?"

"I would say that little encounter with the patrol not long back," Danvers answered dryly.

When he gave the command to charge, a thrill ran along Lieutenant Funston's spine. Would he ever lose that special exhilaration? Stark, white moonlight flooded the valley. Dimly ahead, he could see the battlements erected by the Leatherlegs. Beyond he saw feverish movement, and the flare of torches and several large bonfires.

Fools, he thought, don't they know they are limiting their ability to see at night? So much the better for his platoon, the answer came. Right by the book, Lieutenant Funston led his men down to within a hundred yards of the rifle pits and standing barricades, fired a single explosive volley, and ordered them to dismount.

"Horse handlers to the rear!" Sergeant Gresham bellowed. The remainder of the platoon bellied down, reloaded, and opened fire by Lieutenant Funston's command. After the fourth round, breeches had begun to overheat. His sergeants reported to Funston that a total of seven breech blocks had refused to open. All of the right moves seemed to fly into Funston's head.

"Have those who can fire another volley, then everyone draw sidearms," he ordered.

Quickly, the word passed down the line. "Ready . . . fire!" Funston commanded as he triggered his Sharps, abandoned it at his side, and reached for his revolver. Too late, he heard shouts of alarm and the thunder of hooves from both flanks.

Augustus Moritus had quickly noted the diminished volume of fire from the soldiers. He correctly interpreted the cause and shouted to Danvers. "Now, Quint, have the mounted men hit their flanks!"

Nothing else was needed. Fighting desperately to preserve their lives and freedom, the Leatherlegs acted spontaneously. Howling, the horsemen jumped their mounts to a fast run and streaked toward the edges of the platoon's formation. The revolvers in their hands barked in unison, and gouts of dirt rose around the unprepared soldiers.

Some, with their sidearms already freed, turned to offer resistance. Three Leatherlegs in the lead on the left flank died in the flurry of shots directed toward them. To the surprise of those who followed, panic did not spread through the troops.

Firing as they rose, they fell back in good order to their horses. There they quickly mounted and wheeled about. With a final volley to their rear, the soldiers raced away from the threat.

"Hold up! Hol' up, now." Butch Tucker shouted to the deserters he led on the right. "Let's find out what ol' Moritus wants done next."

To the surprised confusion of Lieutenant Funston, the calamitous events happening around him seemed to go on in slow motion. Still, the right decisions came without hesitation. When he saw the counterattack on his flanks, he immediately ordered his men to fall back.

"Fire as you go," he added. "Fall back and mount up. Keep firing."

They knew, he trusted, to retrieve their carbines. Sergeant Gresham stood at a distance opposite him, urging the lagging troops to pull back to the horse handlers. There he directed a rear guard of kneeling and prone soliders to fire on the converging enemy while the remainder mounted. Funston kept upright, shouting encouragement, calling orders to his sergeants.

"Back to the gorge. Only a few at a time can get at us there. Hurry! Move, dammit!" He looked around. What else to do? "Set up defensive positions to both sides and across the road. Set men to cutting any trees of a size to block the enemy's advance."

Should he have saved that for later? he asked himself. No, he decided a moment later when a bullet cracked past his head close enough for him to feel the displaced air on his ear. He might not be there to give the order. That realization got his foot in the stirrup of his own mount, held in dancing eagerness to get away by an equally nervous private.

Reluctant to leave the field before all his men had been accounted for, Lieutenant Funston sat stoically in the saddle and fired at the Leatherlegs while Sergeant Gresham made ready to mount the rear guard. When the last man's rump filled a Grimsley, Lieutenant Funston fired a final round and spurred his mount toward the gap.

Sergeant Gresham steered over and beside him. "You shouldn't be here, Lieutenant," he shouted over the uproar of battle. "No criticism, sir, but it ain't safe."

"So I noticed, Sergeant, yes, I surely did," Lieutenant Funston fired back, carried away by the wild elation of having lived through the encounter with a superior force and gotten away without a single man left dead on the battleground.

Lt. Segeeyah Oaks halted the Lighthorse detachment at a point along Dardeene Creek that he estimated to be five miles west of Joshua's Mountain. The moonlight provided enough visibility for the horses to make their way safely enough, yet he harbored concern over the condition of the animals. They had been ridden hard and long.

Another worry assailed the Lighthorse officer. Earlier in the day they had come across further signs of white border trash passing through in the direction of the basin. Three frightened Tsalagi women had added verification that the large body of horsemen had been white and a desperate looking band indeed. All they needed, he concluded, was for Moritus to be reinforced.

"It's bad enough," he confided in Wolf Wind, "that we're a day late in reaching the rim of the basin; these new guns, if they aren't delayed, could catch the soldiers between two hostile forces."

"So, what do we do?" Wolf sensibly asked.

"Rest our mounts a while, then keep on through the night."

With the soldiers disappearing into the shadows beyond the moonflooded valley, Augustus Moritus called back his skirmishers. They had done excellently. Some, he recalled, had been among the twenty new men who had ridden in early the previous day. They brought word that more were on their way. Rand Yates led them, he recalled.

"What a grand surprise if our newcomers should reach the gorge in time to come up behind the defenses those soldiers are no doubt preparing right now," he remarked to Quint Danvers and Tom Longdon.

"That would catch them between us," Longdon observed.

"Yes, providing Mr. Yates has intelligence enough to recognize the situation and take advantage of it," Moritus snapped. His patience with the deserter leader had been wearing thin of late. "Have the men stand down, get what sleep they can. I feel tomorrow will be a big day."

"What do you figger to do?" Long Tom asked, aware of the quirks Moritus had been having recently.

"Why, we're going to do exactly what the soldiers expect us to do. We'll assault their positions."

Quint Danvers split his face with a smile. "That way, if Yates an' the new men are out there, stupid as he is, he'll know what's going on."

"Precisely. Get the men ready for an early attack. And . . . we'll use the cannon."

Slouched in a chair, his booted legs spread before him, Col. Owen Bledsoe stared morosely at the decanter of brandy on the table in his quarters. In his mind, fogged by too much imbibing after supper, whirled a review of his actions of the day. He now saw his decisions as unwise.

He had been compelled to send a patrol in search of the missing Lt. Parker Funston. Far too long had gone by without any communication. That had been reasonable enough. And already he had detailed two companies to escort the seditious Indians back to their proper places. That could not be undone. What rankled was that another communiqué from headquarters had forced him to send yet another detachment in search of deserters.

If he had been smart, he would have refused, or at least delayed doing so. It left far too few men to carry on the normal functions of the fort. It also, he realized darkly, placed Fort Gibson in a vulnerable position. What if the Confederate troops in the Cherokee nation learn of his depleted force?

No doubt they would swoop down to capture the post

and crow triumphantly about another victory over the Yankees, that's what, he angrily answered himself. Grunting with the effort, he leaned forward enough to reach the decanter with the cut crystal goblet in his hand.

Shouldn't drink brandy from a goblet, he admonished himself. A small, delicate snifter was what's called for. He shouldn't be drinking this much at all. And alone. People tended to whisper . . . *things* about a man who drank alone. Wouldn't do. Oh, the lonely burden of command, Owen Bledsoe lamented silently.

After a long swallow of the brandy, Colonel Bledsoe continued the grim review of his conduct. In an anxious confusion he had authorized the additional search for deserters. Born of his obsession to attract the positive notice of his superiors and at last achieve his goal of a coveted transfer to the real war that was going on, he had momentarily weakened. Now regret haunted him. A crisp knock at the door startled him into the present.

"C'min," he slurred.

Lieutenant Colonel Kersey, his executive officer, and Major Mueller, the adjutant, stood in the doorway. Each had their garrison hats tucked properly under their left arms; each of their gloved right hands held a bottle of liquor. Their faces bore identical beaming expressions and broad smiles.

"Perhaps the colonel has forgotten, sir," Kersey boomed, "but it is the Colonel's birthday. We came to offer felicitations, and a wee sip of good cheer."

His morose mood banished instantly, Colonel Bledsoe rose, albeit somewhat unsteadily, to welcome them. "Come in, do come in, gentlemen. I'd be delighted to share a toast on such an occasion."

At first sight, each party instinctively distrusted the other. For their part, the Kiowas saw a band of heavily armed Creek warriors, sitting silently and grim-faced in the early morning mist. Touches-Sky, still smarting from his rough treatment at the hands of the Lighthorseman, urged that the Creeks drive the outsiders from their land.

"They come for no good," he stated through split, swollen lips. "These men would make war with us."

The Creek war leader listened thoughtfully. Like Touches-Sky, he had to consider that possibility. He also smarted from the humiliation given them by the Lighthorse. Honor demanded that something be done to recover their self-esteem.

"We could fight them," Touches-Sky prompted, taking the thought from his leader's mind.

"So I thought. We must first ask why they are here."

At the base of the ridge on which the Creeks kept vigil over them, Two Moons and Bullhide also consulted with the other Kiowa war leaders. "Why are they here?" Bullhide asked. "Do they want to make war on us?"

"They see this as their land," Two Moons answered. He considered the armament of the Creeks, head canted to one side, obsidian eyes bright and sparkling. "No. They had no way to know of our coming. They are made up for war with someone else. Before we decide to do battle, we must ask who they are going to fight."

Without waiting for agreement from the other four war leaders, Two Moons heeled his pony forward to a point removed from the body of warriors. There, using the universal plains sign language, he indicated that he wanted a peaceful parlay.

Although not fully accomplished in the silent talk of the plains tribes, the Creek war chief understood the intention of Two Moons and replied in kind. To Touches-Sky, he remarked, "They want to parlay. You and I will go forward and talk."

At the base of the ridge, the two negotiating parties met. Without revealing his thoughts, Two Moons considered that these Creek must have already been in a battle, considering the condition of the big one's face. With signs they identified their tribes. Two Moons and the Creek tried several languages to find a common tongue. To their frustration they found none. Bullhide had joined Two Moons and now tried Chickasaw. The faces of the Creeks brightened, and the uninjured one replied in that language.

"I am called Bright Robe. This is Touches-Sky. We ask what you are doing in the Creek nation."

"I am Two Moons of the Tejas Kiowa. This is my brother war leader, Bullhide. We come to punish the white soldiers."

Bright Robe and Touches-Sky exchanged startled glances. "Why here? Are there not enough blue-legs where you come from?"

Two Moons let a smile show briefly. "*More* than enough. But they are strong and wise from many fights against our brothers the Comanche. We seek the ones who are soft and fat, and lazy from living in a fort."

Again, Bright Robe and Touches-Sky consulted each other with a look. Without need of words they reached agreement. "We have thought to do the same thing," Bright Robe revealed.

Still uncertain as to the intent of these strangers, Two Moons eyes narrowed as he asked shrewdly, "Then why are you riding in this direction? It is said the softest of the white soldiers camp at the fort called Gibson."

"That is so," Bright Robe agreed. "We thought to attack them from the Cherokee nation. The Lighthorse convinced us to do otherwise." He shot a glance at Touches-Sky.

The Kiowas began to chuckle, then to laugh out loud. Touches-Sky joined them, followed by Bright Robe. When the mirth subsided, Bright Robe asked pointedly, hoping he did not sound like a beggar, "You would join us in this thing?"

Nodding and laughing again, Two Moons responded between chuckles, "Yes, yes. We thought to ask if you would join us in a big fight against the soldiers."

Relieved, Bright Robe made signs of agreement. "It is done then. Together we will ride to destroy the fort called Gibson."

Eighteen

Dawn found Lt. Parker Funston pacing with growing pride along the defenses thrown up by his troops during the night. They had done well. He hoped that his planning had been equally effective. The aroma of coffee and frying fatback teased his nostrils. When his stomach gave a mighty growl in response, he turned away and headed for the cookfires to the rear of their position.

"Good morning, sir," Sergeant Gresham greeted him.

"Good morning, Sam," Lieutenant Funston returned. The exegencies of battle, and Sam Gresham's superb performance, had banished formality from Parker Funston's thinking. He eagerly accepted the tin cup of coffee offered by his platoon sergeant. As soon as he touched it, he winced.

"It's hot, Lieutenant," Gresham tardily warned.

Laughing, Funston nodded agreement. "It surely is. I want the men well fed this morning."

"Pardon, sir, but the surgeons recommend very little to eat before battle," Gresham reminded.

"I know that, Sam. I also know that hungry men have other things on their mind besides fighting. Did you know I took up fisticuffs at the Point?"

"No, sir, I didn't."

"Well, I did. The only time I lost a bout was when I had

to study through supper call and went into the ring on an empty stomach."

Gresham chuckled indulgently. "Can't argue with experience, sir. There's fatback, beans, and biscuits. I think we can rummage out enough spuds for fried potatoes if you wish."

"Do it, Sam. I could use some of all of that before we face the enemy."

"They'll come at us soon," Gresham prompted.

"We'll be ready, Sergeant, count on that," Funston answered enthusiastically.

To his satisfaction, Sam Gresham saw a good officer in the making.

Augustus Moritus walked his big horse, Excaliber, along the three-deep lines of mounted guerrillas. He seemed satisfied with what he saw. Returning to the center, he turned left to face them.

"One good charge should do it. Everyone think about getting through their lines and out of the gorge onto the lower plain. Hit them hard, and keep hitting until you break through. Then ride on far enough to reorganize."

"What do we do then, Colonel?" Silas Tanner asked.

"Ride them down again. Coming from the rear, the soldiers will be exposed and easily eliminated. I want you, Mr. Longdon, and three men to continue on through the gorge and locate Mr. Yates and his reinforcements. If they are close enough, bring them on without delay. If they are farther off, hurry them on."

"What's the rush, Colonel?" Long Tom Londgon asked.

"We know where the soldiers are. That leaves the Lighthorse. I for one have no doubts that they will also attempt to attack us here. We need all the men we can get to hold them off."

188

"Thought you said the cannons would hold off anyone fixin' to ride over us?" a doubtful Leatherleg challenged.

Eyes narrowing, Moritus glared at his detractor. "I'll tell you something, mister. When those cannon are out of powder, they're nothing but hunks of iron. There are thousands of Cherokees in the nation. We have certainly riled them with our abortive attempt to take Park Hill. When they come here, and they will, every shot is going to count."

Unintimidated, the argumentative guerrilla countered with a curt suggestion. "Then why don't we jist ride through them soldier-boys and go somewhere else?"

"What? And leave behind all we have gained?" Moritus demanded, scandalized.

"We was lookin' for things when we got this stuff," another uncertain Leatherleg observed.

"No!" Moritus thundered. "Never. We have a paradise on earth right in this valley. Once we deal with the Army and break the backs of the Lighthorse, we can make this a lasting, powerful bastion against savages and soldiers alike. Let me tell you what I see in the future." Carried away by the vision of his ambitions, Augustus Moritus waxed eloquent.

"Some day all of the Indian Territory will become a state. With our power base, we can become the new state's lawmen, judges, politicians. Why, I can be governor, or senator. All of you will be in legally protected positions to reap unbelievable wealth out of the settlers coming into the state. Isn't that worth fighting for? Isn't it?"

"You sold me, Colonel," Long Tom shouted.

"Me, too," Billy White agreed.

Scattered at first, a general cheer roused from the Leatherlegs. Moritus smiled and waved his cockaded hat until the uproar subsided. "All right, then. What's keeping you. Move out in quick order. On to the gorge!"

*　　　*　　　*

Moritus and his Leatherlegs hit the defenses in the gorge while the last of the platoon cleaned their tin plates of food scraps. The guerrillas rushed toward the rifle pits and fallen tree barricade with wild shouts and unaimed shots. Bullets moaned off splintered wood and howled from lead-speared rocks. Bent low, carbines in hand, the troopers manned the positions between lookouts.

"Take careful aim," Lieutenant Funston urged. "Make your shots count. Hold fire . . . hold . . . steady now . . . Fire!"

Their volley seemed to leap out and sweep Leatherlegs from their saddles. Horses neighed in panic and floundered wall-eyed, over fallen men and animals. The second line struck before the majority of soldiers had reloaded. Twenty against nearly seventy attackers, Lieutenant Funston estimated as he watched the mounted guerrillas firing down into his men.

For some unexplained reason, most of their shots went wide of the mark. Here and there a trooper stood, carbine reloaded, and blasted another Leatherleg from his mount. With clubbed butt stocks, those too slow to recharge their weapons fought off the attackers.

"Revolvers!" Sergeant Gresham shouted suddenly. "Draw sidearms. Fire at will."

Shocked to find himself remiss in directing the defense, Lieutenant Funston forced himself to stop gaping at the developing battle and make some decisions. "Sharpshooters, open fire," he yelled to the men he had stationed higher on the walls of the gorge.

By sheer tenacity, the soldiers drove off the second rank. The third hit when every trooper had his Colt Model '60 out and in play. Sergeants bellowed for the men to take their time, to aim their shots. Directing fire, they bounded from place to place, always with one eye on the enemy.

Lieutenant Funston belatedly realized that he, too, had his sidearm out and cocked as a burly Leatherleg with a dark blue Union Army shirt on, obviously a deserter, charged toward an unaware Sergeant Gresham, intent on spilling the NCO's brains. Funston brought up the 7-inch barrel of his Colt and surprised himself when he put a .44 caliber ball in the deserter's ear.

Crazed by the smell of burnt powder and blood, no longer under control, the deserter's horse went berserk. It crow-hopped away from the constant flashes of fire from the soldiers. On its back, the dead Leatherleg flopped back and forth as though still alive. Then his muscles went slack, and he pitched forward onto the neck of the plunging horse.

This rapid departure struck a responsive chord from some of the more faint-hearted. They abandoned the assault and streamed after the fleeing horse with its morbid burden. Lieutenant Funston grasped the fact that they had repulsed the assault at the same time as Sergeant Gresham. In unison, they began to shout a stream of orders.

"Reload! Fresh cylinders only!" Gresham bellowed.

"Horse handlers forward," Lieutenant Funston commanded.

"Load your carbines."

"Platoon . . . pre—pare to mount . . . Mount!" Lieutenant Funston ordered before the smoke and dust could dissipate. "Form column of fours to the front . . . ho!"

With the troops in line, Sergeant Gresham joined Lieutenant Funston at the front of the formation. "Forward at the trot . . . ho!" Lieutenant Funston commanded. Once the platoon had cleared their own breastworks, Funston rose in the stirrups. "Two lines . . . form as skirmishers . . . ho!" When the evolution had been completed with less than parade ground precision, Lieutenant Funston gave a quick glance over his shoulder, raised his arm, and brought it forward with his shout. "At the gallop . . . forward ho!"

Leatherlegs still withdrew in confusion and without positive direction. The thundering cavalry mounts rushed down on the stragglers within seconds. Unable to resist the excitement, Lieutenant Funston bellowed over the rumble of hooves, "Chaaaarge!"

Soldiers seemed to appear out of nowhere. Billy White looked back over his shoulders, and his face blanched. "M'God, where'd they come from?"

"Don't talk, just ride," the man beside him barked.

"B-but it don't seem right. We whupped 'em, didn't we?" Billy bleated.

"Reckon not," the tight-lipped Leatherleg snapped back. Then he stiffened in the saddle, and a bone-distorted Minie ball erupted out through his chest.

Billy gagged and bent over to lose his breakfast. It saved his life as another .54 caliber carbine ball snapped through the space his head had occupied. Right then, all Billy White wanted to do was get as far away from this valley as he could. Sawing on the reins, he yanked his mount's head around and bolted away from the stunned Leatherlegs.

Augustus Moritus watched Billy White defect from the ranks of the guerrillas as he reined in beside Quint Danvers. "They counterattacked," he stated unbelievingly.

"I'd say they have," Danvers answered dryly.

"We've got to do something," Moritus pleaded. "We have to stop this before it becomes a rout."

"Then we'd best get back to those cannon of yours darn quick," Danvers suggested.

"Yes, of course." Augustus Moritus spurred ahead, waving his hat over his head. "To me, men! Rally on me. We'll lead them into a trap. Back to our own breastworks."

192

*　　　*　　　*

Out beyond the gap, to the southwest, along Dardeene Creek, the sounds of battle rolled across the prairie to where Rand Yates and his party of reinforcements sat their mounts. Heck Williams and Butch Tucker had come with him. They exchanged glances and worried frowns.

"Sounds like ol' Preacher Moritus is catchin' hell, don't it?" Heck Williams observed.

"Now, friend Heck, it does indeed," Rand Yates agreed.

"What do you reckon we ought to do about it?" Butch Tucker asked.

Rand cocked his head and listened to the rattle of gunfire. "Seems to me them Leatherlegs have got themselves caught up in their valley. A mighty serious situation, I'd say," he drawled.

One of the new men spoke up. "We'd best ride fast to relieve them," he suggested.

Yates, Tucker, and Williams considered that a moment. "No-o, I don't think so," Rand Yates offered after a long, silent spell. He shared a broad wink and a grimace with his fellow deserters. "What I'd figure to be smart to do, that is if y'all have ambitions to keep yer hair, is cut north and west of here and ride like the devil hisself was after us."

"We signed on to fight with Col. Augustus Moritus," a youthful recruit protested.

Rand Yates studied his boyish face and light blue Union Army trousers. "That's fair an' square with me. You want to go an' die with him, go ahead. There's Union blue mixed up in there with Injun policemen. Not a healthy place for a runner to be, I'd say. Bein' most of us done walked away from the army, I don't reckon any are anxious to meet up with them again." He eyed the kid narrowly, evil green eyes glittering. "Durin' time of war, like now, deserters can wind up facing a firing squad.

193

"You don't 'pear to me to be eager for that, boy," Yates pressed. "Best bet is we push on west, to beyond the forts in Kansas. There's lots of empty out there. A man can carve out jist about anything he wants. Ain't nothin' in Colorado but some militia. Hell, we could live amongst the Cheyenne or the Arapaho and nobody'd give us no mind."

Still doubtful, the youth swallowed and asked the question most pressing on his mind. "Don't they scalp white men?"

"Sometimes," Yates agreed. "Trick is to get on their good side. We bring them some powder and ball, a few rifles, a keg or two of whiskey, an' we're set. At least so's some of the old-timers around the fort tole me." He ran long, thick fingers through his sandy hair.

"Me, I'm partial to keepin' what I got on top, so I figger we can he'p ourselves to a few rifles and some gee-gaws from some of these 'civilized' Injuns along the way. Make big trade talk with the Cheyennes. Once we brew 'em some coffee, eat a bowl of stew with them, they're honor bound to treat us right, least while we're in their camp."

"Don't they eat dogs?" one of the older recruits asked.

"Nope. Not the Cheyenne. The Sioux favor 'em like the folks back East do a sucklin' pig. The Cheyennes only eat their dogs when they're downright starving. So, where do you stand, boys?"

A heated debate followed for five minutes. At the end, the force had split roughly in half. Fifteen of the border renegades and deserters wanted to go on and help Augustus Moritus. Thirteen sided with Yates, Tucker, and Williams.

Yates accepted the division in unusual good humor. "You boys go right ahead. Ride on in. I done told you how to find the entrance to the gap. But, for me, my momma never raised no fools. We'll be off to try our chances with the Cheyenne."

On the northern rim of the basin, Lt. Segeeyah Oaks and his four detachments of Lighthorse waited impatiently. The sounds of heavy gunfire reached them undiminished by distance. Below they could see the lazy layers of powder smoke from the area of heaviest fighting. Midmorning sunlight cast an unreal brightness on the tiny figures darting around over the lush grass. Segeeyah silently cursed himself for having arrived too late.

"How are they holding on?" he asked Wolf Wind. "That many against them should have ended it before now."

"It looks to me like the Leatherlegs are running away from the soldiers," Wolf remarked, his keen eyesight strained to make sense of the confused motion.

Lieutenant Oaks worked to frame the proper terms in his mind. "Attack and counterattack. We did hear gunshots earlier. What's keeping Johnny Walksaround and Squirrel?"

"There is a lot of rim to scout," Wolf reminded him.

As though summoned by Segeeyah's words, old Johnny Walksaround and young Squirrel trotted up on their lathered mounts. "We have a way down," the aged Lighthorseman announced. "It is steep, but we can make it."

"Good," Segeeyah Oaks responded without wasting further time. "Show us the way."

"Everyone has to go slow. It will take longer than this battle will last, I am thinking."

"We'll try to do better than that," Segeeyah voiced his determination.

When the point element of the sixty-seven man Lighthorse unit reached the proper spot, Segeeyah felt some of his anxiety slacken. With the first fifteen riders over the lip of the precipice, he twisted to listen intently to what could have been the sound of rolling thunder. Immediately beyond came a second rumble. Then across the beleagured valley, Segeeyah Oaks saw the flash, smoke, and high gout of dirt thrown up by an explosion.

"Artillery," he announced to no one in particular. "We've got to hurry."

Lt. Parker Funston heard the shriek of roundshot over his head before he heard the flat report of the cannons. To his rear the earth rumbled and heaved and poured a great brown-and-green fountain into the air. Rather than call for an immediate retreat and lose the initiative, he chose the other alternative.

"Spread out! They're shelling us, spread out." *Where in hell did they get artillery?*

His mind reran the question as the platoon fought their sprinting mounts to make more space between each man. Another projectile screamed overhead, along with the angry hornet buzz of grapeshot at shoulder level. Again the six-pounders thundered. A good three hundred yards to where they stood, Lieutenant Funston estimated. Out of range for the carbines.

They had crossed less than fifty of those yards when flame and smoke belched from the muzzles a fourth time. Moritus had some damned good gunners, Funston admitted to himself. Three of his men went down wounded as the grapeshot seethed and hissed around the charging cavalry. Heart sinking, he forced himself to accept that they would never reach the guns with enough effective force to carry the battle and subdue these cursed Leatherlegs.

Blaming himself for their failure, Lieutenant Funston gave the signal to retreat. Bitter and frustrated, he urged a gallop out of the troops as they ran from the terrible punishment of the cannons. For the most part, his men had experienced enough of a charge into the mouths of cannon. They were glad to be headed away. Lieutenant Funston directed the retreat at an oblique angle to make tracking with the field pieces more difficult. They had almost reached the safety of the gorge when new sounds joined the tumult of the conflict.

A crackle of rapid-fire weapons, mixed with whoops and shivering, falsetto cries rose over the now mostly useless parting fire from the Leatherlegs. New hope flared in the heart of Lieutenant Funston.

The Lighthorse! They had gotten there in time after all. Rapidly the shots aimed at himself and his men diminished. Yells of alarm and consternation rose among the Leatherlegs. Along with them came the screams of men wounded or dying.

Thick clouds of dust boiled up around the horses of the Lighthorse as they moved down the steep trail. The men covered their mouths with kerchiefs, still coughing and choking on the effluvium. Two riders lost control and had to spring free of their saddles as their mounts went to their haunches and began to slide and squeal in fright. More dust bloomed. For a painful, fleeting second, Segeeyah Oaks thought they had rushed into disaster.

Then the incline perceptively decreased, the stumbling crush of descent slowed. Rocks from pebble size to small boulders clattered past him as he gained contol of Bashful. He reached out and patted the taut, arched neck.

"Good *Udehosati,* that's good."

Ahead he discerned a clearing of the thick curtain of brown and flying rock. He sat almost level in the saddle. A few mincing steps by Bashful, and he came free of the earthen spill. Others gathered around.

"Form up. Four waves, long guns at the ready. Have reloads in hand to use fast," he commanded quickly. A brief flicker of amusement swam into his mind as he thought of the many and complicated orders that Lieutenant Funston went through to get his men to do the same thing. Satisfied that everyone had complied, he gave the command to set off at a fast run.

They closed on the rear of the enemy positions with surprising speed. Without having to be told, the Lighthorse held fire until they had closed to extreme minimum range. Then, hooting and yipping their individual or clan war cries, they opened up in a thunderous volley.

Cold, genuine fear clutched at the heart of Augustus Moritus. The worst had happened. The cursed Cherokees had joined the battle. A quick look at the far side of their small settlement showed him many more of what must be the Lighthorse than he had expected. How had they gotten in? No time for speculation.

"Turn about," he shouted. 'We're under attack from the rear."

"Holy geez," one of the Union deserters shouted. "It's the Lighthorse."

Men spun about and prepared to defend themselves from this new threat. With a terrible shock, Augustus Moritus realized that the cannons, the heart of his defense, had been abandoned, their muzzles pointed toward the fleeing cavalry.

Nineteen

Segeeyah Oaks and his three subordinate lieutenants led their Lighthorsemen down on the suddenly disorganized Leatherlegs, buoyed with the exhilaration of finally doing something besides riding back and forth over the nation. With a violent crash, the first volley from the long guns of the Lighthorse slashed into men only partly turned to face this new threat. Beyond these rearmost defenses, all arranged to repel attack from the gorge, Segeeyah saw a cluster of guerrillas attempting to turn one of two small cannons.

"Keep going!" he bellowed. "Ride on through them."

Unknown to Lieutenant Oaks, the field piece had been reloaded to fire on the retreating soldiers. The gun crew had no sooner horsed around the six-pounder than the gunner laid a slow match on the primed touch hole. A thin spurt of smoke jetted upward, followed by a flash of fire from the muzzle and a cloud of thick gray-white. An instant before the sound of the discharge reached him, Segeeyah heard the warbling crack of grapeshot as it whipped past the Lighthorse and himself.

Two men he did not know, from another detachment, cried out and fell from their horses. Another volley roared from the charging Tsalagi policemen. At too long a range for his shotgun, Segeeyah drew his long-barreled LeMatt and took aim at the figure of a man bent over the little cannon. The heavy revolver fired with a flat thud.

His sheath of grapeshot in place, the cannon loader raised upward to step clear for the rammer when the .44 ball struck him between the shoulder blades. He stiffened, arched his back, and fell over the barrel of the cannon. Desperate to rake the attacking Lighthorse with grapeshot, the gunner gestured frantically for the rammer to drive the load home. Segeeyah triggered another round, which missed its target.

Down the tube went the grape load. The rammer stepped clear. Instantly the gunner put the slow match to the touch hole. Men and horses went down screaming as the small balls scythed through the ranks of Lighthorse. Segeeyah felt a twitch on the point of his right shoulder joint and a burning sensation. He jinked Bashful to the left and fired at the gunner around the growing balloon of powder smoke.

With a startled cry, the gunner dropped his slow match and clapped his right hand over a spreading stain high on the left side of his chest. His powder-grimed face went chalky behind the smear of black, and he staggered to one side. Segeeyah loosed another round.

At less than fifty feet, the ball entered the gunner's belly and he doubled over in his last agony. A Leatherleg in the gray shell jacket of the Confederate States Army reared up and tried to bring his rifle to bear on the charging Lighthorse lieutenant. Segeeyah shot him in the face.

All but one of the gun crew now lay sprawled, dying or dead. Lieutenant Oaks pointed at the cannon with his LeMatt and watched with satisfaction as four Lighthorsemen reined in sharply and dismounted. They ran to the small field piece and heaved on one wheel until they had overturned the deadly weapon.

"Keep going," Segeeyah shouted. "Get the other one."

"Lieutenant, it's the Lighthorse. They got here," Sergeant Gresham shouted over the din of their rear guard.

"Wheel about," Lieutenant Funston decided instantly. "Form as skirmishers for a charge."

"Best reload first, sir," Gresham suggested.

"Right. See that it's done." He looked off across the valley at the fierce battle developing at the rear of the Leatherlegs. "We have a second chance, Sergeant Gresham. Take charge of the right flank and see we make the most of it."

"Yes, sir," Gresham responded eagerly.

Led by Tom Longdon and the men who had found the deserters outside the gorge, the fifteen reinforcements entered the mouth of the gorge. For a while they rode in silence, then the sounds of battle reached their ears. It grew in volume as they progressed through the two miles of the gap.

"What do you think?" Vincent Butoni asked Long Tom.

Longdon frowningly considered the increasing rumble of gunfire. "There's a hell of a fight going on in there," he stated unnecessarily.

"Maybe that Yates was right," Zack North suggested. "Might be the Lighthorse got mixed into what's going on."

"We saw no sign of anyone entering the gorge in a long time," Butoni objected. "Those Indians can't have gotten in there."

"Maybe you're right," North admitted, sounding unconvinced. "Then again, maybe they did."

"They weren't there when we rode out to find you," Long Tom growled. "I say we go on. Sounds like Colonel Moritus needs us."

"First thing we'll run into is the Army, Vince," North prompted.

"They won't know we're deserters. They're from Fort Gibson."

"Oh, bullcrap, Vince. One look and they'll know every manjack of us has run out from somewhere."

"You want to turn back?" Butoni suggested.

North studied the faces of the men around them. Particularly the hard, determined visage of Tom Longdon. Without some sort of patron, they had little chance of survival in this wild country. "No—no, I guess not."

Vincent Butoni also looked hard at the men with them. He decided that Longdon could probably keep them together. Reluctantly he did something that his limited career with the Union Army had taught him never to do. He volunteered to go on.

"All right, this is the way it is going to be," Long Tom Longdon rapped out. "When we make first contact with the troops, we hit hard and keep on hitting. Ride right through them, and we join up with the rest of the Leatherlegs. You can tell from the sound of it," he added, "that it is going to be one hell of a fight."

On the point of dithering, Augustus Moritus rode through the dismounted Leatherlegs. In a forced tone of calm, he urged them to take hold, turn about, and fight off the advancing Cherokees. While he did, his eyes constantly sought out certain men among the throng. To his most trusted and most skillful followers he gave a single curt message.

"Mount up and pull off toward the south. Wait for me there."

Weary of the desperate fighting, they obeyed quickly. Satisfied, Moritus threaded his way among the disorganized newcomers and sought out their leader.

"Mr. Gore, your men are a rabble. Kindly take firm

command and put them between these barricades and the savages attacking our rear."

Harold Gore eyed Augustus Moritus with stubborn resistance on his face, skewed somewhat by apprehension. "Colonel, we didn't join up to get in the middle of a full-blown war. I'm for pulling out."

"Hey, Hal, what say we light a shuck an' get the hell outta here?" one of his men shouted before Augustus Moritus could bark the hot retort he had framed.

It changed the nature of the response Moritus made. "You will stand fast, or I'll shoot the first coward who turns tail."

Frozen by the heated intensity of Moritus' challenge, the two men stood wordlessly and stared beyond his shoulder as a man at the barricade shouted in alarm. "Oh, God, it's the cavalry. They're coming at us again!"

Wiser now about the defenses established by Moritus, Lt. Parker Funston led his remaining troops at a sharp slant to the enemy front. They swept over the northern flank and turned to the south. With the Lighthorse closing the rear, the maneuver left little choice to the Leather-legs.

"Try to reach that other cannon," Funston ordered the sergeant of the first file when he noticed the Cherokees had put one out of operation.

"Yes, sir." At once he swung his men away from the flank attack and bore down on the gun crew.

Desperate men did one of two things, Lieutenant Funston reminded himself. They broke and ran, or they fought like madmen. Lacking the discipline of regular troops, he observed that the Leatherlegs had about equally divided on those alternatives. Some stood to their guns until they fired the last shot possible, then used their rifle butts as clubs to flail at the troops and the Lighthorsemen. Others ran blindly toward the distant gorge. He failed to note a growing cluster of guerrillas off to the south of the battlefield.

So, likewise, did Segeeyah Oaks. Determined to swiftly end resistance by the Leatherlegs, the Lighthorse lieutenant drove his men relentlessly forward. When they expended their ammunition, they resorted to clubbed rifles and their handy war clubs. Dust and smoke obscured nearly all of the area of combat. To his left Segeeyah noted a new danger.

A tall, rail-thin man had fixed his attention on Oaks. The rage of battle had suffused his pox-marked cheeks and gave Quinten Danvers a diabolic appearance. He had rightly determined the leader of the Lighthorse and struggled through the throng of grappling men to reach a confrontation with Segeeyah Oaks.

Hot with battle lust, Segeeyah gladly obliged him by moving nearer. What happened next took the Lighthorseman by surprise. Rather than strike with the unloaded rifle in his hands, Quint Danvers leaped forward, using his superior height, to reach out and pluck Segeeyah Oaks from the saddle.

Lieutenant Oaks hit the ground hard enough to buckle his knees. Danvers stayed right on him, clamping the Lighthorseman tightly between himself and the heaving flank of Bashful. Belatedly, Segeeyah realized he still held the reins. He released them, and his horse danced away sideways.

That freed Segeeyah, who used the advantage to take two swift backsteps. Still clinging to Segeeyah's shirt front, Danvers came along. Off balance, he was in no position to protect himself from a sudden, sharp kick to the inside of one thigh.

Pain flashed through Danvers, and his leg went numb. He began to sag, which left him open to receive the full force of a solid blow in the solar plexus. Segeeyah Oaks broke his opponent's hold and danced away. Winded, his face gone ashen, Danvers stumbled backward. Not yet on the verge of desperation, he only sought to regain control of the fight. Before Segeeyah could follow up his opening, Danvers left hand dropped to his belt, and he whipped out a long-bladed Bowie knife.

Dust-reddened sunlight glinted off the keen edge. He made two slashing passes, then began a slow shuffle to his right. Segeeyah did the same, eyes on the face of Danvers, as well as on the knife. Danvers made a feint to the left, then drove the point directly toward where he anticipated Segeeyah's reaction would put him.

Only the Lighthorseman no longer occupied that space. Pulled off balance by his momentum, Danvers staggered forward after Segeeyah had pivoted to the side. The Lighthorseman continued his turn and planted his raised foot in the small of Danvers' back. Danvers sprawled face first in the dirt. Bloodwetted mud caked his face when he rolled over, spluttering.

His hand scrabbled over the ground and encountered the plowhandle butt-grip of a Model '60 Colt. Hurting throughout his body, Danvers desperately brought up the revolver, the web of his hand cocking the hammer. Through hate-hazed eyes, he sought his enemy.

He found him too late. Although he had already emptied the LeMatt, Segeeyah still had his .44 Colt. In the instant he saw Danvers reach for the Model '60, Segeeyah groped for his own revolver. He had it steadied now on the chest of Quint Danvers. Danvers had only begun to react to the big muzzle pointed his way when Segeeyah fired.

Deceptively strong for all his thinness, Quint Danvers did not even react to the impact of the bullet. Instead, he fired his own revolver. The .44 slug struck the head of Segeeyah's war club and shattered the smooth stone. Shards of rock and lead bit painfully into the side of Segeeyah Oaks. Pain burned hot channels along his nerves.

For all of the effects of the stunning blow, Segeeyah managed to cock his Colt again and fire a second round into Danvers' chest. This time the ball found, and burst, his heart. Quint Danvers remained sitting upright, an expression of shocked surprise on his face. Feebly he tried to cock his Model '60. The light dimmed in his eyes, and he wavered. Segeeyah Oaks bent and plucked the revolver from Quint Danvers' unresisting hand. Only then did any sound come from the evil-faced man.

"Oh, God—God, I'm killed."

"Sgidv—yes," Segeeyah answered simply.

Segeeyah turned from the dying man to gauge the course of the battle. To all sides, Lighthorse and Leatherlegs flailed at one another. Most had emptied their firearms and fought with knives, war clubs, and rifle stocks. The timely arrival of the cavalry had ended the last organized resistance, he noted. The enemy fought as individuals. Nowhere could Segeeyah discover a pocket of coordinated effort. That didn't mean the Leatherlegs had become much less dangerous.

Two burly Leatherlegs, not more than thirty feet away, drew his attention. They appeared to have cornered someone and were held at bay by a flailing rifle butt. Segeeyah started that way when one of the men groped at the small of his back and drew a short-barreled .45 caliber Derringer from the waistband of his trousers.

With practiced ease, he brought it around his side, cocking the hammer as he moved. Before Segeeyah Oaks could line up on the target, he heard the short, flat report of the small weapon. Laughing, the Leatherlegs stepped aside. Face alabaster with pain and shock, Saloli Juska-jo'i stood before them, swaying slightly. A crimson stain spread from a small black hole over his heart. Segeeyah watched with a growing sense of sorrow and outrage as the slight boy released his grip on the big Dragoon pistol he had carried with such pride. It thudded to the ground a moment before the brave little lad dropped to his knees.

"Uji Uji!" he cried weakly and pitched face first onto the ground.

"Mother! Mother!" The words rang bitterly in Segee-yah Oaks' ears. Sudden fury consumed him. Deep grief would follow, though he knew nothing of it in that moment. Segeeyah raised the Colt and put a .44 ball into the back of the Leatherleg who had laughed and spat on the fallen boy's face. He crumpled as his comrade who had done the killing turned in surprise.

Looking down the barrel of a smoking Model '60, his face underwent a transformation from blood-lust to abject horror. He dropped the compact .45 Derringer and raised spread hands in a pleading gesture. His thick lips worked, and his throat churned as he tried to find the right thing to say.

"I—I—I gi—give up. Don't shoot. Oh, please, don't shoot me. I—I ain't done nothin' wr-wr-wrong." He knelt on the blood-slimed ground. Terror made his eyes dart around crazily.

"Are you a Christian man?" Segeeyah Oaks asked in English, his voice tightly controlled.

Surprise and confusion mingled on the Leatherleg's face. Understanding illuminated his face and eyes with renewed hope. If he answered correctly, it might be a way to get out of this with his life. "Wh—why, yes, brother. Yes, I am."

"Then tell it to your Jesus," Segeeyah snarled as he shot the child-killing Leatherleg between the eyes.

Silence covered the battlefield as both sides recoiled from each other. They made frantic, hasty efforts to reload. Drilled to perfection, the cavalry finished the task first. At once Lieutenant Funston ordered them to their saddles, and they charged the remaining line of enemy resistance.

Lieutenant Oaks and the Lighthorse placed a close second. Immediately, they swarmed over the abandoned and confused Leatherlegs. Witnessing this, Augustus Moritus gave a single, crisp order to those he had hand-picked for survival.

"We leave now."

Behind him he left the screams of his men, dying without hope of rescue. The small band of guerrillas increased their pace to a fast trot. Within five minutes they neared the upper end of the gorge. An unexpected crackle of rifle fire came from within the gap.

"What's goin on, Colonel?" Long Tom Longdon asked uneasily.

"The officer in charge of those troops must have left someone to hold the pass. I would surmise that they have been discovered by some of the replacements due to arrive."

"We gonna go after them?" Silas Tanner inquired in uncertainty.

"Of course. There must not be more than three or four soldiers," Augustus Moritus dismissed. "We'll crush them like grubs under a rock."

Three men had been detailed by Lieutenant Funston to guard the prisoners. The clatter of hooves making a fast pace up the gorge alerted them to an unknown hazard. Corporal Hansen, who had been left in charge, made a quick decision. He came to his feet from where he had been squatting under a low blackjack pine.

"We've got unwelcome company coming. There's some among you who deserted from the Army. I can guarantee that the lieutenant will speak up for you if you choose now to sort of—ah—rejoin and help us stand off any more of these border trash that may be comin' in on our rear. We've got spare rifles. Some we took off you," he added with a hint of mirth.

"Awh, you can stick that," one disgruntled deserter growled.

"D'you mean it? T'lieutenant will see it goes easy on us?" a younger, thoroughly frightened deserter asked.

"Yep," Hansen acknowledged, though he didn't know how he would go about explaining this to Lieutenant Funston.

"I'll do it," the young soldier replied. "Just untie me and show me where to go."

"Any more?" Hansen prompted. Nine more promptly volunteered. "Good enough. Carver, see they get powder and ball, too."

Within three minutes the reinstated soldiers had been outfitted. They took positions to cover the trail and settled in. None too soon it turned out as the lead rider of the new guerrillas came into view around the bend ten seconds later.

"Hold up right there," Corporal Hansen commanded from the center of the trail. He held his Spencer carbine to his shoulder, sights lined on the center of the chest of a squat, swarthy fellow with an impressive expanse of black waxed and curled mustache.

Vincent Butoni eyed him coldly, apprehension rising at the sound of far too many caplocks being cocked from both sides of the trail.

"Get on with it," Tom Longdon shouted at Butoni's side.

Butoni swung his heavy Springfield toward Corporal Hansen, intent of blasting away this solitary show of resistance. Three .54 caliber balls slammed into Butoni's chest and flung him from the saddle a second later.

To his horror, Long Tom Longdon saw that the corporal in front of him had not even fired. He froze. Slowly he lifted his hands. Corporal Hansen made quick work of taking the recruits prisoner. With them disarmed and securely bound, he set four of the volunteers to guard them and took the rest forward to the old breastworks thrown up the night before. They crouched there, ready and waiting when Augustus Moritus and his escaping Leatherlegs came into view.

*　　*　　*

Smoke and flame spurted from at least ten muzzles as Augustus Moritus led the retreat from his once secure basin. Three guerrillas died in that ragged volley. Confused, Moritus spoke aloud his surprise.

"How can this be? The cavalry didn't have that many men to spare."

"We ain't imaginin' it, Colonel," Ed Walsh snapped. "What are we supposed to do?"

Moritus drew a deep breath. "There's nothing for it but to break through and escape out the gorge. Make ready, men. On my command, open fire and keep on shooting until we win free of those soldiers."

Unhappy at the prospect of more fighting so soon, some of the Leatherlegs hung back when Moritus gave the order to charge the barricade. They watched as four more of their number got blown from the saddle. Then the solid thunder of many hooves from back in the direction of the basin convinced them. With a shout, they jumped their horses into motion and, shooting at the smoke puffs from the rapid-fire carbines, they challenged the fates.

Three more of the thirty-two men Augustus Moritus had brought with him died, and thirteen received wounds in the precipitous charge. Fear more than tenacity carried the day for the Leatherlegs. Given the small number of defenders, it made for an easy escape.

Without even looking at the shouting prisoners begging for release, Augustus Moritus led his fleeing Leatherlegs past the cavalry's encampment and off down the gorge. Most could not be more pleased. The Cherokee Lighthorse had shown them the error of resisting a force of vastly superior fighting ability. They and the cavalry had thoroughly frightened the surviving Leatherlegs. No one would be eager to clash with them another time.

Twenty

Racing westward out of the gorge, Augustus Moritus and his Leatherlegs were a bedraggled lot. Several of the men had taken wounds in the confrontation with the army. He had lost seven good men to the marksmen holding the upper entrance to the gap. Of all the prisoners, only one, Tom Longdon, had managed to make good an escape. At the last minute he had leaped on a horse behind its rider and ridden to freedom with Moritus.

Removed now from the pressures of combat, Augustus Moritus had an opportunity to take stock of his resources and options.

He had to consider Quinten Danvers to be dead. At best, a captive. Those confounded Indian savages. Fighting like soldiers, disciplined and deadly accurate with their fire, they had overwhelmed his defenses with even greater ease than the Union troops on the previous night. Disgust boiled in him. How had he let this happen?

He did not find any easy answers. Now he must look to Tom Longdon for subordinate leadership. And how nearly he had come to losing Longdon. He had to accept the fact that Rand Yates, coward that he was, had reached the gorge in time to hear sounds of fighting and chosen to run out on his commitment. Longdon had told him as much, and it put the taste of gall in the mouth of Augustus Moritus. He admitted to himself he sorely needed the reinforcements Yates was supposed to have been bringing.

Without them now, he realized, his situation had become extremely precarious. Where could he go? In what direction lay safety? Or at least obscurity? He would need an answer for the men and soon.

After an hour of fast riding, it became obvious that no immediate pursuit had been organized. Out of consideration for the horses, rather than the men, Augustus Moritus called a halt. The time had come, he grudgingly allowed, for an open assessment of their condition.

Clearing his throat to fix their attention, he addressed his surviving Leatherlegs. "Well, men, we're back to near our original number. In case you weren't aware of it, I chose you out of all the rest because you have been with me the longest, shown the greatest loyalty. What the future holds, I cannot say. Yet, remember, we successfully engaged Confederate troops in Arkansas with fewer in number than at present."

Moritus dismounted and indicated the others to do the same. "This . . . perverse marriage between the Army and the Cherokee Lighthorse cannot last long. Such things rarely do. Our first concern is to find a suitable place to lay low while the nature of human differences takes care of that alliance. After that, we must locate a secure base from which to operate."

"Colonel," Blake Sessions injected, "I can't understand how the Army an' them Injuns got together in the first place."

Moritus let the moment linger. "Nor can I. We haven't any need to ponder that at present. Eventually, it will tell us how to defeat them. For now, I want to find what I believe they call in the vernacular, a hideout. To that end, I will dispatch four groups of three men to scout for some suitable location. The main body will continue westward."

"Why west, Colonel?" one scruffy border ruffian demanded.

"Because it gets us outta Cherokee country, you idiot," Long Tom growled.

"Precisely," Augustus Moritus agreed. "I sincerely doubt that the Lighthorse will pursue us beyond their borders. If we can find a sanctuary outside of the Cherokee nation, I'm certain we will no longer be harassed by the forces of law and order."

"Sounds good to me," the complainer admitted.

"What we gonna do for food?" came a plaintive question. "We didn't take no grub with us."

Augustus Moritus chewed on his lower lip while he assessed this pointed observation. "Surely most of you have been on the run long enough to know to keep a cache of food in your saddlebags?" he prodded.

"Well—ah—right enough, Colonel. But a body gets tired of spoon bread an' overripe bacon. 'Sides, that's for personal use," the first to object remarked.

Eyes narrowed, Augustus Moritus quashed the challenge of his authority. "You've been living too high, Mr. Green. Community meals have spoiled you. We're in this together. We will share and share alike. Besides, once clear of the Lighthorse, we can hunt for fresh meat."

"An' how long will that be?" Green demanded, refusing to let it go.

"Half a day," Moritus snapped. "And I'll thank you to do as you are told from now on, Mr. Green. Or would you prefer to go it on your own?"

Green's normally ruddy complexion paled. "Oh, no—no, sir. I reckon we can share for a meal or two. Then we can hit some Injuns and get us plenty flour, beans, and corn, right?"

"No, Mr. Green," Moritus stated flatly. "We do not wish to offend our unwitting hosts wherever we are going. We will have to buy supplies from a trading post."

"We-ell, gol-dang, I ain't never heard the likes," Green drawled.

"You'll do it, because we have to. And because I say so," Moritus thrust to reinforce his control.

Green took in the grim, disapproving expressions around him and drew back. "Whatever you say, Colonel. Whatever you say."

"Good. Now that is out of the way, Mr. Longdon, select a dozen men to scout for a place to lay low. We'll outsmart the Lighthorse yet."

Good spirits ran high among the Kiowa war parties. They stopped early on the advice of the Creek warriors with them. The fort lay only a short ride away. The war leaders would go on to observe activities and plan their attack. Two Moons delegated this to a trusted warrior in his band and remained to supervise the large encampment.

"We are too close for fires," he decreed. "Surprise is on our side. We want to keep it that way. It is my advice that those who go forward remove their paint. To whites, we all look alike . . . unless painted for war. To them, you will be only another *Indian*," he addressed the group of leaders, putting a bitter, ironic twist on the English word.

"That is wise," a Creek allowed. "Truly, they do not see our faces. Nor do they mark the difference in what we wear."

"I have learned that the whites expect us to attack at dawn," Two Moons shared his knowledge. "We will fool them and strike later. This has worked well for Bullhide and I against the Texicans in the *llano estocado*. There, the whites are most watchful for the Kiowa and Comanche when Father Sun comes up. But when they have passed that gray time, and start to fill their bellies, their caution decreases. That is when we ride down on them."

Chuckles spread through the war leaders. Several nodded wisely. Older men recalled when they, too, had to change their traditional ways to be successful against these utterly different white men. All saw the wisdom of Two Moons and left to scout the fort with new confidence.

Segeeyah Oaks and Parker Funston stood surveying the results of their attack in the basin. They had a lot more prisoners than they had expected. Containing them would be a problem. Segeeyah addressed that difficulty in his usual direct manner.

"We can't keep the prisoners with us any longer," he stated bluntly. "You have taken losses, and so have we. If you agree, I will send them on to Tahlequah to be held for trial."

"What about guards?" Parker Funston asked.

"I have more men than you. Some have no experience at all, except for this battle. They are able to keep watch over unarmed, shackled prisoners," Segeeyah Oaks suggested. "That is, if you have no objection to our taking charge of these vermin."

Parker considered that a moment. "Not at all. I seriously doubt that they could be accommodated at Fort Gibson," he added.

"All the more reason to have them out of our way. We must move quickly. The wounded can go back with the detachment of guards."

"We're going after Moritus?" Lieutenant Funston asked, surprised.

"Of course. We'll burn this place to the ground and be out of the gorge before nightfall," Segeeyah Oaks declared.

"Sounds fine to me." Funston looked stricken for a moment. He slapped a gauntlet against his right thigh. "In all that has been happening, I've completely overlooked advising Colonel Bledsoe of what went on. Forgot it since our first encounter with the guerrillas. I had better send a messenger."

"That might be a good idea," Segeeyah Oaks stated dryly. "I've found that superior officers frequently expect to be informed of what their subordinates are doing."

Lieutenant Funston took the ribbing in the spirit intended and set off to draft a brief report. Unaware of the presence of Sergeant Gresham, Segeeyah Oaks spoke his thoughts aloud. "That man's going to make a good troop leader."

"I agree with you sir, absolutely," Sergeant Gresham volunteered.

Startled out of his pensive mood, Segeeyah Oaks glanced at the non-com. "You've done a great deal toward his education, Sergeant."

"Thank you, sir. I can but try. You've helped a great deal yourself."

Segeeyah produced a smile. "All we can hope for is that he survives the final encounter with Augustus Moritus and his Leatherlegs."

"Right you are, Lieutenant Oaks, right you are, sir," Sergeant Gresham agreed fervently.

Pacing the floor of his small office at Fort Gibson, Col. Owen Bledsoe listened to the reports of the young lieutenants in charge of the patrol screen he had ordered two days earlier. A deep frown furrowed Bledsoe's high brow.

"Yes, sir, we heard sounds of firing in the night, sir, but could not locate any likely place from which it came," Lieutenant Easley replied. "It's not likely that Park—ah Lieutenant Funston and his men were involved."

"What of these border ruffians we've been advised of?" he prodded the second patrol leader.

"Nothing untoward, sir. If they're out there at all, I'd suggest they were Confederates, sir."

A hot light flickered in Colonel Bledsoe's eyes. "You're right!" he barked. "Absolutely. I've suspected it all along. Those scheming Rebels are gathering for an attack on the fort. There's no denying it. No doubt we'll find that this Augustus Moritus is just another name for Bloody Bill Anderson. It's Confederates, I tell you. Now, back to what you were saying, Mr. Easley. Lieutenant Funston is still unaccounted for. What makes you so certain that the sounds of battle you heard did not involve his command?"

"For one thing, sir, the prairie south of our area of operation is swarming with Indians, sir. They are moving around a lot. Lieutenant Funston was looking for deserters, sir. I suspect that he found them and they . . . proved too much for him."

Only four years and one grade superior to Funston, Lieutenant Easley spoke from greater experience on the frontier, Colonel Bledsoe recognized. Surely though, not the entire command wiped out? It had plagued him for the better part of a week. Gunfire in the night, close enough to be distinguished, and yet no sight of muzzle flashes? Colonel Bledsoe framed his next question carefully.

"Lieutenant Easley, in your patrol area did you encounter any large washes, perhaps a wide, deep watercourse?"

"No, sir. Nothing really unusual. Of course, we've never been in that part of the Cherokee nation before. It's all unfamiliar terrain. Our Indian guide told of a gorge that Dardeene Creek is supposed to run through, although we remained north and east of there. We came across the trail of a large party of Indians, sir. Headed west, then south of Joshua's Mountain. They seemed to be headed for—ah—here, sir."

"And you didn't check into this unusual situation, Mr. Easley?" Colonel Bledsoe asked caustically.

217

"No, sir. Our orders said to remain north of Dardeene Creek and to concentrate mostly north of the Arkansas River. If we hadn't encountered the sign left behind by many Indian horses, we would not have gone as far south as we did. We broke off following the trail about two miles north of the creek, sir."

"Very well. With all the Indian activity around the fort, it's a wonder you were not attacked," Bledsoe said thoughtfully. Then his mood changed. "They're all in league with the Rebels, damn their black, savage hearts. I strongly suspect that we are about to be attacked by the Confederate forces and their Indian allies. So certain am I that you will not be going back on patrol.

"You'll hear this at the officers' call I am going to schedule for half an hour from now, but you might as well know it now," Bledsoe went on rapidly. "I want every wagon, board, barrel, bale, and fence rail incorporated into a barricade entirely around the fort. The salute gun and one piece of artillery will be installed on the dirt ramp behind the partial pallisade. The rest of the artillery will be deployed to support the other three sides. Now, see to your men. Get them fed, rested, and resupplied."

"Already taken care of, sir," Easley responded.

Colonel Bledsoe brightened. "Excellent. You're fine, upstanding young officers. Not at all like that bumbling incompetent, Funston. Carry on, then."

Gathering their commands, Lieutenant Oaks and Funston hurried after the fugitives. After leaving the gorge, the trail led northwestward. Four hours of alternating a walk and trot pushed the lawmen and soldiers out of Canadian District and to the banks of the Arkansas River. They forded without difficulty and set off on the wide, obvious trail left by the fleeing Leatherlegs.

Riding side by side, Segeeyah Oaks and Parker Funston

discussed the oddity of this. "Augustus Moritus has so far managed to maneuver around the nation with ease," Segeeyah observed. "Now why would he be headed toward Fort Gibson?"

"I'm not sure. One thing, those Leatherlegs will be in for a nasty surprise if they do come within sight of the fort," Parker declared. "I probably should not sound critical, but Colonel Bledsoe is obsessed with the possibility of a Confederate attack. If he catches sight of Moritus and his guerrillas, he'll be positive that the worst has indeed happened."

"I'd not grieve if your colonel put an end to Moritus," Segeeyah remarked with a straight face. Only . . ." Sadness creased and darkened his face. "I would like to get a little payback for Squirrel being killed. The little rascal made me think of what my son might be like at that age."

"I'm truly sorry about that," Lieutenant Funston stated with sympathy. "Was he a favorite then?"

"Not really. He had spunk, full of vinegar and sass. He would have made a good Lighthorseman." Segeeyah found it hard to swallow.

In a tone of kindness, Lieutenant Funston put a cap on the conversation. "I'd say that was a fitting eulogy."

A scout came up at a fast trot and concluded that line of talk for certain. He reined in and snapped a crisp salute to Lieutenant Funston. "Sir, we've made contact with the enemy. They're three miles ahead, settling in for the night, sir."

Lieutenant Funston smiled. "Excellent. We can hit them before dark."

Segeeyah Oaks nodded in the direction from which the scout had come. "Why don't we wait until later at night? If we create enough confusion, we can get the Leatherlegs shooting at one another."

A tight grin creased the leathery face of Parker Funston. "Now that I like. How do we work it? All go in at once?"

219

"No. I want to send some men around to their picket line. If the horses go charging through camp, it will rile them quite a lot. More distraction. Then, you hit from the east, and we'll take them on their left flank."

"Better and better," Lieutenant Funston praised. "I think we can make an end of Augustus Moritus and his scum before the night's over.

While the camp settled down around him, Augustus Moritus let his mind speculate on the future of his Leatherleg guerrillas. Another day and they would be out of the Cherokee nation. That would end, *should* end, pursuit. Then more northward, toward Colorado and the vast emptiness of the Rocky Mountains. Sound enough, he decided. He came close to cursing the loss of his precious map. None of the men with him had ever been in this part of Indian Territory. He could only guess at where they happened to be.

So far they had seen no sign of troops, Lighthorse or anything significant. They might as well be totally alone on the prairie. It undulated in gold-green magnificence in every direction for as far as the eye could see. At least it allowed for a hot meal and the solace of coffee, he decided. The men were tired, he readily knew that. A fastidious man, in dress and custom, Augustus Moritus did not relish spending a night on the ground, in the open.

His campaign tent was another item he came close to profanely swearing over. It had been his home away from home since back during the turbulent days of the fifties with John Brown and his Jayhawkers. Lost, too, along with their hard-won valuables, the twin cannons and every last bit of reserve powder and ball. His men had only what they carried. Any major confrontation before they reached a place to resupply would be a disaster. In the last red-orange rays of the setting sun, Augustus Moritus lismissed his worries for the time being. He refilled a tin cup with coffee and added a dollop of brandy from the silver pocket flask he had carried of late.

The liquor had its desired effect. It spread warmth and a renewed sense of well-being through him. Tomorrow they would skirt the fort well to the south and find their way to civilization.

Any dreams the Leatherlegs enjoyed shattered in the frightened whinnies of their horses. In seconds the air filled with the undirected pounding of hooves and thick clouds of dust. Crazed animals raced through the camp, followed by yells and ungodly whoops that froze the blood. Rifles cracked aimlessly, men cursed and stumbled or rolled desperately out of the way of the swirl of startled mounts.

Five men materialized to form a protective screen around Augustus Moritus, who had likewise been jolted from his slumber. Leatherlegs ran on bare feet to snag up this or that stomping, dashing animal. In seconds that seemed like hours, they identified the source of the pandemonium and turned as one toward the picket line. Rifles and sidearms rising, they sought targets in the darkness.

A wall of flame erupted to the east of camp. Men screamed and fell to the ground, writhing in agony. Another volley seared the night. Driven by sudden panic, the Leatherlegs fought desperately to subdue their spooked horses. Others hastily slid on trousers and boots and began to snatch at personal belongings. Only a few returned fire.

That brought immediate retribution from the unseen attackers. There seemed to be guns pointing at them from every direction. Confused, sleep-sodden men collided and went sprawling. Two Leatherlegs died under the hooves of tormented horses. Repeatedly shrill whistles and the furry sound of flicked blankets stirred the livestock into new heights of demented fury.

Pure terror momentarily seized Augustus Moritus. "For God's sake, Mr. Longdon, do something! Do something!" he howled in expectation of his immediate death.

Twenty-one

Five carefully selected Lighthorsemen had slipped silently into the Leatherleg camp. Moving with care and confidence, they had freed the horses from a series of four picket lines. When the last of the animals moved about free of restraint, one of the lawmen had thrown back his head and uttered a chilling wolf howl. Nervous whinnies came from the clustered livestock. The other four Lighthorsemen began to whip blankets up and down in front of the milling creatures, and another howl had done the job. In very little time, the whole bivouac had become a bedlam of shrilly screaming horses, shouting, cursing men, and random gunshots. Over the din of the disrupted encampment, Lt. Segeeyah Oaks could hear Augustus Moritus shouting himself hoarse in a vain attempt to restore order.

"Get down!" the guerrilla leader bellowed. "Lay low and return fire."

Enough steady minds and hands responded to end the one-sided nature of the engagement. With his ranks swelled to twenty-eight volunteers among the deserters, Lieutenant Funston weighed the chances of making a charge into the Leatherleg position. He quickly rejected it. The best he could hope to achieve, he acknowledged to himself, would be a stand-off.

So it developed over the next five minutes. Shedding the numbing effects of their surprise, the guerrillas made good account of themselves. Augustus Moritus delegated every fourth man to deal with the horses. They would have to make a run for it. A risky thing in strange territory and at night, yet he had no choice. Somehow the Lighthorse had to have caught up to them. The silent penetration of his screen of sentries and the wolf howls convinced him of that.

Lieutenant Funston, meanwhile, kept up a steady fire. He sought to keep the enemy in one place until his Cherokee allies maneuvered into a position to roll across the flank. He mentally ticked off the time he felt necessary and then filled his lungs to bellow over the crash and thump of gunfire.

"Cease fire! Hold fast now!" the young officer shouted.

A final volley crescendoed, followed by three tense seconds of silence. Then the thunder of many hooves announced the charge of the Lighthorse. The Cherokee lawmen held their fire until they could make out the darker shapes of men against the frosty starlight. Then their weapons spit flame.

Stricken by the ferocity of the charge, the Leatherlegs had no choice but to abandon the ground they held. With wild, desperate grabs at their possessions, the guerrillas made for the recovered horses, mounted in haste and raced into the night. They had only one choice of direction: westward. Immediately, Lieutenant Funston ordered a chasing volley. Then he issued crisp commands.

"To your horses, men. Prepare to mount . . ."

"Not so fast, Parker," Segeeyah Oaks cautioned calmly as he materialized out of the darkness. "There's no reason to get a man's neck broken, or a horse a snapped leg. We'll find them in the morning, nothing to worry about."

"But, they're getting away," Parker Funston protested.

"Not so far and definitely not fast. About a third of them

re doubled up. We've not seen the last of Augustus Moritus, be sure of that."

Indecision smote Augustus Moritus between the eyes when the point rider came back in a mad scramble to report, "There's a lot of smokes up ahead. Some Injun lodges, and what looks like that fort."

How could this have happened? Where had he gone wrong? Plagued by those questions, Moritus remained silent, thin, purple lips down-turned, eyes distant. If only he hadn't been forced to abandon the excellent map of the Cherokee nation back in the basin. They had apparently wandered in the night and come upon the last place he wanted to encounter. The ignominious route of the previous night rankled him. Insult had been added to his basket of woes.

He abandoned worry to consider what chances he had. Still a good hour before sunrise. If they avoided the fort, there would have to be something done to cover their trail. An old trick he learned from John Brown recalled itself.

"We'll change direction, skirt the environs of the fort to the south," he decided quickly. "Wait here and rest your animal. Direct the stragglers to turn some to the south and follow us. Have riders at the end of the column cut sage brush and drag it behind them to wipe out our tracks. Then catch up to the column."

"Yes, Colonel. How long should I wait?"

"Not too long," Moritus said dryly. "You don't want to reacquaint yourself with the Lighthorse."

"No, sir, I sure don't," he agreed enthusiastically.

"He's trying to hide his trail," Lt. Segeeyah Oaks pointed out with a smile. "He might as well have left us an invitation to follow."

Lt. Parker Funston looked blankly at the swept ground "I don't understand what you mean."

Segeeyah pointed to the wide swath. "They dragge brush to wipe out hoof prints. Only it's too fresh. Les than an hour ago, I'd say. Not enough time for the groun to look normal again. If we pick up the pace we can catc them soon."

Parker Funston studied the terrain in the soft, gra predawn light. "This area looks familiar. We're not fa from Fort Gibson."

"No doubt why Moritus turned off the road," Oak surmised. "It won't do him any good, though. We can tra him between us and the fort."

A broad grin spread on the youthful face of Parke Funston. "I have a good idea what Colonel Bledsoe wil think of that."

Segeeyah nodded. "Let's hope he acts predictably."

Half an hour after sunrise, the headquarters' trumpete put the mouthpiece of his instrument to his lips an began the crisp, trilling notes of *To the Colors*. Th salute gun fired from its new position on the artillery ramp behind the token pallisade, and Col. Owen Bledso stood to rigid attention, hand raised to hat brim in salute Everything quite normal, the post commander though with momentary relief.

Something, however, impinged on this calm routine Gradually, Colonel Bledsoe became aware of a faint sound in the distance. It grew in volume while the music sped toward its conclusion. With a start, Colonel Bledsoe recognized the rattle of gunfire. There appeared to be some sort of running fight going on. Alarmed, his obsession with a Confederate attack foremost in his mind, he broke off his salute and hastened to the stairway that gave access to the parade ground.

He crossed directly to the color guard and spoke excitedly to the trumpeter. "Finish that fast. Then sound *assembly* to turn out the infantry, *Boots and Saddles* for the cavalry. We are about to come under attack."

Well trained, the soldiers fell out on the parade with alacrity. As the units formed up, their officers took position in front of their troops. The cavalry came last because of saddling their mounts. When the seriously reduced command finished the ritual of reporting their numbers, the young captains and lieutenants listened in shocked disbelief as Colonel Bledsoe rapped out his orders.

"We are about to be attacked by Confederate forces of unknown strength. Full field kit for all effectives. Fifty rounds of ammunition. Infantry to occupy defenses outside the fort. Cavalry to ride north and conceal their presence. At the sound of our opening artillery, gentlemen, you will attack the enemy on their right flank. Questions?"

"Sir, Captain Morrison, sir. Are we certain that Confederate action is underway?"

"Yes, Captain Morrison. I have suspected this for some time. If you listen, you can hear firing in the distance. If there are no further questions, dismiss the men to outfit themselves, then to your posts. Preserve the Union at all costs!"

With half the fat orange ball of the sun above the horizon, Augustus Moritus and his Leatherlegs considered themselves fortunate to have avoided the fort. Then the Lighthorse and Lieutenant Funston's cavalry rode shouting down on them. Their ease in the saddle converted into another panicked flight.

A running exchange of gunfire ensued. Determined only to evade their enemy, Moritus paid scant attention to the fact they were being skillfully herded north and we[st] toward Fort Gibson. Too late he saw the forlorn gate an[d] incomplete pallisade loom on the horizon. He twisted [in] the saddle and sought some avenue of escape.

He found none. All too clearly then he saw the way the[y] had been driven into this deadly trap. He smashed h[is] small fist on the pommel of his saddle and watche[d] helplessly as his guerrilla band raced toward certai[n] doom.

At a range of some five hundred yards, Augustu[s] Moritus saw the mushrooming spurt of cottony powde[r] smoke and brief seconds later heard the scream of th[e] projectiles over his head. The sharp crack of explosio[n] behind him sent his gaze in that direction. Five horses an[d] their riders went down in the hail of shrapnel. They coul[d] not long endure this, he thought in sinking certainty.

A quick check of his pursuers showed him a possib[le] way out. There was no sign of the Lighthorse, curse thos[e] heathen devils. He raised in his stirrups and began [to] shout to his followers. "Back. Turn back. We can ri[de] right through the cavalry. Smash into them and kee[p] going."

The sudden turnabout by the Leatherlegs caugh[t] Lieutenant Funston and his cavalry by surprise. The la[st] thing they expected was to be attacked by men fleeing fo[r] their lives. Beyond the rise behind them, Segeeyah Oak[s] had swung his Lighthorse to the south to cut off th[e] escape route. Now the massed guerrillas stormed down o[n] him.

Funston heard the bark of cannons from the fort, an[d] two more gouts of turf flew skyward as the shells explode[d] among what was now the rear of the Leatherle[gs] formation. They came on, screaming and firing the[ir] sidearms. In a wild pass, the Leatherlegs streamed throug[h]

thin screen of cavalry. Immediately, without need for
ers, the cavalry troops turned about and fired a volley.
the same instant, the artillery at the fort fired again.
utenant Funston turned to his left, to Corporal
nkett. "Uncase the guideon!" he yelled. "Let them
w we're out here, or the next rounds will reach us."

. Owen Bledsoe stood and stared, unbelieving, at the
tering pennant. It couldn't be, yet it had to be. The
sing Lieutenant Funston and his patrol had returned
ast. Long overdue and engaging the Confederates in
rear. How timely. The lad must be a military genius,
dsoe considered. Then he remembered the artillery.
"First battery," he bellowed. "Cease firing. Those are
ndly troops out there."
"And we were just getting the range," the gun sergeant
mbled to his crew.

the sound of cannon fire, Lt. Segeeyah Oaks turned
Lighthorse northward. They should have Augustus
ritus nicely boxed in now. If Funston could only hold
m, the end would be swift. He could feel Bashful
gging under him as they surged into the incline of the
ge that masked the fort. Too much hard riding in the
t hour.
"Keep pulling, *Udehosati*, we've a ways to go yet," he
ectionately urged the stallion.
n another minute, the Lighthorse crested the rise and
battlefield spread before them. Wolf Wind called to
n from his position nearest the action. "Hey, Bat, the
atherlegs got through your friend's cavalry."
Segeeyah saw it and pulled a grim expression. "We had
ter do something about that. Turn to the right, and
'll cut them off."

Circumstances can and do change so swiftly in batt
that the commanders rarely grasp the turning point. Eve
afterward, in the calm of after-action, they are hard press
to find the reason why the Fates cast the dice of chance
their favor. All Lt. Parker Funston knew was that t
fleeing enemy suddenly halted and deployed for a pitch
battle.

Unable to halt the pell-mell rush of his troops, Funst
barely reached a position to the front center of his platoc
before they crashed into the Leatherlegs. The range close
so rapidly that none had time to reload their carbine
Neither did the Leatherlegs find a chance to charge the
rifles.

Revolvers barked and cracked along the contestin
lines. Lieutenant Funston held his Colt Model '60 in h
left hand, saber bare and ready in the right. He hacke
at one guerrilla who tried to leap at him from the saddl
The keen edge of the sword bit into meat and bone an
cleaved the Leatherlegs' chest. He spilled onto the groun
with a cry of anguish. A quick glance to the left, an
Funston triggered a .44 ball to finish another of th
renegades.

On both sides, men fought with desperate determina
tion. A private in the first file used his clubbed carbine
smash out the teeth and break the jawbone of a Leatherle
who stubbornly persisted in reloading a huge, ancier
horse pistol. The pitched battle grew in fury and, t
Funston's surprise, his men managed to hold their own
He had only fleeting time to wonder where Segeeyah Oak
and the Lighthorse might be.

Moments later he found out when the Lighthorse fell o
the Leatherlegs from the left flank and rear. Terror strod
heavily through the ranks of the guerrillas. Men brok
away singly, then in pairs and threes. With a roar, eigh

forced their way clear of the encircling soldiers and
 en.

 once, a dozen Lighthorsemen split off from the battle
 ase them. Blade dripping blood, Funston wielded his
 to cut a passage to where he saw Segeeyah Oaks
 ged by four scruffy examples of the worst Moritus
 d field. Over the outrageous din, Funston recognized
 ugle call for the infantry to advance as skirmishers.

 Owen Bledsoe stood on the incomplete parapet
 e the main gate. He had just ordered the infantry to
 nce into position to cut off any possible escape of the
 federate irregulars who had attacked the fort. Now he
 d in wonder at the drama that unfolded on the plain
 re him. Who, he puzzled, were these strange troops,
 aned like Zouves, who had so timely arrived to shut off
 sh for the south and safety in Texas?

 e had not received any communication about rein-
 ements. Perhaps they had come from farther south,
 Washita or Towson, following the Confederates. He
 d field glasses to study them. Rather a swarthy lot, he
 rved first. Their features seemed quite like Indians. A
 len suspicion jelled in his mind.

 o, It couldn't be. Were these the infamous Cherokee
 athorse? They certainly fought well for men supposed
 e police. Yet, the Cherokees were on the side of the
 els. Why would they attack their allies? When the
 ting ended, he would make certain, he assured
 self.

 y two of his usual five bodyguards remained on their
 It left Augustus Moritus in a decidedly untenable
 tion. The huge savage who had waded into his
 onal protectors fought like a madman. Even while his

eyes darted frantically around for a means to esca
Moritus saw the revolver in the Lighthorseman's ha
flash again, and another bodyguard fell to his kne
Impossible. Augustus Moritus felt certain he had kept
accurate count of expended rounds, timing his dash
safety on the firing of the last. That would have be
number seven!

Segeeyah Oaks had long since emptied his Colt and h
drawn the LeMatt from its saddle holster. While fie
hand-to-hand fighting went on around him, he loca
the small knot of hard-looking men who surrounded
diminutive figure of Augustus Moritus. Segeeyah shov
his way through the struggling throng and shot the first
the bodyguards to become aware of his intent.

Hurried, the shot went high and left. A shoulder woun
Segeeyah corrected that error with a second round th
drilled into the chest of the burly Leatherleg. He we
down, to be replaced by another. In quick order, Segeey
Oaks accounted for him and another daring rogue wi
three more rounds. Something hot and outraged burn
behind Segeeyah's eyes as he closed on the remaining pa
The LeMatt barked again, and a black hole appear
below the nose of the man to the right of Moritus.

Firing wildly, the last bodyguard sent a .44 ball to bu
a painful trail along the left side of Segeeyah Oa
ribcage. Wincing, the Lighthorseman advanced on h
enemy. The rattled Leatherleg swiftly emptied his r
volver. His shots all went wide of the mark. Determined
reach Augustus Moritus, Segeeyah Oaks continued fo
ward with a fast bound. When his right foot next stru
the ground, the LeMatt discharged. Then, quickly, agai

Segeeyah Oaks watched as his opponent sagged ar
dropped to one knee. The Starr revolver slipped fro
unfeeling fingers and splashed in a puddle of bloo
moistened mud. Dimly, Segeeyah heard his hamm
index. He had only the buckshot round left.

Calmly, he stepped over the corpse and thrust the Le-Matt in his waistband. With one big hand he reached out and grabbed the shirt front of Augustus Moritus. Effortlessly he swung the small tyrant off his feet and shook him like a half-drowned rat.

For the first time in his life, Augustus Moritus knew abject fear. This giant savage, for he was truly that, had the face of a madman. A froth of spittle formed at the corners of Augustus' mouth, and he didn't see the huge hand that so suddenly slammed against his cheek. Before he could recover, it came back from the opposite direction and struck him again. Irrationally, Augustus Moritus thought of the Biblical injunction to turn the other cheek.

He then thought of one he liked better: "an eye for an eye." Recovering his composure somewhat, his free left hand groped for the large knife he wore on his belt. It came free with ease, and he drove it forward at where he expected his enemy's belly to be. To his alarm, it cut only air.

Segeeyah Oaks became aware of the threat of the blade from the grunt of effort and shocked expression of the small man he held. At once he forcefully heaved Moritus away from him. The small guerrilla leader landed on his back near the churning legs of another Lighthorseman and one of his Leatherlegs.

With the breath knocked out of him, he lay there for five seconds. The black curtain over his vision dissolved into a whirling haze, and he saw the big Cherokee leaning down over him. Without warning, Augustus Moritus lunged upward and drove the blade deep into flesh.

A volcano of torment erupted in the side of Segeeyah Oaks. He had never known such agony. Vainly he fought to keep his sight from slipping into darkness. The tumult of battle receded rapidly, and he felt his legs go slack under him.

Twenty-two

Unconsciousness lasted only a split second. Long enough for Segeeyah Oaks to find their roles reversed. Now Augustus Moritus leaned over him, the bloody knife in his hand, ready to strike a slashing blow to the Lighthorseman's throat. Mind still fogged by pain, Segeeyah's body took over control. He moved swiftly, his big right hand closing on the grips of the LeMatt. He pulled it free and eared back the hammer in one move.

Eyes wild with blood-lust, Augustus Moritus bent closer, saliva and blood oozing from his split lips. He never saw the muzzle of the .44 LeMatt clear leather and line up on his middle. Pressed so close together, the blast from the LeMatt put a fiery trail across Segeeyah's belly as particles of powder burned through his shirt and scorched the skin. The three buckshot pellets entered the body of Augustus Moritus an inch above his navel.

He dropped the knife, and his bruised lips formed a silent "Oh!" His body stiffened, and his eyes rolled up in his head. Without preamble, he fell atop the wounded Segeeyah Oaks. Biting his lip against the pain in his side and stomach, Segeeyah struggled feebly to throw off the dead weight. He sensed his consciousness slipping a moment before the pressure of Moritus' bleeding body went away.

"That was too damned close, you ask me," Lt. Parker Funston said cheerily as he gazed down at Segeeyah Oaks.

Slowly the darkness drew back. Segeeyah blinked and studied the powder-grimed face of the young lieutenant. Blood ran from the cut above Funston's left eye. He had a neck scarf tied around a wound in his right arm. With effort, Segeeyah formed words.

"You got a little careless yourself, I see."

"It's nothing," Funston dismissed. Then his eyes went wide as he saw the wound in Segeeyah's side. "My God, man, you've been stabbed."

"Is it as bad as it feels?" Segeeyah asked, trying to make light of his injury.

Lieutenant Funston knelt on the blood-slicked ground at Segeeyah's side. "No. Thank God he pulled it straight out, didn't slash inside you. At least I don't think so."

Only then did Segeeyah Oaks realize that the fighting had ended. Faintly the groans of the wounded and dying came to his ears. With effort he propped himself up on one elbow. Fuzzy vision revealed small knots of prisoners, their arms in the air, guarded by soldiers and his Lighthorse.

"I think that puts an end to Augustus Moritus and his Leatherlegs," Segeeyah opined.

"Yes. But we're not out of trouble yet. Here comes Colonel Bledsoe, and he looks like he could chew horseshoes."

"*Lieutenant Funston,*" Col. Owen Bledsoe thundered from horseback. "First I must congratulate you for your brilliant strategy in luring these Confederates to their destruction. However . . ." Bledsoe broke off as Funston rose to his full height and saluted.

"Begging the Colonel's pardon, sir, but these are not Confederates. They are border trash led by one Augustus

Moritus. He's the dead man at my feet."

Bledsoe bristled. "They are Rebel scum, I say."

"No sir. My men are separating the army deserters from the ranks of the prisoners right now, sir. We, the Lighthorse and my platoon, have been pursuing and engaging them in fights for the past four days. They are definitely not Confederate irregulars or anything like it."

"You dare to contradict me?" Bledsoe rumbled menacingly.

"Yes, sir. With all due respect. The record needs to be straight on this, sir. Without the help of the Lighthorse, we would have been wiped out a long time ago."

Rigid with anger now, Bledsoe raged at the impudent young officer. "That's another matter I wish to take up with you, Mr. Funston. Up until this last inspired move, your conduct in this entire campaign is highly questionable. For one thing, there have not been any timely situations reports."

"I sent a dispatch rider, sir," Lieutenant Funston answered feebly.

"I've not seen the like. Now I find you collaborating with the enemy and denying that these scum are Confederate soldiers out of uniform."

"Just a minute, Colonel," Segeeyah Oaks began as, with the help of Wolf Wind, he came to his feet. "Lieutenant Funston is telling you exactly what has happened. As an officer of the Tsalagi Lighthorse, I can assure you that these men are not Confederates. We have pursued them from Tahlequah District, where they attacked and sacked a town and were in the process of besieging the Tsalagi Insane Asylum. It is true that my people are allies of the Confederate States. As such, there is no hostility between our respective armed forces."

Colonel Bledsoe had heard enough. "I'll see you in chains and hanged for treason, you heathen animal!" he bellowed at Segeeyah Oaks.

He might have said more, only right then the Kiowa decided to attack.

"Now is the time," Two Moons sighed with satisfaction as the battle on the plain below them ended. "The white soldiers think the fighting is over. While they look the other way, we will show them that it is not."

"Why do the white men face each other?" a young apprentice asked.

Two Moons gave him an indulgent smile. "All white men are crazy. Who can say that there is reason behind anything they do. Go now," he commanded the war leaders. "Get your warriors mounted and ready. We strike while their minds are on other things."

Swift as a blizzard wind, the Kiowas and their Creek allies rushed down on the unsuspecting troops from Fort Gibson and the Cherokeee Lighthorse. Excited beyond control at the prospect of spilling much white blood, the warriors could not restrain yips and whoops of jeering challenge as they neared the loosely deployed soldiers. Young Lieutenant Nelson of the infantry saw them first. He gaped in disbelief for valuable seconds before drawing in air to give a leathery shout.

"Indians! We're under attack!"

Wolf Wind had bound the knife wound in the side of Segeeyah Oaks and looked up from the end of his task with surprise. "Our Creek friends?" he asked.

"I don't think so," Segeeyah answered. "They look like plains people. Comanche, perhaps."

Beside himself, Col. Owen Bledsoe could not believe what he saw. First the Confederates attacked the fort, now Indians. They were in league, he knew it. Gulping back his astonishment, he barked orders in a disjointed rush.

"Fall back on the fort. Close ranks. Fall back. Keep these Rebel Indians outside," he blared, hot, hate-filled eyes fixed on Segeeyah Oaks.

Lieutenant Funston shot Segeeyah Oaks a quick glance that implied his sympathy, then his expression hardened. "We're staying. Out here I think your men and mine can make the difference."

"Right you are. Go through the motions, only pull up short of entering the fort. We'll take the hostiles when and where they least expect it."

"Bring those prisoners," Bledsoe went on spewing commands. "Captain Holt, your company to form a rear guard. Cover our withdrawal."

"Yes, sir," a mustached man with sandy hair and sparkling blue eyes responded. Immediately he set about organizing the rear guard. Other infantry took the prisoners from the control of Funston's cavalry and the Lighthorse and hustled them off toward the open gate of the fort.

Funston's platoon, at his command, lagged behind, firing at the rapidly approaching Kiowas. Biting back his pain, Segeeyah Oaks led his detachments away at an oblique angle. The attacking force paid them little mind. When at last the rear guard reached the gate, it swung closed on one side, and they streamed inside. Lieutenant Funston ordered his men to mount, and they rode away from the fort.

A roar of outrage came from inside Fort Gibson. "Traitor! Traitor! You'll suffer for this, Mr. Funston."

Suddenly the artillery opened up with cannister and grape shot. An invisible scimitar, the horizontal layer of moaning small balls cut warriors from their saddles. The second barrage, at near point-blank range, put the Kiowas in dazed confusion. Several spun their ponies in tight circles, yelling insults and vainly seeking any target upon which to vent their fear and wrath. Two Moons and Bullhide swiftly took command.

"Back. Ride back. Away from the long-shoots guns,"

Two Moons shouted.

Bullhide led the way. "Follow me. We must attack their weak points."

Those they soon saw in profusion. Only the headquarters building, suttler's store, quartermaster warehouse, and stables that surrounded the parade ground had been incorporated into the makeshift pallisades. Barracks and other structures remained outside the protective wall. Using flint and steel, the warriors quickly ignited firebrands and rode in, yipping and shouting, to throw the torches into those buildings. Shouts of encouragement came from the watching Creeks and the remaining Kiowas.

Two Moons had wisely selected a rally point outside the range of the cannon. The torch bearers had reached a place midway between when the Lighthorse came up like a whirlwind and swarmed over them. Eleven of the twenty warriors died in the first five seconds of the engagement. None escaped wounds. Fast as they had appeared, the Lighthorse rode out of sight into a large wash that ran parallel with the fort on that side. The surviving Kiowas limped back to where the others waited.

Thoughtful silence greeted them. Without giving time to let the bloody setback register, Two Moons sent out another party to attack the soldiers who had hastened to put out the fires. They did not make it halfway before bluecoat soldiers appeared out of the same arroyo and cut them down with a well-aimed volley.

Two Moons sent another band of twenty warriors around by the west to probe another weak spot. They had barely gotten out of sight when Two Moons heard the muffled sound of gunfire. Silence followed for a long time after. Then, three badly wounded warriors came back at a trot.

"What happened?" Two Moons demanded.

"Lighthorse," a dying brave gasped out.

Beside the older war leader, Bullhide lost control of his hot nature. "We must stop them! Kill the Lighhorse. Who are they but digs-in-the-ground people not fit to carry water to a Kiowa?" He waved an arm to encompass some thirty warriors. "Come with me. We will drive these old women from the battle."

"It is not wise," Two Moons counseled.

"It is the only answer," Bullhide barked vehemently.

At the head of his eager band, Bullhide rode off to find the elusive Lighthorse.

Segeeyah Oaks knew the Kiowa had come after them before he saw them. He felt their approach in the trembling of the earth. He and Lieutenant Funston had joined up again after the defeat of the two skirmish parties. They had agreed to separate and swing in behind the Kiowas and made ready to depart when Oaks noticed the approach of the enemy.

"Wait a minute. There are a lot of horses headed our way," he told Funston.

"Really? I can't hear them."

Oaks smiled. "I can feel the ground shake from their hooves. Let's pull our men back out of sight and surprise them."

"Good idea," Funston agreed.

In less than a minute no sign could be seen of soldiers or Lighthorsemen. Goaded by his hatred of anything or anyone not Kiowa, Bullhide led his men into the deep, wide course of a tributary of the Arkansas River. They rounded a bend in a flurry of hooves and roiling dust. Spears of reflected sunlight stabbed their eyes from the surface of the creek.

While blinded they could not see the men hidden on both sides of the stream. They felt their presence quite abruptly when three warriors flew from their saddlepads a action of a second before the crack of rifles reached the ears of Bullhide. Astounded that he had so easily and stupidly ridden into an ambush, Bullhide yelled at his men to rally them.

The volume of fire increased. In the confines of the banks the fight turned into a wild melee. Powder smoke hung on the lazy air. Its acrid fumes choked men and animals alike. Two Kiowa braves located Robert Runningdeer and leaped upon him at the same time.

He went down with them to roll into the creek. Attracted to the squirming disturbance, Segeeyah Oaks took careful aim and shot one of the hostiles off his Lighthorseman. Runningdeer dispatched the other with a knife thrust to the heart.

"You have to watch them," Segeeyah said tightly. "They're wild Indians."

"*Wado*, Bat. I thought I would suck up the whole creek," a grinning Runningdeer replied.

"Better finish off these hostiles first," Segeeyah quipped.

When the rattle of close-by gunfire reached Two Moons, he quickly surmised that his friend had run into something too big to handle. Quickly he called together the warriors who had followed him from their homes in the wild country of the Texas panhandle. He gestured toward the sounds of conflict.

"We will go and see what is happening," Two Moons stated simply.

They came upon the fight in a rush. Alert soldiers saw the approach and fired a withering volley into the foremost warriors. Four fell from their saddlepads. Two Moons came on, a wicked Kiowa lance brandished as he rose. Nearing the center of the fight, he set the deadly weapon and charged the back of a Lighthorseman.

Lieutenant Funston caught the motion out of the corner

241

of his eye. Without thinking, he catapulted himself from the saddle and knocked the oddly outfitted Kiowa from the back of his horse.

A loud, metallic clang rang from the cuirass worn by Two Moons when his back struck the pebbled area at the edge of the stream. A heavy weight pressed on him, and he knew it did not belong to the Cherokee he had tried to impale on his lance. He turned his head to look into the angry face of a white man. Then a balled fist smashed into his mouth.

Another followed swiftly. Then a third powerful blow brought blackness swimming up around Two Moons. Lt. Parker Funston looked up from his recumbent enemy in time to see Segeeyah Oaks engage the leader of the first war party. Bullhide let out a roar as the Lighthorse lieutenant came at him. Too late he found himself isolated from the rest of his warriors.

Segeeyah Oaks took quick advantage of that. He rammed the broad chest of Bashful into the slighter built pony ridden by Bullhide. While the animals fought each other, the men tried urgently to find an opening that would let the one triumph over the other. Bullhide prodded with his lance while Segeeyah parried the thrusts with the barrel of his shotgun.

Locked in a stand-off, neither man could grasp a moment's advantage. Then Bashful changed the odds by rearing and lashing downward with iron-shod hooves on the forehead of the Kiowa war pony. Stunned, the smaller horse went spraddle-legged and shuddered violently before it swayed to one side and fell to the ground. Bullhide barely had time to jump clear.

Instantly Segeeyah Oaks came out of his saddle and went for the winded, disoriented Kiowa war chief. His left hand held his war club now, while he continued to keep the lance at bay with the barrel of his Parker. Segeeyah's side blazed with the agony from the knife wound Moritus

ad given him. Sweat ran in rivers down his face. Through
the haze and confusion of the battle, Bullhide seemed to
waver before his eyes.

Then the Kiowa struck. The jagged flint point slid past
Segeeyah's rapid parry and hung up in the cloth of his
coat. Reacting with blinding speed, Segeeyah lashed
downward with the barrel of his shotgun. Bullhide jerked
his head aside barely in time. Segeeyah felt a solid jar all
the way up his arm, and it awakened new misery in his
side.

His blow had broken Bullhide's left collarbone. A
torrent of anguish washed through the body of Bullhide as
he rolled on his shoulders and snapped to his feet. He hurt
even more when Segeeyah gave him a butt-stroke in the
gut. Doubled over in exploding torment, Bullhide did not
see the steel butt-plate descending on that vulnerable spot
on his neck at the base of his skull.

Even over his sobbing, gasping breath and the tumult of
the battle, Segeeyah Oaks could hear the dry stick crunch
as bones broke, and Bullhide dropped to the ground to
flop like a headless chicken. He turned away and at once
drew his Colt to put a ball into the fat stomach of a Kiowa
who charged him with the gleaming blade of a tomahawk
raised high.

Another Kiowa saw the flawless, unhurried shot and the
body of Bullhide lying with his face in the water, still
twitching. He shouted something in his own language,
and at once the hostiles broke off their attack. Two of them
scooped up the supine Two Moons, and they all swarmed
from the creek bed.

Panting, his face slicked with sweat and grimed by dirt
and powder smoke, Lt. Parker Funston walked up to
Segeeyah Oaks. "That . . . is the most . . . desperate fight I
hope I am ever in."

"I could have done without it, I'll admit," Segeeyah
informed him.

243

Funston turned a full 360 degrees and surveyed the scene of their strife. "They've gone off," he said wonderingly. "Even that war chief I knocked senseless."

"I killed the other war leader," Segeeyah explained. "They'll have to talk about that, decide on a new chief. I'd say the fighting is over for today. But they will be back."

"We should get into the fort," Funston suggested.

"No. I'd rather stay here. I like fighting in the open."

Funston produced a rueful expression. "I can imagine the welcome waiting me from Colonel Bledsoe. I think I'll stay with you. You do have the strangest affinity for trouble."

Twenty-three

ring the long night, punctuated by the distant,
art-pulse throb of drums and faint wailing chants, the
cupants of Fort Gibson and those outside got little sleep.
e followers of the dead Bullhide elected a new war
der, and the entire Kiowa party made war medicine
th enthusiasm. With the dawn, true to Segeeyah Oaks'
diction, the Kiowas came back.

To the surprise of Lt. Parker Funston, the hostiles threw
ir large force against the fort. They appeared to be
livious to the presence of his troops and the Lighthorse.
called this to the attention of Segeeyah Oaks.

The tall, barrel-chested Lighthorseman produced a
eting grin and offered a suggestion. "I think we ought
remind them that we are here."

By then, the Kiowa had fully committed to their classic
tic of ringing the bastions of Fort Gibson and
changing shots with the occupants. In too close for the
illery to bear, they escaped the terrible punishment of
previous day. For his part, it appeared that Colonel
edsoe had found his element.

He made bold use of his infantry, by far the better
rksmen, and held his depleted cavalry in reserve. With
odigious effort, the small salute gun was horsed into

position to fire downward from above the main gate. Wit
charges of grapeshot it made quick, bloody work of man
Kiowa warriors until on the fifth rapid reload a hea
stressed retaining band broke and flipped the tube off i
carriage. At that point warriors attempted to scale th
ramparts, and Colonel Bledsoe knew a flash of despair.

Then the Lighthorse and Funston's platoon of cavalr
hit the Kiowas in the rear. Spread wide, they streame
across the prairie in a single line, rifles and carbines at th
ready. At a range of less than 100 yards, they swung aroun
to enclose the hostiles between them and the makeshi
walls of the fort. At fifty yards, still undiscovered, th
soldiers and Cherokee lawmen opened fire.

Surprise jolted the Kiowas and Creeks to a confused
milling halt. Another rapid volley cut into their number
and opened the door to panic. Unfortunately, to the troop
behind the barricades, the Lighthorse looked like onl
more Indians. They elevated their range to fire into them
Lt. Parker Funston saw their intent and sprinted forwar
to wave his hat over his head in an effort to attrac
attention.

"Hold your fire!" he yelled. "They're on our side."

Disbelieving faces mirrored the prejudice of Col. Owe
Bledsoe. Several infantry men discharged their weapons
Fortunately the fast-moving Lighthorse provided poo
targets. One young lawman received a painful gouge or
his right shoulder. Otherwise, the balls passed harmlessl
through air.

"Hold your fire, dammit!" Funston roared. "Get th
Kiowas," he added. "They're the hostiles."

While Lieutenant Funston concentrated on lifting th
danger from the troops, Segeeyah Oaks fixed on a knot o
leaders who sat apart from the ring of hostile warriors an
conferred with obvious agitation. With a quick gesture t
Wolf Wind and a dozen Lighthorse, he reined Bashfu
around and sprinted toward the gesticulating chiefs.

f we take them out, it will be over," Segeeyah shouted
he Lighthorsemen with him.

Then less than twenty-five yards separated them from
charging Lighthorse, three of the war leaders looked
and saw their impending danger. Ill-prepared to fight
nst rifles and shotguns, they waved their lances in a
e, but futile, threat and charged.

geeyah Oaks cut down one of them with some thirteen
ls to spare. Wolf Wind downed a second, and an
en Lighthorseman accounted for the third. It didn't
a slacken their pace. With a whoop of exuberance, the
hthorse crashed in among the remaining war chiefs.
eyah found himself squared off against the squat,
warrior in the iron cuirass.

You will die this day," Two Moons growled in his own
gue.

Higigage'i jisuhwisga— I will paint you red," Segeeyah
llenged back in Tsalagi.

wo Moons leveled his lance and charged. Cued by a
cticed knee pressure Bashful made a sudden hop to the
The lance point whistled past, scant inches from
eeyah's body. He made a swift parry with his Parker
then slammed the butt-plate into the iron-clad rib-
e of Two Moons.

o strong was Segeeyah's thrust that it knocked Two
ons off his horse. The point of his lance dug into the
und, and the shaft snapped in two. His small, round
ld dug painfully into his side, and the Kiowa war chief
ed in the dirt until his momentum was spent. Quickly
came to his feet, a bit dazed and disoriented. Not
ugh to prevent him from snatching up the front third
is spear, which he hefted and began to wield like a
g-handled dagger.

egeeyah Oaks sharply reined in and dismounted. His
oaded shotgun abandoned, he let the reins trail on the
und, effectively holding Bashful in place. When he

247

turned to his enemy, Two Moons rushed at him in strangely rolling gait. Unprepared for this type fighting, Segeeyah reluctantly drew his .44 Colt. By count he had but two rounds left.

Two Moons' eyes widened at the sight of the revolv Undaunted, he continued on, fired by the exhilaration battle. Segeeyah Oaks shot him. The round lead b punched through the cuirass and cracked a rib, but fail to penetrate the chest cavity of Two Moons. Swif Segeeyah eared back the hammer and fired again. Anoth hole in the metal covering appeared, and Two Moo staggered and grunted at the pain. Rallying, though came on.

Segeeyah Oaks met Two Moons with the barrel of I Model '60. It parried the first thrust with ease. Then pa exploded in Segeeyah's right side as Two Moons slamm the hard wooden rim of his shield into the Lighthors man's ribs above the stab wound. Segeeyah nearly lost I grip on the empty Colt.

He recovered in time to block another jab of the dead flint blade. His hurried thoughts reminded him, taur ingly, of the .36 Navy Colt in the small of his back. If on he had time to draw it. Inspiration burst on him as parried a third attempt to pierce his hide.

Stooping, Segeeyah grabbed up a handful of loose so and immediately had to roll away to avoid being pinned the earth. Two Moons stood over him, the lance poised f another thrust, when Segeeyah threw the dirt in t Kiowa's face.

Blinded, Two Moons still tried to drive the lan through his enemy's belly. Segeeyah rolled clear and can to one knee, his .44 on the ground beside him. His b right hand darted to his back and closed on the grip of t .36 Navy. He pulled the seven-inch barreled weapon fr and swung it upward. It would have to be a head shot, I figured.

Two Moons pawed at his eyes with the fingers of his left hand. Gradually, washed by tearing action, his vision cleared. He sought the elusive enemy. "You fight well, for a lazy mountain dweller," Two Moons mixed insult with compliment.

Not understanding, Segeeyah Oaks did not waver in his effort. The small pin front sight lined up on the forehead of Two Moons. Hammer back, finger lightly on the trigger. Segeeyah tripped the sear with a soft pressure, and the wedge hammer fell. It produced only a click that echoed loudly in Segeeyah's mind. The percussion cap had fallen off. Quickly he worked the hammer to full-cock.

Swiftly aware of what had happened, Two Moons closed on his prey with his death-dealing weapon tightly gripped. He took a deep breath and raised both arms for a powerful blow when another click sounded from the small caliber revolver. Shoving with his moccasin heels, Segeeyah scooted away from a certain end to his life. He pried the hammer back again.

A smile of almost sensual delight illuminated the face of Two Moons. In hurried but controlled movements, he positioned himself to dispatch this irritating Cherokee. Then his eyes perceived a momentary flash of orange before his head exploded in bright white light. The lance still clutched in one hand, he fell heavily, face-first onto the ground.

Slowly, Segeeyah Oaks rose to his feet. He bent over the dead war chief and used his belt knife to slit the leather straps that bound the cuirass to the body of Two Moons. Grunting at the effort his exhaustion caused him, he stripped the two-piece metal armor from the corpse. He staggered as he walked to Bashful and painfully regained the saddle.

Then he rode toward the ring of Kiowas still engaged in fighting the soldiers in the fort and his Lighthorse. In his right hand he held high the battered chest plate. He called out in Tsalagi that the chief war leader had been slain. None of the hostiles understood his words, yet all could see the evidence of his deeds.

Suddenly demoralized, the word spread among those on the far side of the fort. Without a backward look, the defeated Kiowa and Creek warriors dashed through the gaps in the thin line of cavalry and Lighthorse and sprinted off across the prairie. Silence fell as gunfire from the pallisades dwindled. Lt. Parker Funston róde up to a chest-heaving Segeeyah Oaks.

"I think the battle is over," the young Union officer observed dryly.

"This time I'd say you are right," Segeeyah panted out.

A protesting creak came from the huge iron hinges of the main gates to Fort Gibson some ten minutes after the Lighthorse and Funston's cavalry secured the area outside the hastily erected pallisades. Rigid in his fury, Col. Owen Bledsoe, his staff in tow, rode out to confront the deliverers of the fort.

For a man just spared a disaster, he had an odd attitude. Determined to reprimand Funston for collaboration with the enemy, he retained the realization that not only his errant cavalry officer, but these sneaky-eyed Indians, had been responsible for lifting the attack on his command. He approached the two youthful leaders with a thunderous expression. Slowly, words began to form for what he wanted to say.

"My compliments, Mr. Funston. It seems your timely actions have lifted the investment of the fort."

Funston stiffened to attention in the saddle and saluted. "Not mine alone, sir. This is Lt. Segeeyah Oaks, of the Lighthorse, whom you have met before. His men outnumbered mine and fought courageously. We are all in his debt, sir."

Bledsoe turned a hate-iced gaze on Oaks. "Oh, yes, the Rebel savage. That recalls to mind your dereliction, Mr. Funston. I am entering notation of it in your efficiency report. It might also be that a general court-martial is in your future. Collaborating with the enemy is a serious charge."

"Colonel, I—"

"Silence, Mr. Funston," Bledsoe snapped.

"Yes, sir," a chagrined Fuston responded.

Not in the least cowed by the bigoted colonel, Segeeyah Oaks determined to get the true story out regardless of consequences. "Colonel, no disrespect, but you've had your say. Now I'm going to have mine. I want the truth on the record, not just your wild, erroneous speculations."

"How dare you, sir!" Bledsoe blurted in outrage.

Major Mueller muttered wise advice. "You had better listen to him, Owen. His men fight like demons, and they did save our bacon."

Unswayed by Bledsoe's outburst, Segeeyah answered hotly. "I dare because we are on the soil of the Tsalagi nation, my country, and technically you are a trespasser. You will hear me out. And then I think you will offer an apology and a commendation to Lieutenant Funston."

Only then did it register on Bledsoe that this savage spoke in flawless English. Different circumstances, he admitted, required different responses. "Very well," he grated tightly. "Have your say."

"First off, Lieutenant Funston did not collaborate with us," Segeeyah hammered out, shading the letter, if not the spirit, of the truth. "My Lighthorse detachments were pressed into federal service by Lieutenant Funston in order to apprehend suspected deserters in the nation. Since their presence was a violation of Tsalagi law also, I agreed to collaborate with him. He had recently engaged in a brief skirmish with some of the border guerrillas known as

251

Leatherlegs and had suffered a large number of casualties. Our reinforcements were necessary for him to carry out his mission."

Segeeyah paused a moment and sucked in air, wincing at the pain the effort brought. "From that point on, we were in nearly constant contact with the enemy. Lieutenant Funston attempted to disrupt the advance of the guerrillas outside the Tsalagi Insane Asylum. With our help, he devastated their ranks and sent the rest fleeing. Again, seriously outnumbered, Lieutenant Funston led an assault on the stronghold of the Leatherlegs. We were able to attack from an unexpected direction and again broke their fighting spirit and caused the remainder to flee.

"By some misdirection, they wound up outside the fort yesterday. You are aware of the result of that. These men are guilty of violating the laws of the United States as well as the nation," Segeeyah pressed on rapidly. "In the case of the deserters, we are more than willing to leave their disposition up to the Army. Those who belonged to the guerrilla band of Augustus Moritus, outside of the deserters, should be turned over to me to be taken to Tahlequah for trial and punishment."

Eyes narrowed, Owen Bledsoe still tried to retain a scrap of his delusion. "There is still the matter of Lieutenant Funston's failure to keep me properly informed."

Segeeyah sighed heavily. "At the beginning, he was too busy and undermanned to send off messengers. Later, he did so, though the man has not as yet arrived. Perhaps I should have sent one of my own men. From what I've been told, though, he would not have received a cordial welcome."

Moved by this candid response, Colonel Bledsoe replied dryly, "Point well taken. This punishment you refer to for those other than military prisoners, what will that be?"

"Since they have no papers to prove their legal status as irregulars for any participant in the current war, they fall under the current conditions of Tsalagi law. If found guilty, which I have no doubt they will, they will be executed," Segeeyah informed the colonel.

Cooled down, and somewhat mollified by this rendition of Funston's activities, Bledsoe at last admitted to himself that it was indeed the presence of Funston's troops and the Lighthorse that saved the fort. Grudgingly, he acknowledged that the plan sounded good enough. "By what method of execution?" he concluded.

"Firing squad, no doubt," Oaks answered.

"Won't do," Bledsoe responded in his old tone of disapproval. "It would be better if they are turned over to the Army," he insisted, "to be hanged."

Segeeyah Oaks eyed the colonel speculatively. He wondered what advantage the caustic officer angled after. Bledsoe didn't leave him guessing long.

"Under those conditions of cooperation," Colonel Bledsoe added, "I would seriously consider allowing the Lighthorse to go freely about its duties of policing this God-forsaken land."

That concession, from such a man as this, jolted Segeeyah Oaks. Although his mind had not been keenly honed in political maneuvering, Oaks quickly came up with the proper gambit. "If you will put that in writing, sir. For my report to my superiors, you understand," he added placatingly. "I think we have what you *diyoniga* call a deal."

Tension sloughed away. Segeeyah smiled first, followed by several in the staff. Then, as though it pained him, Colonel Bledsoe crooked a small grin. Laughter followed, and the principals shook hands around on it.

After order had been restored, Colonel Bledsoe dictated a document to his clerk. It read in part that on behalf of the United States of America he placed himself on record as applauding and approving the peacekeeping efforts of the Cherokee Lighthorse. It further gave his bond that Union troops would not interfere in the enforcement of Cherokee law within the nation.

When it had been signed and sealed, Segeeyah Oaks and the Lighthorse made ready to depart. Lieutenant Funston found his new friend outside the symbolic gates to the unwalled fort. He spoke hesitantly.

"I was looking for you. To say good-bye. Where are you headed, by the way?"

"Why, back to Tahlequah to make my report."

"What about your family? Won't they be worried about you?"

"Oh, I think not. Besides, I'll see them on the way," Segeeyah volunteered.

"Really? Where are they?"

"They're in Park Hill," Segeeyah answered lightly and turned to step into the saddle.

"But, wait a minute," Funston recovered his sagging jaw enough to blurt. "Park Hill? That's the town Moritus set out to sack."

"Yes. Only nothing to worry about. Everyone who lives there is Tsalagi."

Laughing, Lt. Segeeyah Oaks shook Funston's hand, and his Lighthorse rode away from Fort Gibson highly pleased with themselves.

Author's Note

In order to avoid confusion, we have chosen to use modern terms for distance and time (e.g., miles, yards, feet, hours, minutes, etc.) rather than early Cherokee words. Also, so that the reader may follow along on a modern map, most place names have been rendered in their contemporary form. Park Hill does not appear on any modern map. By judging its indicated location on an 1896 map of the Cherokee nation, it appears that Park Hill currently rests below the waters of Tenkiller Lake. The wide basin on Dardeene Creek is an invention for the purposes of the story.

It has been necessary, to meet typesetting requirements, to omit the A prefix on nouns used as names in Tsalagi. It also prevents a plethora of confusing "A" surnames. The prefixes "j," "d," "di," and "u" have been omitted where confusion would result from similar word beginnings. For those of our readers who have written to remark on the use of *Ani-Waya* for the Wolf Clan in *Prairie Fire*, this has been looked into and found to be a North Carolina usage. The Oklahoma Nation usage is, properly, *Yvwi-Waya* (People [of the] Wolf).

Finally, a note on the use of "v" as a vowel. In Tsalagi, the Roman character "v" has the sound of "u" in *but*.

Likewise, "ge" is sounded like the "ge" in *get*, "gi" as the "gi" in *git*. An "s" appearing in a word such as *didehlogwasdohdi* (dictionary) is asperated in a hiss. I hope that this will aid those who like to subvocalize dialogue, and make Tsalagi words simpler to read in general.

MKR